The Scandal of the Vicar's Wife

QUENBY OLSON

The Scandal of the Vicar's Wife is a work of fiction. Names, characters, places, and incidents are products of the author's imagination or are used fictitiously. Any resemblance to actual events or locales or persons, living or dead, is entirely coincidental.

ISBN-13: 9798842259328

Published in the United States of America by World Tree Publishing

First Edition: March 2022

1 2 3 4 5 6 7 8 9 WTEP B2211

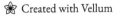 Created with Vellum

To my children, for making writing sex scenes in the same room as you extremely awkward.

Contents

One

Not once in her seven years of marriage had Julia loved her husband. She had married him because she was the oldest of three daughters, because her fortune upon her father's death had not amounted to more than forty pounds a year. Because she had been twenty-nine years old and desperate to be out and away from her family's home with the promise of being mistress of her own household.

It had been a careful, logical decision. Like the choice between throwing oneself onto a piece of flotsam or going below the waves with the rest of the shipwreck. Mr. Frederick Benton had been her flotsam, and she had clung to him with everything she had. Everything but love.

Perhaps if she had loved him…

Ah, no. Now was not the time to sink into such a maudlin quagmire. Perhaps if she had loved him more. Perhaps if she had been able to do her duty and bear him children. Perhaps perhaps perhaps. The last five years of her widowhood had been framed by nothing but the possibility that if she had done something different, if she had not rushed into a marriage with a man for whom she felt nothing more than a mild affection, then perhaps…

Damn. There was that word again.

She sighed, and she put her hand up to her brow, and she squinted through the winter sunshine at the small crowd gathered outside the church. A small wedding it was, complete with a beaming bride and red-faced groom, the both of them gazing at one another with the sort of blushing looks that made one suspect their time in the marriage bed tonight would not be an inaugural visit.

Julia dropped her hand back to her side and wished them well, her whispered words caught up by the cold wind and torn from her lips. "May you have a better time of it than I did." Nothing particularly poetic or worth having penned in fine calligraphy on a card or letter. But any penchant she had ever possessed for pretty sonnets and pretty words had been scrubbed away by too many years of disappointed hopes and harsh realities.

The marriage celebrations carried on after she turned and walked away. She hadn't been invited only, only a common bystander happening by at the proper moment. She didn't know the groom and the bride had never been one of her pupils. Not a remarkable thing, the latter, seeing as how the majority of Barrow-in-Ashton's inhabitants still looked down on the idea of educated women, as though imbuing half the population with a knack for reading and writing and independent thought was a sin left off the list of Ten Commandments simply because eleven would have made too awkward a number.

Her mouth twisted at the direction of her thoughts. She sounded bitter to her own ears. Nothing like how a former vicar's wife should think or feel. An interesting thing, how seven years so closely knit with the church could harden her heart against so many of its tenets. Or rather, how so many inhabitants of the world in which she lived chose to shape those tenets to suit their particular wants and needs.

She dipped her head down as she walked, away from the church, past the vicarage that had once been her home, through a town that hardly acknowledged her existence now that her husband was dead and buried and they had no use for an aging widow with nothing more than forty pounds a year to her name.

There was still the teaching, of course, but the town barely paid any notice to that either. Sometimes she suspected they only allowed the school to remain open in order to give her something to do, her few students like offerings of charity to make them feel as if they were doing right by the former vicar's wife. A vicar who had been well-liked. Tall and handsome, a man who had delivered his sermons with a wit and fervor that spoke of a true calling to his post; instead of the truth of the matter, that Frederick had been a second-born son with few prospects and a remarkably hale older brother who had married young and produced enough heirs to ensure that only a dire catastrophe of historic proportions would see the family estate tossed over to another branch of the tree.

A few people nodded their heads to her as she passed, but most failed to notice her. She did not take their lack of interest as an offense. She truly believed most people simply didn't see her now. Before, she'd had the status of her husband to lift her up to the attention of others. But now she was a widow, a widow well past the age of marrying again, and a widow who had failed to produce a single living child while her husband had been alive.

And she was plain. It would not do to forget that, either.

She pulled a key from her pocket and let herself into Mrs. Cochran's house. To tell the truth, Mrs. Cochran only laid a claim on the lower floor, leaving Julia to pay for the use of a small set of rooms above. The stairs were dark and narrow and announced her arrival with numerous creaks that reverberated through the building's bones. At the top she went through another door, and... there. She was home.

It wasn't much to boast about. A small sitting room, a sort of pantry off to the side, and then a single bedroom. Nothing more. Julia did not mind the lack of space. If she needed open air or time to herself, away from the clatterings of Mrs. Cochran down below, she could go for a walk. Mrs. Cochran, on the other hand, rarely went out, preferring to remain at home with her letters and her tea and the occasional visits from the other ladies of the town who paid homage to her and the status she had once held before her own widowhood had rendered her a person of steadily diminishing wealth and importance.

"Mrs. Benton, is that you?"

Julia smiled. Of course it was her. Who else would it have been? And then she winced as she reached up to the ribbons of her bonnet, her fingers stilling over the knot. "Oh, I forgot your letters," she called down the stairs. "I meant to stop at the post office, but it seemed I was distracted." The wedding had distracted her, and then the mire of her own thoughts following swiftly upon its heels. "I will go out again directly, if you wish. I do not mind."

She went downstairs again and found Mrs. Cochran seated in a chair by the fire, her legs tucked beneath a knitted blanket, the upper half of the blanket still in the midst of production by a pair of clacking needles. "I wish you would not trouble yourself. It is much too cold for you to be constantly going in and out between the cold and the heat. You'll catch a fever or worse!" She gestured towards another seat — one of only three in the room, apart from a sofa bearing holes in the upholstery and damage to the legs from decades' worth of brooms knocked against them. "Have some tea, warm yourself up. And if you look on the shelf in the kitchen, there might be a bit of cake leftover from what Mrs. Oakhouse brought to us yesterday."

But Julia shook her head. The chair looked too comfortable and the fire too bright and inviting. If she divested herself of her bonnet and gloves and pelisse, if she pushed her feet towards that fire and found a piece of Mrs. Oakhouse's cake to accompany the tea, she doubted she would be willing to stand up again before bedtime.

"Save some of the cake for when I return," she said, and gave her gloves a tug. She went out of the house again, something sharp and bitter pushing her along, like a finger prodding her in the back.

Because the cake had not been brought for the both of them. It had been a gift for Mrs. Cochran. The tea, as well, all belonged to the older gentlewoman. Julia had little in her budget for tea and cakes and other delicacies. And she did not inhabit the same charitable circle as Mrs. Cochran, visited by the ladies of the town and brought small parcels and baskets of comfort to carry her through the declining years of her life.

Julia did not blame them. She had not done much during her time as mistress of the vicarage to endear her to the town's female population. She had been too ill, her attention always fixed inward on her own cares and troubles. And then her husband had died and what was left for her? A set of rooms at the top of a drafty house and one day a week of teaching a handful of young girls to read and to write, to learn their sums and memorize a litany of kings and queens. All so they could grow up and marry and bear children and see themselves existing forever as only a support for their husband. God help them should they fail in that task. The blink of an eye, and they would cease to exist as living, thinking things. That is, if they ever had ever been allowed to in the first place.

She walked back along the street, her head down, her cheeks stinging with the cold. The sun had already disappeared, clouds sweeping in across a blue sky that had been brilliantly clear only a quarter of an hour before. A proper English sky, changing its mind faster than a lady could exchange one bonnet for another. Julia stepped into McKinley's Fine Teas and Other Goods (the 'Other Goods' of its title covering everything from fabric to sugar to perfumes) and went up to the counter, asking for Mrs. Cochran's letters.

Mrs. Cochran always had letters. She was in possession of a plethora of nieces and cousins who wrote to her regularly, and she wrote back to them with assiduous care. Julia, on the other hand, heard from her sisters about once a year, and it usually took her months to work up the courage to send at least a brief note in reply. What closeness she had shared with them had deteriorated over the course of her marriage. Years of illness and misfortune and misery... How could she share that with others? They had their own lives, their own happiness. Why should she send her anguish to them in little bundles through the post?

Mrs. McKinley gave her a small packet of letters for Mrs. Cochran, asked after Mrs. Cochran's health, if she (Mrs. Cochran) was enjoying the cake, and that was all. Julia turned around, tucking the letters into her reticule before she went out again. There had been no inquiries as to her own health and well-being, as though she had been perfectly invisible whilst standing directly in front of the other woman.

But when had Julia shown a tremendous measure of interest in the people who she had lived near for the last dozen years? As the wife of the Vicar, she'd been expected to make regular calls around the village, to visit the sick and others in need, to organize charitable events and help with the running of various fetes and gatherings throughout the year. Whereas she had spent most of her time sequestered in her own home, tired and ill and in no mood to tolerate the inanities that seemed to fill so much of everyone else's days. It did not help that she failed to ever acquire the talent of conversing easily with others, to inquire after various family members about their rheumatisms or the state of someone's kitchen garden after a late freeze.

But there was the school, at least. Her paltry collection of students, meeting every Sunday afternoon. A handful of girls learning to read and to write, risking a chance of no one wishing to employ them later on as servants simply because they wanted to scratch at the boundaries of what was traditionally allowed to them and their class. Oh, no. That had not warmed Julia to the hearts of Barrow-in-Ashton's society, her efforts to blur the lines between the gentlefolk and everyone below them taken as a mild offense at best, and a war on the fundamentals of British society at worst.

Well, it was too late now. Too late for Julia to ingratiate herself into the town, to feign interest in people who had whispered behind her back about her numerous attempts at motherhood that had never come to fruition, about the frigidity between herself and her husband in a marriage that must have appeared to others to only be in name only. About how scant her public show of grief had been when Frederick had died, only a quiet resignation that her life would no longer be what it had been before.

She had considered, briefly, returning to her family in Sussex. But it had felt too much like a defeat, dragging herself back to her childhood haunts, her sisters having all gone off and married, raising families, fulfilling all of the duties set out for them. And what had she to show after seven years of marriage? A broken womb and a festering resentment towards a dead husband who had made it crystal clear he had married her because he had wanted a wife and nothing more.

And then he had died, fool that he was. During a snowstorm, a carriage accident sending him down an icy bank, his neck broken the moment they struck a tree. At least it had been a quick, pain-less death, she mused. As though means of death could be sepa-rated into classes and genuses, and he had been blessed to garner one from a higher level.

It had begun to rain during the time she'd been inside McKin-ley's, a chill drizzle that stung like ice but threatened no danger of freezing the ground beneath her feet. She turned down a side lane, one that would return her to Mrs. Cochran's with greater speed and also provide a few extra eaves to protect her head and hat from the weather.

It was not even fully winter yet and she was already tired of it. The cold seeped into her bones more than it had in her younger days, taking up residence in her hips and her knees and the tips of her fingers. And her rooms at Mrs. Cochran's were not as warm as

7

the vicarage had been, drafts slipping in around the windows and under the doors, the fire in her grate always struggling to burn properly on the windiest days. A sad thought that what she should miss most about marriage was a lack of drafts and a coal scuttle that had always been full.

Another turn and she was nearly home. She kept her chin tucked down to keep the rain from blowing past the brim of her bonnet, and to prevent her from having to make unnecessary eye contact with anyone she might pass along the way. For how better to avoid the pity in someone's gaze if she simply failed to meet their eyes at all?

The unfortunate side to walking with her attention pinned on the ground was that she hardly saw the child before she stumbled over her. Julia bit back a curse and grasped at thin air to stop herself before she fell over the girl completely. Because it was a girl, a slip of a thing, her skirts streaked with mud and her dark hair hanging lank and wet and very hatless around her head.

"Goodness," Julia amended, before the first two or three unsuitable declaratives had a chance to fall out of her mouth. "What are you doing there?"

The girl had been tucked beneath one of the eaves, clearly sheltering from the weather as aside from a lack of millinery she was also devoid of a shawl or coat to help keep out the cold. At first, Julia thought the girl to be an unfortunate, some child stricken by poverty and left to wander the lanes of the town alone without anyone to look after her. But that thought only lasted as long as it took for Julia to take a measure of the girl's gown. An impeccably made creation, fine blue wool and edged with ribbon and piping and most likely better than anything Julia had ever worn in her life.

"Are you lost?" It was the second question Julia asked, as the first had yet to receive a reply.

The girl looked up at her, dark blue eyes that might have been mistaken for gray in a different light. She could not have been older than seven or eight, her figure and face displaying an upbringing that showed she was well fed, even if her natural build gave her an overall appearance of slightness.

"No," came the girl's answer. And that was all.

Not a talkative sort, this one.

Julia did not recognize the girl on sight. She had never seen her at school — though that much was not surprising as the child would most likely have a governess or at least a nurse to look after her — nor at church on Sundays. But still... there was something familiar about her face, like a hazy memory prodded back towards recollection. "Don't you have a cloak or an umbrella?"

The girl shook her head. Ah, so a step backward on the speaking front.

"Where is your mother? Does she know where you are?"

Another shake of the head. "Of course not."

As though Julia was a simpleton and of course this child was out on her own in an icy rain without a hat or coat to protect her from catching her death.

"Where do you live?"

The girl's gaze jumped towards the west.

Julia sighed. Adults tended to frustrate her and make her feel as though she was lacking some innate quality that other women possessed in surfeit. But children did not stymie her the same way, nor did they make her feel lesser for failures of adulthood that still lay so far ahead in their own futures. "My name is Mrs. Benton, though years before that I was known as Miss Cooper. But when I was younger even than that, when I was just about your age, most people called me Julia."

The girl's mouth puckered. It was a thinking face. And then she nodded once, as if she had arrived at a decision, and she tipped her head to one side and said, "I'm Zora."

"Zora? That's an unusual name. I like it very much."

"It's not my real name," the girl stressed, leaning forward and lowering her voice to a loud whisper that carried farther than everything she had said before. "My mother named me Isadora, but when I tried to say it — when I was really very little, still a baby, I think—" she hastened to add, "all I could manage was Zora. And so that's now what I am."

"Zora," Julia repeated, and smiled. "It's lovely. May I call you Zora?"

The girl — Zora — nodded.

"Excellent." Julia took a step back and quickly unbuttoned her pelisse. Before Zora probably even knew what was happening, she wrapped the coat around the girl's slender shoulders, dragging the collar up high enough so that it protected the back of her head from the worst of the rain. "There. That's much better. Now, do you know where your mother is?"

Another pucker. This one accompanied by a brief wrinkling of Zora's nose. "Yes."

"Should we go and find her then? She might be wondering where you are."

"I don't think so," Zora said, while her fingers fussed with the buttons on Julia's coat. "She's dead."

Oh. "At this moment? I mean, when did she...?"

"I don't remember her." And that was enough to answer the question Julia hadn't been able to finish.

"We should get you home," Julia said, and held out her hand. "Do you know how to find your way back?"

Another nod. The girl was made of nods and puckers and blunt statements of fact presented in a way to knock the wind out of someone's lungs.

Julia was about to prod further and ask if Zora would allow her to accompany her home, but without another word the child slipped her hand into Julia's and tugged her along.

The rain did not let up. Julia was thankful for her bonnet and gloves but grit her teeth to keep from shivering at the loss of her pelisse. Zora trudged onward, dragging Julia out of the town and along the road that led them past fields lined with jagged stone walls and copses of trees that dipped down into hollows where small streams burbled out of sight. If it had been a fine day it would have made for a pleasant walk, but as they began a steady trudge uphill Julia noticed the heavy wetness of her gown, the loose tendrils of hair clinging like icicles to the back of her neck. And her toes... well, if she was capable of feeling them, no doubt they would complain to her of their discomfort inside her sopping boots. (And thank goodness she'd thought to put on her sturdiest pair of shoes before heading out, for anything less would have been shredded to ribbons a half mile behind her.)

It was just as Julia began to worry that Zora was leading her to the middle of nowhere when she spotted twin stone columns flanking a set of gates, and beyond that a long gravel lane leading to the right and away from the road.

"Langford," Julia whispered, and she cleared her throat and spoke again. "You live at Langford?"

Zora only led her onward, cutting across the lawn and towards the main house, a sprawling two storey-edifice made of crenellations and diamond-paned windows hidden behind layers of ivy thick enough to fool Julia into believing the land was in the midst of reclaiming the place for its own.

"Over here," Zora said, pulling Julia around the side of the house and towards a stable that opened onto a cleared, fenced-in area beyond. A few servants milled about in the rain, none of them remarking on Zora's appearance there, as though it was only a matter of course for her to stride determinedly past them all in a borrowed pelisse and soaked through to the bone.

They ducked inside the building, Zora finally letting go of Julia's hand to race towards a ladder and begin scurrying up it, as nimble as a mouse.

Julia stood at the bottom of the ladder, gazing upwards as the girl shimmied out of sight. The smell of animal and hay was strong, despite the chill in the air. "Zora?"

The child's dark head peeped out over the edge of the loft. "Come up, Mrs. Benton! Come and see my kitten!"

Julia looked at the ladder, eyeing it as she would a challenge. There was no one else in the stable, at least no one else she could see at the moment, and so she tugged on the hem of her gown and set her foot on the first rung.

The wood let out an ominous creak. She was not as slender as she had once been — and she had never been what one would describe as 'willowy' — and she could only hope the ladder wasn't infested with some kind of rot or woodworm that would turn it to sawdust as she climbed upward.

"Isn't she darling?" Zora announced as Julia arrived at the top of the ladder and stepped into the loft with greater grace than she would have expected of herself. The girl held a small puff of orange fur that mewed helplessly, while Julia unwound her skirt from around her knees and plucked damp bits of hay from her sleeves. "Here!"

Julia reached out as the girl passed the warm, blind ball of kitten into her hands. "Goodness. It's so easy to forget how helpless they are when they're first born."

"I'm to have her when she's weaned," Zora said, and pushed her shoulders back with parental pride. "I've not thought of a name yet, though. Maybe Ellen? She was a Celtic goddess, you know, with three heads! Or perhaps Boadicea, but I don't know if that one would suit her as well. Does she look brave enough to face a Roman army?"

The kitten's fur was short and still damp in places where its mother must have cleaned it only moments ago. "Perhaps you should wait and see. Not all cultures name their young at birth. You might have to give her time, allow her to earn her name rather than foist one upon her, hmm?"

There was a step on the floor below. The strike of boots on swept wooden boards. Julia assumed it was one of the servants coming to check on something, but Zora's posture underwent a subtle change, her shoulders rounding forward again as the happiness that had illuminated her face a minute before turned her mouth into a flat line.

"Isadora?" came a voice from below. A man's voice, deep and laced with a sternness that made even Julia's breath catch at the sound of it. But she recognized it, no matter that it must have been years since she had last heard him speak. "Isadora, come down here at once!"

"Oh, no." Zora returned the kitten to its hay-lined crate. She picked up Julia's abandoned and dripping pelisse and held it out to her. "Papa's home," she said. "I'm sorry, Mrs. Benton. I hope you don't get into trouble, too."

Two

Zora climbed down first. Or rather, she slid down, her shoes propped on the rails as she bypassed the rungs entirely and landed with a soft flump at the bottom.

Julia slung her wet, mud-streaked pelisse over one arm and hoisted up her skirts again. The ladder was twice as treacherous on the way down as it had been going up, her boots threatening to slip and her hands gripping the sides with white-knuckled strength. She couldn't pause long enough to consider how she must look, her damp hem pulled up to show off stockings no doubt snagged with runners and clinging bits of hay. At the bottom, her feet again on solid ground, she turned around and looked steadily at Mr. Alexander Halberd.

He was taller than she remembered. A silly thought, as he couldn't have grown since she'd last seen him, only that her memories had proved faulty. There was gray in his hair that hadn't been there before, streaks of silver starting at his temples and weaving through the dark waves that threatened to curl at the ends from the humidity.

"M-Mr. Halberd," she said, her teeth chattering. And then she swallowed. Loudly.

"What are you doing here?"

Not the most pleasant or polite of greetings, but Julia couldn't fault him for his dereliction of etiquette when she had just climbed down a ladder in his own stables while also sharing a close resemblance with a drowned thing lately rescued from the nearest pond. "Your daughter," she said, holding her arms tight to her sides, the pelisse tucked against her. "I came upon her in town and I offered to accompany her home."

"Mrs. Benton," he said, as though he was already several beats late in the conversation. "I beg your pardon. I confess I'd not expected you of all people to be traipsing about in my stables."

You of all people... What on earth did that mean? Though before she could decide if she should take offense at it, she understood why he had said it. For what connection did she have to him, aside from occasional greetings and the trading of mundane pleasantries when she had still been installed as mistress of the vicarage?

Oh, only the fact that their respective spouses — her husband, his wife — had both died on the same night, in the same carriage accident five years before.

Since then, she had hardly seen him. Rumor went that he had taken his daughter to London and had spent most of his time there, only returning to Langford a few times a year to make certain the place hadn't crumbled to pieces in his absence. Since then, he had abstained from church and the general events of the town while they had both carried on with their roles of widow and widower.

So what was the proper greeting when happening upon one another after such circumstances? Perhaps he did not wish to see her at all, considering the very sight of her might do nothing more than remind him of the death of his wife, the loss of the mother of his child. It was why everyone said he'd escaped to London, to try and run from the grief that lay over Langford and Barrow-in-Ashton like a heavy fog.

"I was showing her my kitten, Papa," Zora spoke up, her voice reduced to little more than a whisper now that she stood in the presence of her father.

"You've driven the entire household to distraction with your disappearance," he said, though the scold was delivered in a manner that sounded to Julia as if he'd made the speech at least a time or three before. "But we shall speak of that later." He slipped out of his coat and draped it over her shoulders, the garment nearly drowning her in its layers of wool. "Now, back up to the house with you and put yourself in order. Go!"

The girl darted away, her damp hair streaming out behind her in inky ribbons. Julia watched her depart, suddenly wishing she could shuffle away in her wake. She did not want to be there alone, alone with Mr. Halberd, trawling her mind for something to say to him that would not sound as though she was doing everything in her power to avoid speaking of the only thing she knew they had in common.

"I'll have the carriage made ready for you," he said, his eyes giving nothing away. Or perhaps there was nothing to give away. Perhaps seeing her there did nothing to dredge up memories of his wife, of what he had lost the same night she had lost her husband. "Why don't you come inside and warm yourself by the fire while you wait? You must be freezing."

"No, I..." But her arguments faltered to nothing when she realized that she was, indeed, freezing, and there was no need for her to risk her health for a show of pride or an overwhelming desire to escape his presence. "Thank you, yes. That would probably be best."

He caught the attention of one of the men in another part of the building and ordered a carriage to be prepared. After that, he began to lead her out of the stable, but when they arrived at the door he stopped short, so suddenly she almost ran into his back. "Hmmph," he said, or something very much like it, and shrugged out of his jacket.

Julia didn't understand what his intentions were at first, until he gave the jacket a brief shake and held it out to her. "It's raining harder than before," he said, as though she couldn't see the puddles forming in the yard in front of them, couldn't hear the raindrops striking the roof above their heads.

She blinked at it. At *him*. Standing there in his shirt and waist-coat, all of him slightly damp around the edges, like a wilting neck-cloth in need of some starch and a hot iron. "But you'll get wet," she told him, while in the back of her mind she wondered why she felt the need to fight against this one simple kindness.

"Yes," he agreed. "And yet I will still not be as drenched as you are. Please, Mrs. Benton," he added, when she continued to hesitate.

It wasn't the please that swayed her. It was the look in his eyes. No, not quite that. It was the way he looked at her. His jaw was set, carving out defined hollows beneath his cheekbones. A deep line cut a fissure between his brows. But his eyes — a brown like honey and chocolate swirled together — held no pity in them. He didn't look at her as though all he could see were her failures. Instead, he saw her. A woman, cold and tired and quietly dripping, in need of a jacket and short spell before a warm fire.

"Thank you."

He placed it around her shoulders, raising the collar so that it would protect her neck. His fingers brushed her jaw as he worked, a quick touch of skin against skin that he probably didn't notice. She noticed, though. And so she closed her eyes and held her breath until he dropped his hands and took a step back from her.

Julia tugged at the edges of the jacket, pulling it closed around her. It was still warm from him. She turned her head into the collar, breathing in the mingled aromas of soap and sweet cherry tobacco.

"Come along," he said, and gestured for her to follow. He didn't offer his arm. She didn't have a spare arm to accept such an offer, cocooned inside his jacket as she was. She ducked her head as she walked, only looking up again as they went indoors, through a back entrance of the house that led them past the kitchen and several other rooms set aside for the servants and the general running of the household.

She wasn't familiar enough with the layout of the house to know where he was leading her. She had been here only once before, nearly a decade ago, to a Christmas party to which she and her husband had been invited. But a Christmas party had only allowed them access to a few of the more publicly-oriented portions of the house, not the kitchen nor the servants' stairs nor the book-strewn study into which he brought her.

He turned an armchair towards the fire, a crackling blaze that almost made her forget about the ice and the rain currently assaulting the outer walls of the house. "Sit." He gestured to the chair. "At least see if you can warm yourself before I have to send you out again to the carriage."

She sat. She was still wrapped up in his jacket, the bundle of her pelisse and her reticule shoved into the chair beside her. He made no move to relieve her of her things and she did not trust the shudder of her fingers to tussle with even the knot of her bonnet's ribbons. Behind her, there was the clink of glasses before Mr. Halberd reappeared at her side, holding out a crystal tumbler filled with-

"Sherry," he said. "To stave off the worst of the chill."

"Oh." She took the glass from him, unsure of whether or not to tell him she did not make a habit of imbibing spirits. Not from any religious or moral standpoint, but merely because fine alcohol was not something one could indulge in when one adhered to a budget of only forty pounds a year.

The first sip seemed to go directly up her nose and lodge there, but she breathed slowly and allowed the next sip to settle on her tongue, to lend that subtle burn to the back of her throat as she swallowed and filled her stomach with a pleasing warmth.

Mr. Halberd stood in front of the fire, a glass in his own hand, though he seemed more content to stare into its depths rather than raise it to his mouth and take a drink.

"Thank you," she said again, just as he said-

"I'm sorry for the trouble my daughter has put you through."

"It's no trouble," she assured him, and took a third sip. She wondered what would happen if she let herself drink the entire glass, and the imagined possibilities made her clutch it between both hands and lower it to her lap instead. "I was already out on an errand for Mrs. Cochran, fetching her post for her, and..." She cleared her throat. What would Mr. Halberd care about Mrs. Cochran and her letters? "I came across her just after it began to rain. I offered to escort her home, though I will admit I..." She glanced down at her glass, reconsidering whether or not she should have that fourth sip. "I failed to recognize her, at first." *Or at all,* but she would not say that. "There was something familiar in her looks, but I did not put it together until she brought me to Langford's gates."

Mr. Halberd sighed and scratched at the groove between his brows with the side of his thumb. "Zora is..." But whatever she was, he did not seem capable of shaping it into words. "This is not the first time she's escaped from the house. Though, I will admit it's less worrying when she does it here than in London."

"Escaped?" She knew he did not mean it as it sounded, as though the child was locked away in a prison or an asylum and had managed to slip past her guards. But still the word put a stutter in her thoughts, and she watched his own expression crinkle as he realized what he had said.

"She has a tendency to wander," he explained, and set his untouched glass of sherry on the mantel above the fire. "It's not deliberate. She simply loses focus on her surroundings, I think. If one does not keep a close eye on her, she'll venture halfway across the county without pausing to look back."

Julia ducked her head and hid a small smile. "Children can be like that. To be honest, I suspect many adults still possess the same trait, only we have more freedom to roam around as we please and no one thinks anything of it."

"Perhaps you are right."

He made no move to further the conversation after that. Julia kept her attention directed towards her knees and the floor, where the hem of her skirt had begun to send up small tendrils of vapor as the fire drew up the moisture from the fabric.

A light knock on the partially open door broke the awkward silence that had sprung up between them. A manservant stood there, looking only at Mr. Halberd, as though Julia was not even present in the room. "The carriage, sir. It's ready."

"Ah, good." His relief was a palpable thing. Julia wanted nothing more than to withdraw into herself at such a reaction, that a mere ten minutes in her presence was something from which he was clearly so eager to retreat.

She set her unfinished drink on the nearest table and slid forward in her seat to stand up. Before she could do more than place her hands on the arms of the chair, Mr. Halberd held out his own hand to her, palm turned upwards.

It would be rude to refuse. And then the questions remained of why her instinct was to refuse him in the first place. But she placed her hand in his, his skin so warm against her chilled fingers she nearly pulled away for fear of being scalded. As soon as she was on her feet, she began to shrug out of his jacket to give it back to him.

He shook his head. "Keep it for now. You can return it at your leisure."

At her leisure. She almost laughed at that, as though she was a fine gentlewoman with nothing better to do than to loll about on overly upholstered furniture and send servants scurrying away to return borrowed jackets that smelled too much like their owners.

"I don't know when I will see you again," she said, and let the jacket slip off her shoulders before she handed it back to him. "But thank you, Mr. Halberd."

She gathered up her pelisse and her reticule, carrying them in a bundle as she followed the servant out of the study and towards the front of the house. With her shoulders rounded forward, her chin tucked down against her chest, she watched the damp tips of her boots appear and disappear again beneath the stained hem of her gown. The carriage was already outside and waiting for her, the poor driver hidden beneath hat and coat and scarf, a collection of wool and knitted things hunched against the weather.

"Mrs. Benton?"

Julia stopped before she stepped out the door and onto the first stair leading down to the drive. Mr. Halberd came up beside her, the breadth of his shoulders easily filling up the rest of the doorway. "Yes?" she prompted when he did not speak again right away.

He hesitated. She would wonder about that hesitation later, if it occured because he was reluctant to say what was inside his head, or because he had stopped her before he had fully considered what he wished to say to her. "I, uh... I wanted to thank you for your care with Zora this afternoon. She does not take kindly to many people, but she appears to already hold you in high esteem."

Julia chuckled. "I'm not sure how you can tell from so short a time of seeing her with me."

"She showed you her kitten, did she not? Ellen, is it?"

"Ah, but I'm not certain she's fully decided on Ellen yet. Boadicea may still be a contender."

"Well." Was that a touch of a smile at the corners of his mouth, or merely a trick of the light? "She does not introduce her kitten to everyone. Apparently she has appointed you as someone special in her small circle of acquaintances."

Despite the dampness of her clothing, the chill seeping through the layers of wool and chemise and stockings to reach her skin, a soft warmth spread through her at those words, like a flame licking outwards from her abdomen.

"And I wanted to apologize to you," Mr. Halberd continued,

this time speaking with his gaze directed downwards, as though the scuffed edge of the step had become the most fascinating thing in the immediate vicinity. "For any brusqueness I displayed when I came upon you and Zora in the stables. I was... I was caught off guard by your appearance there, and I hope you did not take my surprise for incivility."

"No, not at all. I doubt you have many older widows tramping about on your property, so I understand if I caused any confusion."

She looked away from him then, unsure of what else to say. A history lay thick between them, and she could not honestly class Mr. Halberd as much more than an acquaintance, as far as their past interactions had gone. "So," she said, because there were no other words within reach that came along to help her. "Thank you, again."

She moved to walk out beyond the shelter of the house, only a few quick steps needed to cross that small portion of the drive and step up into the carriage that sat waiting for her. Mr. Halberd came up from behind, holding an umbrella over her head. At the carriage, he again offered his hand to her as she climbed into the vehicle. And there was his bare skin against hers, the warmth of his fingers spreading across her palm like water spilled from a jug.

It should not have affected her, she knew. It was surely only a courtesy on his part, basic manners put on display. Had she been without the touch of another person for so long that a few brushes of his fingers against her jaw, her hand, should imprint themselves on her skin as though she'd been burned?

Ah, but it wasn't as simple as that. She looked at him through the carriage window after the door was shut, his face and features blurred by the rain-streaked glass. Yet her memories were clearer, her mind slipping back a dozen years to when she had first been introduced to him, had first laid eyes on him. Not in church, but at the vicarage, when Mr. Halberd and his wife had come to welcome the new vicar to the village.

Julia remembered Mrs. Halberd. A beautiful creature. Julia had always been aware of the loveliness of others in comparison to herself. It was a practice she had tried to fight, that constant urge to set herself against other women and discover where she placed. Mrs. Halberd had been all that was kind and welcoming, her smile bright and her eyes glittering as she asked questions about their wedding, about Julia's plans for the roses that grew on either side of the front gate, about recipes that Mrs. Halberd promised to have her cook send on to the vicarage for them to sample.

She was like a light walking into the vicarage, settling on their threadbare chairs as though she had wandered into a palace. Even Frederick had come out of his shell in Mrs. Halberd's presence, discussing his ideas for that week's sermon and listening eagerly as she pointed out which biblical excerpts and verses would best accompany his chosen topic.

But Julia had been flustered at the unplanned arrival of their guests. They had hired no maid yet, and Julia had taken the full weight of the cooking and housekeeping upon herself until they acquired help. And so she had been in the kitchen, clad in an apron covered in a mingling of flour and lard and dirt, her hair twisted up into a serviceable rather than fashionable style, her gown something she had plucked out of her wardrobe because a few more stains wouldn't mar what was already halfway towards ruined.

There had been no time to go upstairs and change. No time to even remove her apron, as the knot had stuck and all of her frantic pulling at it had only tightened it further. She stood beside her husband, offering tea when she could not recall if they had purchased any yet, or if the tea service still boasted its full set of cups after their move. Mrs. Halberd had behaved with perfect grace, as though the prospect of tea with neither tea nor cups was exactly what she had wanted and nothing more.

Julia had escaped to the kitchen in an effort to assemble a tray from the few things she had in the pantry. She had no desire to return to the parlor again, to stand there in her plain, frayed gown while Mrs. Halberd twinkled like a star dropped down from the firmament. It was the jealous, bitter side of her coming through, the side that always reared its head when she was tired or anxious or beset with worries. She had only been a wife for a few weeks, wed to a man she had accepted only because she had been too old and too desperate to wait for someone she might eventually come to love.

And she had told herself she would try to love her husband, while understanding that those things could take time. Even as she had looked at Mr. Halberd as he entered the vicarage, as she had wondered what it would be like to have the ability to flit and flutter like Mrs. Halberd and gain someone such as him for a partner instead.

Julia pressed her head back against the seat, hoping the jostling of the carriage would shake her free from her thoughts. Old thoughts, they were. Ones that had circled around and around inside her head until they'd been worn down to the smoothness of a pebble. And perhaps soon, with more tumbling and more wearing, they would disappear entirely. And she would cease to think of what could have been, how her life might have turned out differently, when indeed no such privilege as options or choice had ever been available to her.

Three

The schoolhouse was built from a converted barn that sat at the edge of the vicarage's property. The current vicar, Mr. Parker, taught his more esteemed pupils in his study, those few boys that came from both affluent or minorly-titled families, the ones who would need their grounding in Latin and declensions and a fair bit of history and arithmetic before they were bundled off to a proper educational institution where their places in the world would be carved out for them in those hallowed halls.

Twice a week, the local boys from the village, the farmers' and tradesmens' sons, bundled into the damp, drafty schoolhouse for a basic education in reading, writing, and numbers. Everything that was necessary for running a farm or a business, for totting up figures and filling out sales orders.

And on Sundays, Julia taught the village's daughters.

There were not many to teach. Not that the village boasted a remarkable disproportion of young ladies to young men, but rather that the majority of families did not believe their daughters to be in need of an education beyond what the tutelage of their — mostly — illiterate mothers could provide.

Julia sat on a bench with Lilith, one of the older girls who had started to come for lessons only because her younger sisters were now grown enough to help with the various chores around the house, giving her leave to come to school for an hour every week and practice her reading.

"Every time you arrive at a word you do not understand, I want you to write it out on your slate, hmm?"

Lilith nodded, her bright, freckled face already screwing up in concentration for the task ahead.

There would be no sending the girls home with additional work to tackle during the week. Most of the poorer families did not own books, had few means of practicing their letters over and over for memorization. Sometimes there was not even a family Bible, the sort bearing the names of their ancestors scrawled down in increasingly faded ink on the front pages. So their studies had to be done during that single hour when Julia had them in her care. Primers and prayer books and slates were passed around, the half dozen girls who made up her class sitting together on one bench at the front of the room, closest to the pot-bellied stove and its radiating heat.

"Mrs. Benton!" A younger girl seated at the end of the bench raised her hand, fingers waggling.

"Oh, Esther! Your spelling words. I nearly forgot! Let's see how we fare with those today, shall we?"

Julia took the primer from Esther and stood facing her so the girl could not see the words. "Now, spell 'fountain'."

"F... um, O... U..."

A noise at the back of the room dragged Julia's gaze away from Esther as she forged her way through 'N' and 'T'.

Mr. Halberd stood there, just inside the door, a broad smudge of black in his layered greatcoat and hat. There was sunlight in the room, pockets of it coming in through a few small windows spaced at intervals. He raised his hand to remove his hat as he stepped sideways and away from the door, into one of those pale rays of sunlight that limned him in cold illumination.

"... I ... N," Esther finished, displaying a grin that sported no less than three missing teeth.

"Very good. Only nine more to go. Next is 'establish'."

She would make him wait until her hour with the girls was up. She had so little time with them already, and that was taking into account the fact that a few of her pupils could not make it every week, their responsibilities at home sometimes preventing their parents from sparing them."

"Wipe your slates before you leave!" she reminded them as the clock ticked into a new hour and she declared their class finished for the day. "And Kit, don't forget your hat!"

The fair-haired Kit grabbed her squashed straw bonnet from a peg on the wall and dashed around Mr. Halberd as she ran to catch up with the rest of the girls.

And then Julia was alone with him.

Mr. Halberd closed the door behind the nimble Kit. To keep out the chill, Julia reminded herself. But still she looked at the rows of benches between them as though they were bulwarks erected in her defense.

"Mr. Halberd," she said, pleased at how calm and easy her voice sounded to her own ears. "What brings you here today?"

He took a few steps forward. She watched his gloved hands as he slowly turned the brim of his hat between them. "My daughter."

Julia waited for him to elaborate. When he did not, she moved along the front bench and gathered up the scattering of slates abandoned there. "Is something wrong? Is she unwell?" It had been three days since she had met Zora in the village and accompanied her back to Langford. Had the poor girl caught a chill since her jaunt in the inclement weather?

"No, she's... I mean, she's quite well. But she is why I'm here."

Julia set the slates on a table in the corner, along with the small stubs of chalk she did not want to lose. Supplies were expensive, and most of them were purchased from her own meager savings. She turned to him with her hands buried in her apron, wiping the chalk and the smears of graphite — along with the agitation — from her fingers. "Well, Mr. Halberd?"

He took another step towards her, out of the shaft of sunlight that had drawn him as an imposing figure only a moment ago. Now, he appeared to be just a man, his dark hair flattened from the weight of his hat, the lines at the corners of his eyes and mouth carving deeper as his jaw set. "You live in the village. I believe you rent a set of rooms there?"

It was hardly a question. "Yes. From Mrs. Cochran."

His gaze darted away from her, skimming the corners of the schoolroom as if he might find something of interest there, hidden behind the stacked benches and crates of old books and a few buckets of coal set in from the weather. "You were fortunate then, to find a place to stay after the death of your husband. But you do not have family nearby?"

"Not nearby, no." She swallowed and lowered her head before his attention could find its way back to her. "And I had no wish to inflict myself on them, the poor and recently widowed relation. At least here, as things are, I feel I can retain some small portion of freedom. Or at least the illusion of it."

The truth spilled from her lips before she could stop it. And so she breathed, and she smiled, and she looked up again to find Mr. Halberd watching her.

"I must admit," he said, and gave his hat another turn. "I came here today believing I already knew how best to phrase my request, but..." He cleared his throat, his lips tightening into a line so thin they almost disappeared. "Zora has reached an age when she needs someone. More than a mere nurse, and I never found her a new one ever since we left London. No, I've been remiss in seeing to my daughter's care, and I realize now she is in need of a governess, or something very like."

"And you wished to approach me concerning this matter because...?" Julia left the question to hang in the air between them.

"I know the role of a governess can be repellant to some." He spoke slowly, deliberately, and Julia wondered if this was the part of his speech that had already been composed in his head. "It occupies an unusual place between family and servant, and it is also a paid position, so some would denigrate it as employment. But you've already shown that you're not hesitant to work," he said, gesturing around the empty schoolroom. "And you say you have no family here, no one who might argue against you taking on such a position in a household."

No family here...

His words hurt more than she thought they would. But then he couldn't know how much his words could harm her, could remind her of the family she had never been able to provide to her husband while he had been alive. She eased the tension out of her shoulders and reached behind her back to fuss with the knot of her apron. "You wish for me to be Zora's governess?"

"You are educated, are you not? You are... I mean, you were a vicar's wife. So I suppose reading, writing, embroidery... Do you speak any languages?"

"French," she admitted. Though as the wife of a vicar in a small English village, it had never done her any good. "And some Latin."

"Music? Drawing?" His eyebrows rose higher with each word, and she began to suspect he was simply pulling items out of thin air. "I know a few of those things are usually required as well."

This had to be one of the strangest conversations Julia had ever taken part in. With a slight shake of her head, she hung up her apron and took her pelisse down from its peg. "I play the pianoforte, yes. I wanted to play the harp, but my youngest sister, well..." She bit off that tidbit of sibling rivalry before it could advance any further. "And I draw, embroider, all of those things.

29

With varying degrees of success," she added, before it could sound like she was boasting.

"And you're not..." He tilted his head to one side as he regarded her. "You're not about to be married again, are you? No suitors clamoring for your hand?"

She couldn't decide whether to laugh outright at the notion of someone seeking her out for a wife, or to take offense at the surety in his tone that she had no plans to marry again in the near future. "No suitors, Mr. Halberd. None at all."

He blew out a breath. "I apologize if the question sounds officious, but I'm reluctant to bring someone into the household only to have them leave again a short time later in order to be married."

She smiled to show him she was not perturbed. "I understand."

"Then you will consider it?" He took a step forward. There was still half the room between them — the schoolhouse was not a small room — but Julia felt the space slipping away from her as though the floor had tilted beneath her feet. "Zora needs someone to teach her, to exert a healthy influence on her. I am not home nearly as much as I would like, and without her mother—" He cut himself off suddenly, his words tumbling away from him, leaving an echo like rocks falling down a cliff.

"I will give you time to think it over," he continued. His voice, she noticed, had taken on that same edge of gruffness it had exhibited when he'd first encountered her and Zora in the stable at Langford. "As much time as you need."

He bowed stiffly then and retreated a step towards the door. "I'll not keep you, Mrs. Benton. Good day."

He turned and walked away from her. He was almost to the door before she found her voice again, lodged as it was beneath a knot in her throat.

"Yes," she said, the single word sounding through the room like a rifle shot.

Mr. Halberd's progress halted, his fingers still reaching for the door, his hat still dangling from his other hand. When he turned, his lips were slightly parted, his brow furrowed over eyes that seemed to have grown darker over the last minute.

Julia swallowed. "I accept." She did not need time to think it over. She did not want to think it over. Thinking would lead to weighing her options. When all she could see was an opportunity for change, one she knew she needed to grasp as soon as possible. "But on one condition."

The line between his brows smoothed out. But he licked his lips and he batted his hat against his thigh. "And what is that?"

"That I continue to teach here. Every Sunday. As long as I have pupils who wish to learn, I will not desert them."

Her voice did not shake. It would have, she thought, years ago. When she had been so determined to be a good and compliant wife, and hopefully a mother-

"I wouldn't have asked you to stop teaching, Mrs. Benton. I hope you did not mistake me for someone who would have required you to leave your post here."

But she did not fully know what sort of person he was, really. Only that he had lost his wife in the same accident that had taken her husband, that they had existed on the periphery of each other's lives for a dozen years. Acquaintances at best, she told herself. A nod to one another at church, or if they passed each other in town. A rare occurrence even then, as Julia's circle of society had shrunken to nonexistent dimensions after Frederick's death, and Mr. Halberd had spent the majority of the last few years in London with his daughter. And yet...

She wanted to think well of him. There he stood, offering her a position as a caretaker to his child. And who was she to gain his attention? Who was her family? What connections did she have? Nothing worth garnering notice, at least as far as the previous four decades of her life had demonstrated. And she was poor, that greatest of social sins. And she would be poorer still as the years went along. Fading into a creature who might finally acquire a dose or two of charity from those around her in the twilight of her life.

"Thank you," she said, suddenly aware that his offer of employment could be construed as an act of charity towards her. A way of making amends for her loss, though she knew he was not at fault for what had happened that night, five years before. Unless he could claim power over the very skies and had ordered the ice and snow to fall heavily upon that narrow road. "I expect this means..." Her fingers tangled together after she slipped into her pelisse. "Am I to live at Langford?"

It hadn't crossed her mind until that moment, that he would expect her to move into the great house on the hill. A sudden worry struck her, that she would be giving up some of her independence with such a move, but then she was a poor widow of no account. Whatever independence she thought she'd achieved after the death of her husband no doubt measured at a higher level in her mind than in reality.

"I would anticipate it, yes." His eyes widened, and Julia considered that until that very moment, he had neglected to consider the fact of her living at Langford, as well. "I suppose I shall have to arrange for your things to be brought to the house."

"Well, I don't have much." She tried to laugh, and hated how forced it sounded. "Probably one fair-sized trunk should be enough." And she pressed her lips together into a tight line, holding back a slight prickling behind her eyes at the thought of how her entire life could be packed into a single trunk and trundled across the countryside.

"I will have a room made ready for you and alert the staff about having another person living beneath our roof. Mrs. Holland, my housekeeper... she will manage everything, I'm sure." He lifted his hat, still in his hand, and looked at it as though he'd entirely forgotten its existence while he had been speaking with her. "And I'll speak to Zora as well, let her know that she will be welcoming a new governess soon."

He settled his hat on his head while Julia fiddled with the buttons of her pelisse. She realized that he might expect her to leave the schoolhouse at the same time as him, might expect to offer his arm to her or even walk her back to Mrs. Cochran's, all behavior typical of a gentleman. So she ignored her bonnet hanging on its peg and instead turned around and walked back to the table where the primers were stacked. "When do you wish for me to come to Langford?" she asked, and sorted through the thin books in a way that she hoped made it seem very important that she should sort them.

Mr. Halberd tipped his head an inch to one side. She noticed he did that, when he was thinking. "Three days? I can send a carriage for you on Wednesday morning."

"Yes, that will do."

"Wednesday, then." He raised his hand to the brim of his hat. "Good day, Mrs. Benton."

"Good day, Mr. Halberd."

She watched him leave. It wasn't until he had stepped through the door and closed it behind him that she realized she had been holding her breath, waiting for him to be gone. She abandoned the primers then, checked the remnants of the fire in the stove, and plucked up her bonnet and fit it on her head. She went through all the motions of leaving for the day as if she was striking things off a list, even though she had done all of it so many times before she should not have had to think about it.

But her mind was occupied with too many new things for the mundane activities of her everyday life to take their proper place in the forefront of her thoughts. She would be living at Langford in only three days' time. She would be in charge of the care and education of a child she had only met a few days before, a child she would no doubt be expected to raise through to adulthood.

A daunting prospect, that. And she would be living beneath the same roof as Mr. Halberd, a fact she saved for last as it was the one most likely to send her racing out the door to catch up with the man himself, to refuse his offer and tell him that she couldn't...

She couldn't...

She tied the ribbons of her bonnet beneath her chin, tight enough to make the sides of her jaw ache. She was being nonsensical, she realized. The very true, very real facts of the matter were that Isadora Halberd was in need of a governess, and Julia could not live in Mrs. Cochran's cramped upper rooms forever. She would have steady employment, steady income, a fine home in which to live, and perhaps most importantly, she would have company to keep her from sinking into the quagmire of her own thoughts. A young girl and her father and a houseful of servants. People to talk to, and something with which to occupy her days apart from her scant hour with her Sunday pupils.

The air outside the schoolhouse was crisp and bright, like an early apple just picked from its branch. Julia blinked at the onslaught of sunlight, even the brim of her bonnet failing to adequately shield her face from the full brunt of the cloudless sky.

She would walk home, she told herself, sketching out the rest of her day as though she was paving the very road in front of her feet. She would begin to sort through some of her belongings, see what should be kept or discarded, what was worth having transported all the way to Langford. And no, it would not be much. She had brought so little to her marriage with Frederick, having had to cobble together a dowry from what had to be shared among three sisters and an inheritance that would go to none of them upon their father's death.

Ah, but enough of that.

Three days, and today was already waning. And then she would be living at Langford, looking after Zora.

She quickened her pace, the chill in the air reminding her that she hadn't eaten anything since breakfast.

Three days...

And despite all of the tasks to be done during that time, the lesson plans for her new charge that she should already be outlining inside her head, the packing and speaking to Mrs. Cochran about leaving her rooms, Julia found she could concentrate on little more than a tall gentleman standing in a shaft of sunlight, the dark blue of his gaze shining almost black as jet as he watched her.

Four

Wednesday morning came, and the carriage arrived at ten o'clock. Julia had been ready for it. Indeed, she had been ready for the last two days, living out of her single trunk and two small bags. Everything else had already been packed and sorted since Sunday evening, ready to be carried downstairs the moment the servants from Langford appeared.

And they announced their arrival with a knock on the door, two smart footmen climbing up the narrow staircase to help her carry down her things and load them onto the carriage. Julia kept to the background, putting on her bonnet and gloves, making her farewells to Mrs. Cochran. Mrs. Cochran gifted her with a small basket of cakes for the drive, as though she was departing on a long journey across the country and not merely shifting her things from one side of the parish to the other.

She sat in the carriage surrounded by fine upholstery, by velvet curtains framing the windows. She had been in this same carriage only a few days before, but there was a different aspect to it now, a feeling as if she belonged in it, even if the sensation was only a fleeting one. Mr. Halberd was not the wealthiest gentleman in Lancashire, but he was the wealthiest gentleman in all of Barrow-in-Ashton and its immediate surroundings, and so of course his carriage would be outfitted with fine upholstery and fine curtains. Of course he would even have a carriage to upholster and curtain in the first place.

She was sure there were people of greater means who would look down on the small, faded patch on one corner of the seat, the scuff marks on the floor as evidence that his wealth was nothing of a remarkable sort. But as Julia's upbringing had never been marked by extravagance, and her years as Frederick's wife had always included strict adherence to a budget, to ride regularly in a private carriage was a luxury she had not often enjoyed over the previous four decades of her life.

It seemed as though she had hardly settled in her seat before they'd already left the bulk of the village behind them. Up the long drive to Langford, the gravel crunching beneath the wheels of the carriage while Julia forced herself to sit still, her hands clasped tight around her basket of cakes, her gaze pinned to the view outside the window as the house came into view.

The same gravel ground beneath the soles of her shoes as she stepped down from the carriage. Her arrival had ignited a small storm of activity, the footmen unloading her trunk while another servant came to unhook the horses from the carriage. And amid all of that, an older woman stepped out from the rear entrance of the house to greet her.

Or rather... to stand and survey the work of the servants before her gaze cut towards Julia with the swiftness of a scythe.

"Mrs. Benton?"

The questioning tone seemed superfluous, as Julia doubted the carriage had been sent into the village multiple times that morning to pick up frumpy widows and bring them back to Langford. "Yes," she replied, and took a few steps forward. "And you are...?"

"Mrs. Holland."

Right. The housekeeper.

There was an undercurrent to the moment as both women

faced each other. There had been a shift, Julia realized, since the last time she had been to Langford, only the week before. Then, Julia had been a guest of sorts, the daughter of a gentleman and the widow of the former vicar. Now, she arrived as a governess. An employee. And worse yet, one who would hover between the worlds of paid subordinate and member of the family without being fully accepted into either sphere.

And in the flash of Mrs. Holland's eyes, Julia saw that same knowledge come to life in the housekeeper's thoughts. She would not be invited to the drawing room for a round of tea and cakes and idle gossip. She was not a guest. Nor was she a part of the family, no matter how close she would undoubtedly be to Zora over the upcoming years. Even looking at the house, she noticed that she had been driven around to the rear of the building. To the servants' entrance.

Julia raised her chin an inch and set her shoulders, despite the gathering of sweat on her palms and the pounding of her heart like a child's toy drum behind her sternum.

"I am the housekeeper here at Langford," Mrs. Holland said, her own chest puffing up as if to assert herself at the top of the household. It was a superfluous statement, but she seemed determined to wear her position like a sash across her chest, greeting Julia as though she saw her as a usurper. "I am not sure how much Mr. Halberd has told you about the running of the house or the schedule we adhere to, but you will always come to me if and when you are in any need of assistance."

Julia did not know what was expected of her. Did the housekeeper wish for her to cower beneath the older woman's age and experience? Or would Mrs. Holland prefer for her to assert herself as someone on equal standing? There would be politics here, but Julia had no interest in treading the maneuvers of some silent war between the upper and lower levels of the house.

She had come here for employment, to help Zora, and also for something she had not been privileged enough to experience for some time: a purpose.

"Come along," Mrs. Holland gestured her forward. "I will see to it that you are properly warmed up by the fire while they take your things to your room." She spared another glance for the servants then, her gaze narrowing on the trunk they had already unloaded from the carriage. "Is that everything you've brought?"

"Yes," Julia said, and as pleasantly as she could manage. "Only the one trunk." She owned only a few gowns, a few books, a few personal possessions. It was an odd thing, how each time she left one home for another, she seemed to slough away more of her worldly goods until she suspected another decade or so of living would see her with nothing but the gown on her back and a single, dog-eared book tucked beneath her arm.

She was led through the same back corridors of the house Mr. Halberd had taken her through the week before, but instead of veering off towards the family's rooms, Mrs. Holland escorted her to a small sitting room tucked away at the end of the hall, lit by a single high window and a desultory fire crackling limply in a narrow fireplace.

The housekeeper's room, Julia guessed, taking in the mixture of old and mismatched furniture, a writing desk stacked with well-wor ledgers and neat lists, and small bits of comfort tucked in wherever they would fit.

"We do not yet have a full complement of staff here at Langford," Mrs. Holland said after they were both seated in front of the fire, Julia still holding onto her basket of cakes as though it was a lifeline. There was no offer of tea, she noticed. No offer of anything stronger, either, though she doubted the housekeeper would dole out glasses of sherry at half past ten in the morning. "Mr. Halberd spends the majority of his days out with his steward, seeing to the improvements that need to be made to the estate since he has been away in London. He'll often be gone before his daughter has risen and sometimes does not return until well after dark. We do not entertain yet, and we have only a small kitchen staff. Most of the rooms are still closed up, so if you came here expecting balls and dinners to be held every few weeks as they were in Mrs. Halberd's time, then I am afraid you will find yourself to be sorely disappointed."

Julia tried not to let her astonishment show in her face. Did Mrs. Holland truly believe her to have taken on the position as Zora's governess in order to gain some sort of proximity to a more glittering style of life?

"I expected nothing of the kind," Julia remarked, while keeping her breathing even. "I was taken on as Miss Halberd's governess, and so I was not anticipating any additional frills or extravagance, as you might put it."

Mrs. Holland's expression grew tight, as if someone had sprinkled her with starch and pressed a hot iron to her features.

Julia wondered if the housekeeper had thought she would be a quiet, biddable sort; the former vicar's wife left to molder away in her small set of rooms at the top of Mrs. Cochran's house. The previous years of her life had set such an example, all the way back to her childhood when, as the eldest daughter, she had recognized acquiescence as bowing to the responsibilities laid on her shoulders in that role.

But despite the fact less than an hour had passed since Julia had left Mrs. Cochran's, a strange feeling of liberty stole over her. She was glad to hear that Mr. Halberd spent most of his daylight hours away from the house. It would give her more freedom, she hoped, with Zora's education and care. And the less she saw of him overall...

"Miss Halberd has been without a nurse for three months," Mrs. Holland continued, breaking into Julia's thoughts. "The girl needs proper looking after. She has been given too much independence, far too much. I do not envy you your task. But if you can take her in hand, all the better. She will make a fine match when she is older, especially considering the dowry her father plans to settle on her."

Julia bit down on the inside of her cheek to keep her teeth from grinding themselves down to dust. It was crass to speak of Zora's value, as though she was a horse or a plot of land to be portioned off and sold. As though there was nothing else of worth about the girl beyond what she could provide to the world as a wife and potential mother.

"Well, let us see about your room," Mrs. Holland said, and rose from her chair, indicating that Julia should follow.

She was led up the servants' stairs, a narrow climb that twisted steadily upwards and smelled faintly of damp. The housekeeper took her to a room at the back of the house, past furniture hiding beneath dust cloths and shadowed portraits bearing the haze of a half dozen years' worth of dust and smoke on their surfaces. "You will be warmer here in the coming months. The front of the house takes too much effort to heat, and better for you to be nearer the nursery and all of Miss Halberd's things."

Mrs. Holland opened a door at the end of the corridor. Despite the dimness behind her, the room Julia stepped into was suffused with light. The curtains had been drawn back, and a bright fire crackled as if the flames themselves wished to welcome her.

The room was larger than all of the space she had rented from Mrs. Cochran, and even twice as large as the bedroom she had shared with her husband at the vicarage.

"I will leave you to wash up and settle your things how you would like them. Miss Halberd is in the nursery, and you may attend to her as soon as you are ready. Dinner will be served at five o'clock, though I am sure you will be comfortable taking it in the nursery with Miss Halberd, as that is where she has most of her meals when her father is not at home."

And that was all before Mrs. Holland stepped out of the room, shutting the door behind her.

"Well." Julia turned around slowly, surveying the room again without Mrs. Holland's gaze upon her. She walked to one of the windows — because there were two windows to choose between, such extravagance! — and looked out across the grounds. She knew the dips and hollows of the land, the streams that threaded through the trees and flowed between the various fields stretching off into the distance towards Barrow-in-Ashton. They were the unchanged borders of her world, her life for the previous dozen years.

Yet amid all that sameness, so much of her life seemed to be in constant flux. She had come here as a new wife, had spent her years at the vicarage attempting to run a household and build a family. But the family had never arrived as planned. And then her husband had been taken from her. For the next five years, she had scraped through her existence, renting her small rooms and teaching her small class every week at the schoolhouse. And here she was, over four decades into her life and at the start of another change; now a governess, set to mold the life of a little girl into what society would expect her to be. A wife. A mother. And little else.

Julia exhaled slowly, her breath blasting onto the glass and leaving a cloud of vapor behind.

So, what of her, then? What of Mrs. Julia Benton? She was no longer a wife. She had brought no living children into the world. Had she failed as a woman?

She was not young anymore, either. Especially not according to the standards of local society, a sort that prided itself on pink-cheeked maidens and lusty young farmers. But she was still here, with the same hills fading from green to blue in the distance, the same rocks worn smooth by the same run of water tumbling over them. Should she have been allowed so many chances in her life? Or was it rather a symptom of having made so many mistakes that fate would not cease giving her opportunities to rectify them?

She pushed away from the window, her eyes blinking away a

burning at the edges she wouldn't allow to progress into any further show of emotion. She saw her trunk sitting at the foot of the bed, but she had no desire to unpack yet, to sort through her meager things and scatter them about the room to mark it as her own. Later, she told herself, before she opened the bedroom door and went off in search of her charge.

* * *

Zora was not to be found in the nursery.

Julia had no wish to alert any of the servants about the girl's sudden talent for invisibility, so instead she granted herself leave to wander through the house, checking under furniture and dust cloths and inside closets in case Zora had taken to hiding away somewhere. Then, she remembered the kitten in the stable, and so Julia donned a shawl and went outside.

But she didn't have to go as far as the stables. Julia spotted her not far from the house, just beyond one of the outbuildings. In a tree. Dangling upside-down with her legs hooked over a branch, her skirt bunched up around her knees.

Julia said nothing as she approached. But Zora saw her, and with the wiry strength of her arms and torso alone, she pulled herself up to grab the branch and swung herself down to land in a heap of skirts and pinafore on the mossy ground between the tree's roots.

"Mrs. Benton." Zora straightened up and executed a flawless curtsy, as though she was being presented at court and not standing in the dirt, her gown and her face streaked with mud and grass stains. "Papa says you're to be my governess now?"

"Yes, Miss Halberd." And she bit her lips. "Zora," she corrected, and watched the girl's face lighten with a smile. "Your father has declared that you are grown too old for a nurse. You're to begin a proper education, one better suited to your status and future prospects."

Zora shifted her weight, her body twisting from side to side while her feet remained planted on the ground. "You mean, that I'm to grow up and marry a rich gentleman and converse with him in French while I paint a watercolor of a barn?"

Julia choked on her next breath. She covered it with a cough behind her hand, then cleared her throat and moved further beneath the tree. "What makes you say such a thing?"

Zora shrugged as she plucked a small twig from the ends of her hair, curling dark and tangled over her shoulder. "I hear them talk about me. The servants, I mean. And Mrs. Holland."

Ah, the precarious existence of a child, to be spoken about as though one was nothing more than a mere piece of furniture in a room, rather than a living, thinking person.

"That is one future you could have, yes." Unless she wanted to grow up to be labeled as a spinster or cloister herself away in a nunnery, marriage to a rich gentleman would be the first choice foisted upon her once she came of age. And so Julia tried to think of other lives Zora could lead, anything more than the slow whittling away of herself until she was shaped into the young lady society would expect her to be.

Julia lowered her head, a rush of warmth flooding her cheeks at the fear she was allowing her own experience with marriage to color her opinion of the union in general. She knew there was happiness to be found there, for some people. Her own mother and father had been content enough together. Though if contentment was the most a couple could aspire to, she wondered why marriage had proliferated in as many cultures as it had.

"Will we begin today?" Zora did not look up as she asked, instead bending down to watch the progress of a caterpillar on one of the tree roots at her feet.

The rapid change in subject left Julia reeling for a moment. "Tomorrow, I think. After breakfast." There were no benches or seats beneath any of the trees, so she drew her skirt forward around her legs and sat down on the thickest patch of moss she could find.

"Though we could make a bit of a beginning now, if you'd like. You can tell me something about yourself, something you believe I might not already know."

"And will you tell me about yourself, as well?"

And there was the rub. "Of course!" Julia smiled, despite the tightening in her abdomen as she considered what truths an eight year old girl might wish for her to divulge. "As much as is polite to share," she added, hoping to stake some boundaries around their impending conversation.

Zora walked in circles around the base of another tree, one hand gripping the trunk, her arm stretched taut as she moved. "Will there be lots of reading? I don't much care for reading. At least not any of the books Miss Trask used to give me. All of them lessons about naughty children being pinched and scolded and set up as an example against all of the naughty things they'd done."

Julia raised her eyebrows but did her best to hide her smile. "And what would you prefer to read about?"

"King Arthur and his knights," came the reply without hesitation. She had begun to walk faster around the tree, nearly spinning around the entire trunk in only a single step. "Lancelot and Guinevere. The Lady of the Lake. Oh, and Merlin, of course."

"Of course," Julia nodded.

"I quite like birds, as well," Zora said, now grasping the trunk with both hands and arching backwards to peer up through the branches. "Have you ever climbed a tree to see a bird up close? A baby starling in its nest or a robin's egg when it's about to hatch?"

"Not since I was about your age," Julia admitted. She looked up at the tree under which she sat, eyeing the spindly branches near the top with no small amount of trepidation. "I'm afraid most trees would fail to support me now."

"And I have drawings, too. Do you draw?" Zora stood up straight again and studied Julia from the other side of the trunk. "I hope you do."

"A little," Julia confessed. Though what she did not confess was that she had not picked up charcoal or paint since Frederick had died. Those things had all been packed away and then lost in the move from the vicarage to Mrs. Cochran's house, and she had not since found herself in a strong enough financial position to see them replaced.

"Oh, that's what everyone says." Zora let out a sigh as she knelt down and began plucking at rocks where they were lodged between the roots of the tree. "They draw a little or play a little or speak a little French or Italian. You'll have to show me what you've done and then I can tell if you only draw 'a little'." She picked up another small rock and tossed it up above her head, snagging it out of the air again with a practiced snap of her hand. "But I've done a sketch of an owl, one I found up in the hayrick. They're difficult to hear, you know, when they're flying? They have soft feathers all down their legs and along the edges of their wings, all so they can come out at night and hunt without being heard by their prey."

Julia listened with interest as Zora continued on with the subject of owls before she leapt to a tale about a sheep that had stranded itself in a stream a few weeks before, the rescue requiring her father and a half dozen other men to wade in and coax the poor, frightened animal out again.

A curious mind, that was what Zora possessed. And one that bounded from subject to subject at a dizzying pace. She would be a bluestocking in no time if left to her own devices, though Julia couldn't decide if that would be a hindrance or a help to the girl's future success in life.

Because success for the daughter of a gentleman would no doubt be measured in the quality of husband she could obtain, in how many children — sons, especially — she could provide. Whether or not the daughter in question was knowledgeable about nocturnal birds or King Arthur's Court was irrelevant. Only her potential for breeding along with her fortune would be taken into account. As though she was an animal sent to market for purchase.

"We can begin with studying birds, if you would like," Julia ventured to say when there was finally a lull in the conversation. "Perhaps there are even some books in your father's library that would help us with our studies."

Zora began circling the tree again. "What sort of stories did you like when you were a girl?"

Julia tucked her ankles further beneath the edge of her gown and pulled her shawl more tightly around her shoulders. A breeze shivered through the branches above them, and while Zora did not seem to notice the chill, Julia felt it sinking into the muscles of her thighs and lower back. "Any stories that had to do with horses," she said with a light shrug. "I was absolutely obsessed with them for a time. I even went so far as to beg my father for a pony — an extravagance we could not afford — and when my dream was thwarted, I began to paint and draw and read about them as much as possible, as though I could will one into being with the combined strength of my imagination and my watercolors."

She laughed at the memory, at how simple one's desires could be at such a young age. "I was also determined to learn to ride. And I did, when I was older. But our only horse was an old mare fit for little more than plodding walks and pulling a wagon laden with hay or wood for the fires."

"Do you still ride?" Zora had ceased her spinning again, but her fingertips continued to slide over the bark in small whorls.

"No, not since—" Not since she was married, she stopped herself from saying. "Not since I was younger," she amended lamely.

"You should begin riding again," Zora told her, wholly unaware of Julia's discomfort with the direction the conversation had taken. "Papa has more horses than he would ever need, so I doubt he would care if you were to take one out. And he's hardly at home since we came back from London, always out visiting his farms or working with his manager. I hardly see him most days now that we're at Langford again."

Julia pounced on the opportunity to change the subject. "And do you wish to see him more?"

"I don't know." Zora wrinkled her nose and pushed a dark lock of hair behind her ear, only to have it slip out again as she bent forward to watch the progress of a beetle on the ground. "Sometimes I think he doesn't like to see me. And then other times I think he wishes he could spend an entire day at home playing toy soldiers with me."

"Well." Julia blew out a breath and tried to conjure up a response that wouldn't make the conversation as uncomfortable for Zora as it had been for herself only a short while before. "Perhaps he—"

"I think it's because the house reminds him of Mama," the girl went on. She straightened up, her expression solemn. "I think I remind him of Mama. It's why sometimes he wants to be with me and sometimes he doesn't."

Oh, the utter frankness of a child. Julia pushed her hands down the front of her skirt, smoothing out the fabric from her hips to her knees. She could have sat there for hours and mired herself in parsing out the similarities between Mr. Halberd, Zora, and herself, all of them tangled up with a single accident that had irrevocably changed their lives forever.

"Come along." Julia stood up, brushing a few leaves from her shawl that had fallen from the branches above. "You must show me to your room, hmm? I would love to see it."

She held out her hand to Zora. Without pause, the girl slipped her small, warm fingers into the curve of Julia's palm.

"I can show you my doll, Polly. She was a gift from my Mama, you know. I've had her since before I can remember."

Julia tightened her grip on Zora's hand as they walked back to the house. "I very much look forward to meeting her."

Five

It took three slices of cake with currants and orange peel, two stories from a book of Celtic myths found in the library, and a fictitious tale about a dragon with a heart of coal Julia created out of thin air before Zora finally closed her eyes and fell asleep.

She had fallen asleep on top of the covers, and so Julia carefully tucked her in, shifting the pillow beneath her head and sweeping the dark reams of hair back from her cheeks and forehead. There was a moment, as she reached towards the nightstand to turn down the lamp, that the shadow's flickered across Zora's face, throwing the girl's profile into sharp and familiar relief.

Julia blinked at that, something in the curve of the child's jaw making her breath catch, as though she had traced that same curve with her gaze a dozen — no, a hundred times before. And then she looked again and... there. It was gone. A mere trick of the light. A crumb of anxiety triggered by this sudden change to her life. Shaking her head, Julia gave the corner of Zora's pillow a last, gentle plumping and turned away from the bed.

It took her a few minutes to tidy up the nursery before she retired to her own room for the evening. There were drawings scattered on the table, and little dolls whittled out of pegs that bore tufts of cotton wool for powdered wigs on their heads. Tomorrow, Julia planned to begin proper lessons with her. There would be reading and arithmetic and geography, French and piano and sewing...

There was an excitement that bristled through her at the prospect, of teaching someone new, introducing them to a broader world of knowledge. She was limited in her instruction of the girls at the schoolhouse, by time and by the support — or lack thereof — from their families at home. It was a victory if she could instill in them the rudiments of reading and a little bit of writing, perhaps even some finer needlework beyond the basics of mending and a foundation in arithmetic for the girls who attended week after week and did not disappear again after only a few months of instruction.

But with Zora, she had access to an entire library of books, to materials for writing and drawing and music she had never been able to afford for her other pupils. And now with an income that wouldn't go towards paying for a roof over her head and other essentials, she could begin to purchase new things for the school- house — new books, actual paper for them to write on, maybe a globe so they could see just how large the world around them really was — and no longer worry about straining her own budget to breaking.

She took the small oil lamp from the nightstand and carried it with her into the corridor. Her own room was two doors down from the nursery, and she counted them just to be certain, her unfamiliarity with the house and its layout especially strong with only the shifting glow of a lamp to guide her. But she would learn her way around soon enough. She would have to, as this was to be her home now for the next...

Oh. Years, at least.

Her room was warm and quiet, illuminated only by a low fire burning behind a painted screen. She set down the lamp, adjusted the wick to give herself enough light by which to read, and picked up a book she'd fetched from the library only a few hours before.

And then there was a knock at her door. With a sigh, she returned her book to the nightstand.

It was only a few paces to take her back to the door, but in that time she wondered if it was Zora, already awake again and in need of something. Or perhaps it was Mrs. Holland, come to sneer at her in thinly veiled disdain.

"Oh," was the sound that dropped out of her mouth at the sight of Mr. Halberd in the hall, framed by the darkness behind him.

"I beg your pardon," he said, his gaze flicking towards her and then away, down to his clasped hands in front of him.

Julia took in the sight of his clothes and the general state of him. He looked mussed and tired, his jacket dusty and creased, his neckcloth a rumpled bulge of fabric that appeared to have been already halfway through removal before he knocked on her door. "My pardon? For what?"

"I've disturbed you," he said, and took a small step back from the door. "It's late, I know. And for that, I apologize. I was hoping to make it back to the house before Zora went to bed, but I just looked in on her and saw that she's already sound asleep. Many thanks owed to you, I'm sure."

"And a story about a dragon," she said, and fought to pull in a full breath. She wanted to pretend that she didn't know why the unexpected sight of him at her door should rattle her nerves, but that much would be a terrible falsehood. Her gaze caught on the narrow expanse of his bare throat above his collar and disassembled neckcloth, snagged there like a scrap of cloth on a patch of thorns. There was the shadow of a beard beginning to grow on his face, and a smudge along the edge of his jaw like dirt wiped from the back of a sweaty hand. "Though I'm sure the three helpings of cake she had after dinner played their part as well."

And he smiled at that. Only for a moment, before the corners of his mouth sagged again as though drawn down by the weight of an emotion she could not begin to recognize. "I thought I might..." He cut himself off, shaking his head. "I'm sorry," he apologized again. "I had hoped you would not already be in bed for the night, but—"

"What is it?" She stood up straighter, prepared to help him with some emergency pertaining to the house or his daughter, though she wasn't sure why one of the other servants — someone more acquainted with the house and its surroundings — could not help him with what he needed. "Is something wrong?"

"No, not at all."

"You're not keeping me from my sleep, if that's what you're afraid of. I had planned to sit up and read for some time yet."

He shifted his weight as though he wanted to look around her and into the room, but held himself back. "Mrs. Benton, I wondered if you would join me for a small supper."

It was not what she had expected him to say. Or rather, she hadn't really any idea of what he'd been about to ask of her, but an invitation to share a meal with him was the least likely of candidates.

"I—" she managed, before her tongue seemed to adhere itself to the roof of her mouth.

"Forgive me." He retreated again. Another step, and Julia feared he would sink into the shadows entirely. "It was an impertinence. As I said, it's probably too late, and I was selfishly in want of some company at the end of a long day."

He began to turn away from her. She didn't raise a hand to stop him. Her arms seemed frozen at her sides. "Wait," she said, before he could leave her completely, that single word a tremulous creature, tip-toeing out on a thin crust of ice.

Mr. Halberd stopped and looked back at her.

"Yes, I-I'll dine with you." If you wish, she nearly added, but kept those words to herself. Because they implied she was only agreeing in order to please him, as a sort of favor, when that wasn't at all the truth.

He brushed his knuckles along the side of his jaw, demonstrating how that streak of dirt must have found its way to his skin. "Does my study suit? I usually take my meals in there when I'm alone, but if it's too... private," he said, in a way that sounded as though he had sorted through and discarded several other choices before settling on that one. "I can arrange something else."

"No, that will be fine." She knew what he alluded to, that it might be unseemly for them to spend any extended amount of time together unsupervised. But they were neither of them particularly young anymore, and she doubted that anyone could take a single look at her and derive something scandalous from her presence.

"And you remember how to find your way there?"

"Yes." Or, at least, she hoped she did.

He nodded. "Allow me a few minutes to, um..." He gestured vaguely towards himself, the dirt and the sweat and the creases highlighted with that sweep of his hand. "... slough off the work of the day and I'll meet you there in... oh, shall we say twenty minutes?"

"Twenty minutes," she echoed, and waited until he had turned away again to shut the door behind him.

For a full minute of the twenty still before her, she stood with her back against the door, one hand at her throat. Her pulse fluttered beneath her fingers, too fast, too erratic. She wanted to close her eyes, to squeeze them shut until she saw stars. But she feared if she blocked out the world for too long, what had just happened would pass into something out of a fantasy, out of her imaginings, and it would slip away from her as quickly as the last dream of the night upon waking.

It was absurd, she thought. He had only asked her to eat with him, nothing more. No doubt he was lonely, and tired, and simply wanted someone to talk to while he ate his final meal of the day.

But still, she looked down at her dress, plucking at her skirt and its faded flowers, its thin spots where stains of years' past had been diligently scrubbed away.

Her gown, her hair... She reached up and tugged at a loose strand that had worked itself free of the pins she'd pushed into place that morning. She wasn't presentable. It was one of the things her husband had used to lament, that she would not take the time for elaborate hairstyles, to dress herself as an important personage in the town. As though she had failed him, by not gilding herself in lace and ribbons and intricate braids.

Did Mr. Halberd expect her to change? She opened her wardrobe, more out of curiosity than with any real intention, and searched through the gowns there. The same gowns she had worn for years, done over again and again, the hems repaired and the sleeves trimmed shorter to disguise the fraying and...

She shut the door to the wardrobe with a snap.

Whatever he expected, he would get Mrs. Julia Benton in her decade-old gown, with the smudges of ink still around her fingernails, with her hair simply brushed and braided and pinned like a pork pie to the back of her head.

When she arrived in the study, it was empty. The servants, however, must have already been directed to prepare the room, as a bright fire had been built up in the fireplace and a half a dozen candles burned in various places, lending their additional light to the space.

Julia breathed. Slowly in, and slowly out again, her fingers twisting and twisting until she thought she might pop her knuckles irrevocably out of place. She had seen little of the house so far, only a brief tour provided by Zora on their way up to the nursery. But now that she was here again, she realized how different Mr. Halberd's study was from the other rooms, as though the hand responsible for decorating the rest of the house had not been granted access here.

It was Mr. Halberd's space. It smelled of him, of smoke and

soap and the heady, rich aroma of leather. Another breath and she caught that bright tang of tobacco she had noticed the other day, an undercurrent of cherry sweetness threading through everything else.

And there, just as if she had conjured him through her senses, she turned and saw him standing in the doorway, watching her.

"Ah," he said. "You came."

"Did you think I wouldn't?" She had not meant it to sound so much like a challenge, a forced battle waged between them despite the fact she had no idea what they could be fighting over.

He shook his head, and it took her a moment to realize that was all the reply to her question she was to receive.

She studied him then, taking in the dampness of his hair, the rumbled cleanliness of his shirt and waistcoat, the simplicity of his neckcloth, seeming to be there for no other reason than because it would have been less respectable of him to be without it. He hadn't shaved though, and there was still tiredness evident beneath his eyes, smudges of shadows resting atop both cheekbones.

He looked his age, she thought, and not unkindly. The gray in his hair stood out more in the glow of the candlelight, fanning out from his temples. He was older than her, but she wasn't sure by how many years. A half dozen, perhaps. That would place him only a few years shy of fifty. But he was fit yet, regardless of the lines and the gray and that subtle exhaustion that made his shoulders round slightly forward when he thought she wasn't gazing at him.

She knew she carried it herself, the weight of all the years she'd endured up until that moment. She felt it in the tightness of her joints in the morning, the slow and subtle rounding of her figure, the silver in her own hair as she brushed it out every night before bed. An amazing thing, how her body could display the signs of so much experience when her life had only ever felt like a thing half-lived.

Mr. Halberd moved further into the room as a servant came in behind him, a young woman bearing a large tray laden with more food than Julia thought it would be possible for two people to eat in one sitting. "Set it near the fire," he instructed her, leaving Julia to wonder why it wouldn't be placed on a table or even the desk at the other end of the room.

"My meals are generally informal," he explained, as if he had the power to delve into her head and read her thoughts. "At the end of the day, I've no wish to burden the household with the effort of preparing an elaborate supper, nor do I want to burden myself with the task of digesting it." He walked towards the fire and knelt down by the foot of it, where the tray had been placed. "Tonight we have bread and cheese for toasting, fresh mushrooms, some sort of sausage..." He picked up a chunk and smelled it, then popped it into his mouth with a low sound of pleasure. "And if we're fortunate... ah, yes." He lifted the lid off a small dish. "Some of Mrs. Bastion's famed pickled eggs." He replaced the lid and glanced at her over his shoulder. "If you've suddenly changed your mind after encountering tonight's menu, I will take no offense if you turn right around and make a hasty retreat to your room."

He was giving her an excuse to leave, should she desire one. Did he sense her hesitation? She still lingered only a few paces from the door, her hands clasped together, fingers tangled in knots at the front of her skirt. If they had been in the dining room, or the drawing room, or some other place less intimate and with servants lurking in the background, she might not question whether or not she should stay.

On the other hand, she reminded herself they were both older, a widow and widower, an employee and her employer. Weren't they beyond the age of being touched by scandal and gossip and impropriety? Between the two of them, they had accumulated nearly ninety years of experience. She could have some toast and cheese with him and not need to feel guilty about it.

She walked further into the room, that first step alone a show of her decision. She thought she saw Mr. Halberd's shoulders sag as she sank into one of the armchairs near the fire — near him. From relief or some other emotion, she couldn't tell. But he worked quietly, fixing slices of bread onto toasting forks, doling out small plates and bits of food with all the care and attention to detail of a servant working for his mistress.

"So, how do you find Langford?" he asked once the first slice of bread was toasted with a hunk of cheese melting atop it.

Julia took the toast, waiting for it to cool on her plate before eating it. "I've been here before," she replied, unaware she'd avoided answering his question until after she'd finished speaking. "Your wife, Mrs. Halberd. She always hosted a Christmas party. I attended at least one of them, if my memories haven't yet failed me. But it's been some years since I was last here. Well, for longer than it takes to warm up in front of the fire."

What she refrained from saying was that she hardly retained any memory of the Christmas party in question. A few words exchanged; the heat of the fire and the candles and the assembled guest; Mr. Halberd himself, catching her attention with greater force than any other ornament put on display. Despite the party being an annual event for Barrow-in-Ashton, Julia could only recall that single season when she had been well enough to attend. All of her attempts to carry a child had not been kind to her health. Sometimes she wondered how much of her own life she had missed during her struggles to bring another life into the world.

"My room is very comfortable," she went on, when the lull after she had first spoken became an awkward silence between them. She glanced at Mr. Halberd. He sat with his toast near the fire, turning it slowly at the end of his fork so it would not burn. "The nursery should do very well for Zora's lessons. Though I wonder if we would be permitted to extend our studies into other areas of the house and grounds? For a change of scenery, so to speak. Children do not always do well when confined to one place for an extended period of time." She had learned this lesson from her own pupils, discovering that a few of them were able to hold a stronger focus on their work if given leave to pace around, to prac- tice their reading outside, with the sun — when it deigned to make an appearance — and all of nature acting as a backdrop to their education.

"Oh?" He shook his head, his expression one of someone extri- cating themselves from a deep thought that had nothing to do with the conversation at hand. "Of course you may study wherever you wish! In here, the dining room, the library... I've no desire to place any boundaries on your teaching, Mrs. Benton. The house and its grounds are entirely at your disposal."

"Thank you." She finished her toast and cheese and began on another slice, despite the fact she had already eaten with Zora only a few hours before. "I was wondering," she began again between bites. "I would like some supplies for drawing and painting. Brushes and paints and fine paper. Your daughter shows an interest in art, and I should no doubt sharpen my own skills as well if I am to teach her."

Mr. Halberd took a bite of his own food and chewed thought- fully. "You've not made a habit of drawing recently?"

"No, I..." It would not do to prevaricate with him, she decided. Better to speak the truth and leave it for him to parse as he would. "While I lived with Mrs. Cochran, I could not afford the supplies I needed. I had little income and less to spend on frivolities." She bit back a scoff. "Nothing for frivolities," she amended. "And the few times I was able to save an extra coin or two, I would spend it on new primers for the school. New slates. Coal for the fire. Other things they needed."

He blinked. "I see," was all he said, and Julia wondered if he did. "Well, speak to Mrs. Holland about anything you need and she will see that it's provided for you. Not only supplies for Zora's education, but new clothes for her, for yourself—"

Julia drew back in surprise. "Oh, I don't need anything for myself. Thank you."

And there, his eyes found her again, beneath graying brows

arched high on his forehead. "I don't consider myself any sort of expert as to ladies' fashions, but when did you last purchase a new gown for yourself?"

"I..." she said, and stopped. She pinched the fabric of her skirt, the faded blots that had once been roses. Or perhaps nasturtiums. "I don't know," she admitted. "Not since before..." Before her husband had died. Before she had tried and failed to begin a family. "Well, at least ten years or so."

She wanted to look away from him as the warmth increased in her cheeks. She knew the gown she wore was old, that it neither suited nor fit her properly. She also knew that everything else in her wardrobe was old and faded and years out of fashion. If they had even been in fashion when she'd first acquired them. But still, the fact that he had acknowledged it, that he had even noticed in the first place made her quaver between a thrill at being seen and a fear that he would see even more the longer he should look.

"I'm sorry," Mr. Halberd said. "I didn't mean to..." He closed his mouth, shaping his lips into a tight line, a slash of discontent cutting the lower half of his face in two. He reached up and rubbed the back of his neck above his collar, then ran a finger beneath the edge of his neckcloth as though he wanted to tear off the offending thing. "I'm sorry," he repeated. More urgently, in case she had not believed his sincerity the first time. "My wife..." He paused, his gaze darting towards her. For a moment, Julia thought he was attempting to communicate something more to her in that glance, but she didn't possess the power to decipher it. "She took care of the running of the household, from top to bottom. There is, of course, still Mrs. Holland to see to the managing of things, but I cannot leave Zora to be raised by a household of servants. She needs—" *a mother,* was the phrase that filled the heavy silence he created. "Guidance," he said instead. "And of a sort I don't feel fully capable of providing. She's a child yet, but it won't be long before she is a young lady. I trust you to help her, to teach her how best to navigate her future life."

Julia shook her head. The food, the warmth from the fire, her own fatigue that had crept up on her in the last hour all worked together to blur the edges of her thoughts. "I feel I should be flattered you've put so much trust in me, but... in all honesty, we hardly know one another."

And they didn't, really. No matter that she had lived at the vicarage for seven years, that she had continued on in Barrow-on-Ashton for another five years after that, their paths had seldom crossed during all that time. More often than not, it had been her husband who had worked with the Halberds on various charitable projects and events, regularly venturing up to Langford to discuss his sermons or other important happenings in the parish.

But Julia had always remained at home. At first, because the difficulties of pregnancy had confined her there. And then, because attempting to make social calls while everyone around her politely and obviously refrained from speaking about why she was always so ill and tired and reclusive... Well, it was infuriating.

"Should I have hired someone else, then?" He almost smiled, but not quite. "Placed an advertisement in the papers for a young woman, fresh from the schoolroom herself? That's how it's usually done, is it not?"

"No, I mean..." Why couldn't she stop talking? Was it the comfort of both the meal and the room? Or was it him? Every time she looked at his face, every time their gazes caught, she wanted to speak to him, to tell him things better kept to herself. "Why me?" she asked instead. "Why come to the schoolhouse and make the offer you did?"

He sighed. At first, she did not think he would answer. Perhaps she had gone too far, asking questions of her employer to which he might not believe she had a right to a reply. He glanced away from her, towards the open door of the study, but there were no footsteps to interrupt, no sounds of anyone near them.

"There is something in you, Mrs. Benton." His voice was low, as if he spoke more for his own benefit than even her ears. And so she found herself leaning forward in her seat, straining not to miss a single syllable. "A reserve of strength, I think, that has carried you through. I can only know a portion of what you've endured, and I won't claim to know the precise measure of your suffering. But you've come through it better than I. Of that much, I'm certain."

No doubt he referred to that night, five years earlier, when he had lost his wife and she had lost Frederick. She hadn't considered his own difficulties during that time, leaving him the sole parent of a young child. Perhaps she should have done more to reach out to him during the years, but she had been so wrapped up in herself, mourning not only the loss of her husband but the loss of who she had been. Or who she had spent so many years trying to be.

No longer a wife, and with that the quick demise of any hope she'd ever maintained about becoming a mother.

But if she were to be honest with herself, that particular realization had wrapped its fingers around her long before Frederick had breathed his last. Though it wasn't until she'd watched them pile the damp, loamy earth onto his coffin that she had finally accepted the failure for what it was.

"I will do my best with Zora," she said, her fingers busy tearing the last crust of her toast to crumbs on her plate. "And I thank you for... thinking of me. For her."

Mr. Halberd finished off a bite of sausage, the back of his hand held to his mouth as he chewed. "I wouldn't have considered anyone else," he said, once he swallowed. He looked at her from his place near the fire, the black and silver of his hair catching the shifting light of the flames so that he almost appeared an otherworldly creature. "You are..." But whatever he'd been about to say, he didn't seem inclined to finish. Instead, he twisted around and tipped his head back, seeking out the clock on the mantelpiece. "I fear I've kept you up too late."

"Oh, no. Not at all," she said, without bothering to check the time herself. She could've stayed there all night, she realized, just warming herself by the fire, eating such simple and delicious food prepared by the man in front of her. Wasn't this what she had always wanted with her husband? An uncomplicated existence, filled with quiet moments fueled by mutual respect and...

She smiled to herself, lowering her chin as she did so. No, it wasn't only respect that she felt for Mr. Halberd. Because she remembered all too well that day she had first met him. He and his wife sitting in their front parlor at the vicarage, Frederick taking on the effort of entertaining them while she bustled about in the kitchen, trying to put together a tray for their unexpected guests. And then she had spotted him stepping out of the parlor and into the hall. Mr. Halberd. His gaze darting around as though he was searching for something.

Searching for her.

He wasn't, of course. He couldn't have been. What impression could she have made on him in only a few minutes that he would even bother to spare a thought for her when she was no longer in the room?

But he had followed her into the kitchen, dipping his head as he passed through the low doorway. "Are you in need of any assistance?" he had asked.

She had stood there, in her drab gown and her stained apron, her hair already slipping out of its pins. The new vicar's wife, already a disappointment before she had even begun.

"Thank you, no," she had said. Twelve years later, and she could still recall every — brief — word that had passed between them, every glance as he had stepped around the table to where she stood, that quick brush of his hand against hers as she had reached for the teapot and he for the matching cups.

She raised her chin, and there he still sat before her. Deftly arranging the tray that held the remains of their supper, as though hardly a minute had passed between when he had helped her in the vicarage kitchen and today.

"I am usually up quite late," she assured him, stepping back into their previous conversation as though her mind had not tripped back a dozen years. "It's all too easy to fill those midnight hours with books and my own repetitive thoughts. And I must confess, I don't sleep for as many hours as I did when I was younger."

He chuckled at that. His attention switched from the tray to the fire, which had begun to burn down as they'd eaten. "When I was a child, I did everything within my power to avoid naps or going to bed early. And now that I am an old man, I spend half of every night wishing for rest as it continually eludes me."

"You are certainly not an old man," Julia protested. "For if you are an old man then I am not far from becoming an old woman, if I'm not already there. And I am not at all prepared to view myself in such a declining light."

She had spoken in jest, but his smile faded. It was an abrupt change, like a cloud sweeping into the room, casting its shadows on his features. "I fear that might be part of the curse of growing older, that we struggle so hard against it only to find it has already washed over us before we'd noticed." He gave the fire a particularly forceful prod with the poker and scattered the coals as the sparks snapped upwards. "And here, I've asked you to distract me for an evening and in exchange for your company I infect you with my own dismal musings. Forgive me, Mrs. Benton."

"There is nothing to forgive, Mr. Halberd." She reached out and returned her plate to the tray, then brushed her crumbs from her skirt for no other reason than to give herself something to do. A reason to avoid looking at him now that the mood in the room had undergone such a drastic alteration. "You say you were in need of company? Then I was pleased to provide it. We cannot be left alone with our own thoughts for too long, I fear. Even speaking them outloud to someone else is often enough to release us from the burden of them. At least for a little while."

He stood up, and she hated that he did, that it signaled an end to their time together for the evening.

"Here," she said. She stood up as well and moved to pick up

the tray. "Allow me to take this to the kitchen. My room is on that side of the house, so it will not be far out of my way.

But he stopped her, one hand on her forearm. A gentle touch, but enough to make her pull back from him as if she'd been burned.

"I'm sorry."

Julia shook her head. "No, you startled me." And he had, but perhaps not in the way he might have thought. She picked up the tray, holding it between them, an unbreachable wall of bread crusts and cutlery.

Not because she was in need of protection from him. Oh, no. Though she did worry he might take it that way. Instead, she wanted that barrier there, something to prevent her from leaning in to that touch on her arm, from wondering what it would feel like for him to touch her elsewhere.

"Goodnight, Mr. Halberd." She said it quickly. Too quickly. As she backed away from the chairs and the fire and him. "And thank you for the food. It was delicious."

She took the tray to the kitchen, then went up the back stairs to her room. It was dark there now. Her fire had burned low while she was gone, and she had blown out the lamp before she'd gone downstairs. She looked at her book, still sitting on the nightstand where she'd left it, the evening she had planned before Mr. Halberd came to her door still spooling outwards as though she'd never left the bedroom at all.

"I shouldn't have come here." The whispered words landed dully in the dim, empty room. The room that was so much larger than any other room she'd ever had to herself before, with its fine furnishings and its lovely prospect from the twin windows.

Because all this time, she had told herself that she had accepted the position as governess here for Zora's sake, or for the extra money she would be able to earn and put towards her school. But in the end, she knew the truth of her own heart and her own desires. In the end, she had come here for him.

Six

Before she had come to Langford, Julia had set about putting together a curriculum for Zora, one that she had altered slightly after their meeting beneath the trees, to incorporate the girl's budding interests in mythology and ornithology (and most likely some other -ologies she had not thought of yet).

By the end of the first week, her carefully designed lesson plan had evolved into something else that bore little resemblance to its origins.

To begin with, Zora never ceased moving. Her mind worked best when she was permitted to walk, or to sit on the floor with an old box of her father's tin soldiers, her fingers occupied with the task of arranging them into neat rows and formations. And so more and more of their lessons found them moving about the house, often working their way out of doors earlier every day. While Julia concentrated on a piece of embroidery or a small sketch of the landscape surrounding Langford, Zora would lie on the grass, her feet kicking lazily behind her as she plucked blades of grass from the ground and plaited them into small baskets and wreaths. And all while reciting French verbs or a litany of multiplication facts.

Zora, Julia had quickly discovered, was imbued with an affinity for numbers. She could work out large sums in her head with greater speed than Julia could, even with the help of a chalk and slate in front of her. She had no interest in studying arithmetic, however, only completing enough work in the subject as was required before turning her attention to something that held more appeal.

They commemorated the end of their first week together by spending the afternoon in the apple orchard, tucked into a corner of Langford's grounds. Julia sat on a cushion she'd had the forethought to bring outside with her, while Zora dangled upside-down from a low branch on the nearest tree. Julia paused in her work — a ball of yarn and a hook were all she needed to begin on a new shawl for winter — and watched as Zora pulled herself up and climbed higher into the tree. Nimble hands and feet were all the girl needed to seek out the most secure holds before she settled herself on a sturdy branch, her legs stretched out and ankles crossed in front of her.

"Do you miss him?" came Zora's unprompted question.

"Hmm?" Julia sought out her hook and ran the thread of wool between her fingers. "Who should I miss?"

"Mr. Benton. Your husband. Do you miss him terribly?"

Julia's hands stilled. There was perspiration on her palms, though the afternoon was fairly cool. "Of course I do." As soon as the words were out, she realized how trite they sounded to her own ears. But they seemed to succeed in satisfying Zora's curiosity for the moment.

"I should like to miss my Mama," Zora went on, head tilted up to peer at the leaves drifting down from the topmost branches. "But I think it's hard to miss someone you cannot remember. There is a portrait, you know, hanging in one of the sitting rooms we haven't used since coming back from London. It's of Mama and Papa together. I look at it sometimes and imagine what it must have been like to be held by her, and played with. I wonder what she smelled like? There's an old bottle of perfume in her room, smells like roses. I don't care for the smell of roses. It makes me think of old ladies. But it's all just fancy, I suppose. I was only three years old when she died, and I can't recall anything about her, not for real."

Julia let herself wonder what sort of person she might conjure up in place of Frederick if all she had was a few pieces of his life with which to create. A few letters, perhaps. A miniature portrait. A pair of gloves. What manner of man would she paint on the canvas of her imagination? A kind man? Or perhaps a passionate one, someone who nurtured a fire within them like a light hidden under a bushel. And a bitter part of her envied Zora the ability to fabricate the mother of her dreams, dressing her up like a doll and bringing her out to play whenever she wished.

Zora slipped down from her branch, onto another and another, until she dropped from the tree and landed with a bit of a stagger as she brushed bits of dirt and bark from her hands and her skirt. "Would you like to see it?"

For an instant, Julia recoiled at the thought. She told herself she had a very clear memory of Mrs. Halberd's appearance and was certainly not in need of a reminder. The woman had worn beauty and elegance as easily as other women donned their hats. But it was an image that had faded into mist over the last five years, especially when she reminded herself that she had never been particularly close with Mrs. Halberd in the first place.

"Very well." She gathered up her crochet work and handed the cushion to Zora to carry. With a flick of her fingers, she knocked a stray leaf from the girl's unraveling braid. "In one of the parlors? Perhaps we can stop in the library on the way there and search for a few new history books, since you've already read through everything I could find pertaining to Hadrian's Wall."

They trooped back to the house, Julia stopping to leave her

things in her room before Zora led her to a portion of the house populated with covered furniture and darkened windows. The parlor door was unlocked, and Zora opened it slowly, allowing the whine from the hinges to lend a touch of the dramatic to their entrance.

The room was dark. Zora went up to one of the three tall windows and dragged the heavy drapes open, letting a broad shaft of daylight into the dusty air. Julia found the painting at once. It was difficult to miss, as the portrait was enormous, taking up a large section of one wall.

She recognized Mr. Halberd immediately. It was the version of him she had met a dozen years before, or rather an artist's interpretation of that version. His shoulders were a touch more broad than reality afforded, and his jaw more set. Hard, she thought. No, haughty. And it was jarring, seeing such an uncharacteristic expression on his face. Nothing like the man who had crouched in front of the fire in his study, toasting bread and cheese for her while the glow from the flames licked across his features.

There was none of the gray in his hair, all of the lines of age and grief that filled out his face like a map of his life were wiped clean away. And his hair was neat and short, his clothing brilliantly tailored and impeccably styled. Nothing rumpled or worn, his neckcloth tied in intricate folds and layers that would have made a geometrician salivate. It was like him but not like him. A paper doll facsimile, one that lacked all of the necessary components to render him human.

Her attention drifted to the woman in the painting, Anna Halberd. Dark hair, shining green eyes that matched the emeralds dangling from her neck and her ears...

They made a handsome couple. A stunning couple, Julia amended. She remembered that much of them when she had seen them together, how like two pieces of the same puzzle they had appeared to be.

"Everyone says that I look like her," Zora said, interrupting

Julia's thoughts. "And perhaps if I didn't look so much like her, Papa wouldn't spend so many hours away from the house every day."

Julia placed her hand on the girl's shoulder. "Your father is seeing to the care and running of an entire estate. It's a role that takes a considerable amount of time and effort, especially as you've been away in London for until recently. But I'm sure he wishes he could spend more time with you, if possible."

"Do you think I look like my Papa?"

She was caught off guard by the question. "What do you mean? Of course you do." Julia answered without thinking, because it was the correct thing to say. And then she hesitated, because the query made her study Zora's face more carefully than before, searching for some aspect of Mr. Halberd's features that was not immediately visible.

"I hear the servants talk, you know." Zora looked up at her, golden brown eyes glinting like honey in the light from the windows. "They sometimes talk as if I'm not even there. Probably because they wish that I wasn't. But I've heard them mention how Papa must not be my real father since there's nothing of him in my face. What do you think, Mrs. Benton?"

No amount of teaching or lesson planning could have prepared Julia for such a question. *How...?* was all she could think before her mind stuttered to a halt. How could she answer that question? And how could she speak clearly and calmly while her anger at the servants who had spoken of such things in front of an impressionable child roiled like a storm-tossed ship inside of her?

"It doesn't matter whether or not you resemble your father," she said, choosing her words with so much care she thought she might never pick her way to the end of the sentence. "He is the one who is here, seeing that you are cared for, making certain there is a roof over your head that you have everything you should need as you grow."

Zora pursed her lips, a habit she had when she took a rare

moment to consider something before saying or doing what she wanted without any prior thought. "Perhaps we should do something. For Papa. Make him a present, or... something kind."

"Something kind." And Julia smiled. "I cannot think of anything better."

* * *

They sat outside together the next morning, accompanied by easels and watercolors and stubs of charcoal that stained their fingers black. Zora decided she wanted to sketch a picture of Langford to give to her father, and so they made a circuit of the house, trundling across the lawns with all of their supplies, stopping every minute or so to see if that was the prospect they wanted to record. At long last, they found a shaded area beneath a small copse of elms giving them a view of the front and the western corner of the house at once.

Julia worried that Zora wouldn't be able to sit still for long enough to render an image with any measure of great detail, but the constant working of her fingers kept her focused on the task, but continued to chat and ask questions with all the energy of a hummingbird flitting around the petals of a brightly colored bloom.

"What will *you* draw?" Zora asked once she had the first strong lines of the house's walls and foundation marked in brief sweeps of charcoal on the page.

"I'm not sure." Julia stared down at the box of pencils and pastels, her mouth pinched in a tight line. It still felt so unusual to be able to have so many tools and supplies at her disposal, after years of barely doing even the simplest of sketches. She hadn't wanted to waste the paper — which cost money to replace, money she did not have in abundance — and so it was a frivolity that had been put away along with so many other things during her time living at Mrs. Cochran's house.

Her own fingers fluttered before she picked up a pencil and placed the sharpened tip of it to the page.

She'd never cared much for still-lifes, painting vases filled with flowers or bowls of fruit arranged on a tabletop in the golden light of the sun. And so the lines flowed across the page, faint at first as she began with setting the marks of eyes and nose and mouth, bolder with the slant of cheekbones and brow.

The morning slipped away as they worked, as they talked, as the sun slipped in and out behind the passing clouds. A chill threatened to penetrate the wool of their shawls and stockings, but Julia hunched her shoulders against it. She finished first, her hands aching from working for so long without a break, and after so many years without steady practice.

It was not her best portrait. Several places were fudged and shaded where she had made a mistake and not been able to fix it as she'd wanted. But it looked like Mr. Halberd, or it looked as he had the other night, crouched in front of the fire, turning back to gaze at her with a ghost of a smile playing about the corners of his mouth.

"You've made his ears too small."

Julia glanced at Zora, who had abandoned her picture of Langford to peer at the portrait of her father. "I'm afraid I have, yes. But I haven't drawn regularly for several years, so my hands are a bit clumsier than I would like."

Zora tilted her head. "But I like how you've done his eyes and mouth."

"Thank you." Julia slid the portrait beneath another clean sheet of paper. "May I see your work? Are you finished with it?"

Zora stepped back, hands clasped behind her. She was proud of what she'd done. Julia could see that in the girl's posture, in the pursing of her lips as though she was disguising a small smile. And the sketch was rather good, especially considering the age of its artist. There were awkward parts, of course, and she would need instruction in showing the perspective of things, but there was also a natural talent there in every line and stroke.

"I like it very much," Julia told her.

Zora scuffed the sole of her shoe across the bulge of a tree root. "Will Papa like it? I want to give it to him."

"I think he will be extraordinarily pleased to receive such a gift from you."

Zora smiled, and a little bit of tension released from her face and shoulders.

They gathered up their things and returned to the house to eat. Marching around outside and sitting in the chill of a sunny autumn morning had given them both a hearty appetite, so they tucked themselves beside the fire in the nursery with bowls of hot stew and thick slices of bread and bacon. Lessons renewed after that, mathematics and French as clouds moved in and the light from the windows grew dim.

It was already dark when the first strike of rain landed on the nursery room windows. Julia added another log to the fire as the wind picked up and batted against the side of the house. She planned to crochet until it was time for dinner, while Zora shuffled a worn deck of cards and began to build a house with them in the middle of the floor.

A quiet and cozy evening was all that Julia anticipated for the two of them. What she didn't anticipate was a knock on the nursery door before Mrs. Holland stepped into the room. Julia winced at the housekeeper's expression, as dire as if she had come to announce a recurrence of the Black Death sweeping through the village.

"Mr. Halberd has returned early for the day, due to the storm," Mrs. Holland announced. "He hopes the two of you will be free to join him for dinner this evening."

Zora scrambled to her feet, her half-finished house of cards tumbling down at a sweep from the edge of her skirt. "Mrs.

Benton!" she cried, and clapped her hands together. "We can show him our pictures!"

"I think you can show him yours," Julia said with a smile as she set aside her crochet, dropping it into the basket she kept beside her chair. "I don't believe mine is fine enough for display." That, and she had no need for it to become common knowledge that she had begun sketching portraits of Mr. Halberd in her spare time. "When are we expected?" she asked Mrs. Holland.

"Six o'clock, in the dining room."

"Very good. Thank you."

If Mrs. Holland bristled at this brief dismissal, she did not show it beyond a tight nod and the sharp snap of the door as she shut it behind her.

"Six o'clock," Julia echoed, and checked the time. "You should wash up and change before you go down. Your dress is still smudged with evidence of your artistic exploits this morning."

Zora pouted, but it seemed a superficial reaction. The girl's eyes sparkled in anticipation of having dinner somewhere that wasn't her nursery, and Julia could not help but share a little in her excitement. She had tried not to dwell on what Zora had told her the previous day, the suspicion that Mr. Halberd might not be her true father. Servants' gossip, she hoped it was, and nothing more. For both Zora's sake and Mr. Halberd's.

"Now, let us choose a dress for you," Julia said. "It is already after five o'clock and we don't want to be late!"

Seven

They walked downstairs together, Julia and Zora, through corridors paneled in dark wood, past tapestries of golds and greens that fluttered lightly as their hems swept past. And then they were in the dining room, the long table suffused with the light of over a dozen candles, while a large fire crackled in the wide fireplace on the other side of the room.

"Mrs. Benton."

Julia had not sought him out at once. There had been the table, the flickering light, the strange cloistered vastness of the room with the dark colors of the wood and the furniture threatening to close in around her despite the height of the ceiling above them.

"Mr. Halberd." She placed her hand at Zora's back, between her shoulders. It had been an instinctual thing, to reach out and touch her at that moment. To crave the contact and support of another person, even someone as diminutive as the child beside her.

He looked different from when she had been in the study with him, enjoying a small meal toasted over the fire. He was dressed well, as though he expected finer company than a small child and a drab governess. Zora stepped forward and dropped a quick curtsy, then held out the roll of paper she had carried beneath one arm.

"What is this?" He took the proffered paper from her, his brow furrowed.

"A present." Isadora rocked back and forth from her heels to the balls of her feet. "For you."

He unrolled the picture, his eyes gleaming as he studied his daughter's sketch. "I had no idea you could draw so well." His smile broadened. "You certainly didn't inherit your skill from me."

Julia inhaled sharply at his choice of words. Did he know about the gossip trailing through the edges of the household, the suspicion Zora held that he wasn't really her father? If he was aware of it, he made no further sign as to his intelligence as he rolled up the picture again and placed it on the edge of the dining table.

"I'll have it framed, hmm? And may I hang it in my study so I will always see it while I am working?"

Zora nodded sharply. "And perhaps you'll want to frame Mrs. Benton's picture as well."

His attention leapt to her. "Did she draw a picture of Langford, as well? I would like to see it, if she's willing to share."

"Oh, no. No, it's—" Julia stammered before Zora interrupted.

"She drew a portrait of you!" The girl nearly bounced out of her slippers. "It's very good, but I think she made your ears too small."

"Thank you, Zora." Julia placed her hands on the girl's shoulders before she could jump out of her shoes entirely. "But I'm sure your father has other things with which to occupy his time."

Mr. Halberd cleared his throat. "Well, I—"

Julia looked at him, her jaw set. If she had been a bolder woman, a different woman, the expression on her face might have been mistaken for determination, for courage. But it was fear that set her teeth together, that he would somehow be able to decipher her thoughts at that moment. He had faltered into silence at that look from her, but still he regarded her, and in a way that made her draw in a long, slow breath. Because her heart had begun to beat faster, because — for a moment — she thought she might burn up at the heat of his attention.

And then he blinked, and he looked away.

Had she imagined it then? That look...

No, no. Of course it hadn't been real. It couldn't be. She was a fool to think he would look at her in such a way. As someone to be wanted, desired. It was only her own lust clouding her judgment, making her believe...

Julia closed her eyes, her cheeks flooding with warmth. *Her own lust.* No, she couldn't think like that. She couldn't continue to acknowledge how much time she spent thinking about him, how she had always thought of him. Even during the years her husband had still been alive.

"Shall we be seated?"

For a moment, Julia couldn't move. She felt tremendously fragile, that a single step or tilt of her head would crack her open like an egg, and every part of herself she'd kept hidden for the past twelve years would spill out in front of him.

Zora took her hand, giving her a tug towards the table. Julia stumbled on her first step but recovered quickly, allowing herself to be led forward. Mr. Halberd took the seat at the head of the table, while Zora and Julia sat across from one another on his left and right-hand side. There was soup, to begin with. Something that smelled strongly of leeks and chicken. And there was wine, a servant stepping up from behind Julia to fill her glass with the jewel-red liquid.

She had not touched wine for years. Yes, she had sipped some sherry in Mr. Halberd's study, but that had been more medicinal than anything. As the wife of the vicar, Frederick had admonished against her ever imbibing too freely, claiming that it would be unseemly for her to drink, even a small glass with dinner. She had wanted to bristle against his ruling, but then she had discovered that even a single swallow of wine while she was pregnant had always left her violently ill, and so it had become an easy thing to leave behind. And after he had died, wine and other spirits had simply become a luxury she could not afford.

She picked up her glass, breathing in the scent of it, as heavy as a perfume. One sip, rolling back across her tongue, and she told herself she would drink no more than that, rather than worry about losing her head.

"So what are you learning?" Mr. Halberd asked his daughter between bites. "Will we be able to converse with one another in French soon?"

"I don't like French." Zora sniffed her soup before she took a tentative sip from the edge of her spoon. Her eyes brightened and she slurped up the rest of it noisily. Julia made a small sound in her throat, and Zora shifted in her seat, her expression guilty but twinkling. "Sorry," she said quickly, and took a less hesitant — and less cacophonous — second bite. "I like Latin, though. I like to pretend I'm Merlin and can say a few words of it to work some great, deep magic over the land."

Julia dropped her chin to hide her smile. Mr. Halberd raised his napkin to his mouth, taking a remarkably long time to wipe a few imaginary drops of soup from his lips. When she looked up, it was to find him watching her again, this time with the unmistakable glint of humor in his eyes.

"And what else has Mrs. Benton been teaching you? Tell me everything."

It was a daring invitation. Zora rarely needed prompting to speak, and so the majority of the dinner conversation came from the child's detailed descriptions of life under her new governess's tutelage.

Julia kept waiting for the moment when Mr. Halberd would grow tired of his daughter's chatter, to scold her for being too loud or to speak over her about things he deemed more important. Children were to be seen and not heard, were they not? It was the belief Frederick had held, one that he often prefaced with the statement of "When we have a child..."

But their child had never arrived. And with each failed pregnancy, Julia craved the sound of a bright young voice in the house, one that would never cease with their questions and observations. She'd had enough of the loss of babies who had never found their voice, never found their breath. Let the living ones talk and giggle and shout as much as they wished. She was not sure she had it in her heart to tell them to be quiet.

They retired to the drawing room after dinner, Mr. Halberd walking Zora through the finer points of backgammon while Julia set herself apart from them in an oversized armchair with her crochet in her lap. She had made the mistake of taking too much wine at dinner, and she felt a bit too warm and a bit too fuzzy, as though her mind was made of the same wool that slid through her fingers with every stitch.

An ache settled in her chest as she watched father and daughter play together, a twinge of grief at the loss of something she'd never had. But what if one of her children had lived? Would the roads of fate still have taken Frederick from her? Would she have still been a widow, but with a child in her care, living in Mrs. Cochran's spare rooms with a babe on her hip?

Ah, no. If there had been a child, no doubt she would have gone to live with one of her sisters. Those happy women with their living, loving husbands and their passels of children and-

She stopped crocheting and looked down at her work. Her last row of stitches had come out too tight, and she was pulling on the yarn hard enough to nearly break the thread. She unraveled the ruined part, considered trying again, then gathered it all up and set it aside before she could be tempted to toss the lot of it into the fire across the room.

"I think it's time for Zora to prepare for bed." She didn't check to see what time it was, but the storm outside had yet to abate, and between the sounds of the rain and the wind lashing at the sides of the house, Julia wanted nothing more than to be tucked up warm and comfortable in her bed. Preferably with a book. Or just blessed solitude.

Zora said goodnight to her father, giving him a kiss on his cheek before he could stand and see them out of the room and upstairs. Julia nodded her own farewell without meeting his eyes, holding her crochet to her chest and rushing to keep up with Zora as she rushed up the main staircase two steps at a time.

Julia helped her undress and wash and change into a clean nightdress. There would have to be stories, then. There were always stories, Julia found. It had swiftly become one of her favorite parts of each day, tucking Zora into bed, settling in beside her with a book from Langford's library or maybe only the spark of her imagination fueling tales that would slowly, eventually lull the child into a deep slumber. But the excitement of the evening must have exhausted Zora more than usual, and after only a few minutes of reading she was snoring softly with her head pressed against Julia's arm.

It had been a long day. Julia set aside the unfinished book, her head tipping back against the headboard while the sound of the rain worked as an accompaniment to the slowness of her breathing and the steady beat of her heart. She closed her eyes even as she told herself she shouldn't, that she should return to her own room and lie down in her own bed. But it felt good to remain where she was, with the warmth and peace of a sleeping child beside her.

And of course, as her eyes drifted shut and the first threads of sleep wove through her, all of the questions and anxiety that had been held at bay for the majority of the day bombarded her. That perhaps it had been a mistake to come here. That perhaps she should have remained where she was, snug in her tiny rooms at Mrs. Cochran's house, teaching weekly at the school, counting her pennies over and over until she'd rubbed their surfaces smooth. It hadn't been much in the way of a fulfilling life, but perhaps she didn't deserve more than that. She who had never really loved her husband, who had not mourned his death but for the loss of home and income that came with it, who had found herself looking at another man with lust in her—

"Mrs. Benton?"

Her eyes flashed open. Had she fallen asleep? She blinked rapidly and tried to catch her breath. Above her stood Mr. Halberd, a candle in his hand as the lamp beside her on the night-stand had run out of oil.

"Oh." She sat up so quickly she nearly struck her head against his arm. "I'm sorry. I must have dozed off. I didn't realize how tired I was."

He stepped back to give her room as she stood up, her hand gripping the edge of the bed for a moment as she waited for a brief spate of dizziness to pass away. The wine, she thought, and regretted that second glass.

"I glanced in to check on Zora," he explained as she rubbed the sleepiness from her eyes. "I couldn't decide whether or not to wake you, but in the end I was worried you might roll off the edge of the bed or wake up with a ferocious crick in your neck."

There was a cramp in her neck, or at least the beginning of one. She poked at it self-consciously, then found that several pins had fallen out of her hair, leaving her braid to slide out of its bun and trail over her shoulder like a tangled horsetail. "I'm sorry," she said again, unaware she'd taken to repeating herself. "I shouldn't have…" She cleared her throat and tried to take a step back from him, but ended up knocking the backs of her thighs against the side of the bed instead. "What time is it?"

"Er…" He pulled his watch from his pocket, flicking it open with his thumb. "Not quite eleven o'clock. You've been up here for several hours."

"Well, then." She moved to step around him, keeping her head down so she wouldn't look at him, wouldn't even breathe in the scent of him if she could avoid doing so. "I should be off to my own room. Th-thank you for waking me. Um… goodnight."

It was the wine, she would think later. She caught her foot on the bottom of the nightstand, jostling it and setting the lamp to wobbling. Mr. Halberd reached out and placed his hand on her arm to steady her, but she recoiled from his touch before she could stop herself.

"My apologies." He held his free hand up between them, as broad as a white flag. "I didn't mean to—"

"Goodnight," she said again, cutting him off. But she didn't move. The candle he held guttered from the movement of their mingled breath, and she watched the light of it shine in the darkness of his eyes like a living thing.

The wine, she tried to tell herself. Only it wasn't the wine, not at all. Her thoughts were as sharp as the air on a clear winter's day. She knew very well what she was about as she stepped up to him, as she rose onto the balls of her feet, as she placed her hand on his cheek and brought his mouth down to hers.

He tasted of whisky and a hint of the cherry tobacco she so often smelled on him. She wanted to savor him, like the wine she had drunk at dinner, the flavor of him flowing over her tongue until she was intoxicated by it. Her thumb traced the line of his jaw, the prickle of unshaven hair there. And his lips...

It was such a hesitant kiss, and she didn't want to be hesitant. She had spent all of her life being hesitant, holding back. So she pulled him closer, her fingers sliding into his hair at the nape of his neck, her teeth nipping at his bottom lip before he opened his mouth to her, before she touched her tongue to his.

A moan came from the back of his throat, and Julia heard it like the sounding of an alarm bell. She broke away from him, swallowing, gasping for a proper breath. "I'm..." She shook her head, putting her hand over her eyes. "I'm sorry. I'm so sorry. The wine..." she lied, and rushed out of the room.

She couldn't return to her own room fast enough. She shut the door behind her and immediately paced away from it, needing as much space between Mr. Halberd and herself as the bedroom could provide. She stopped at the windows, pushing back the curtains so that she could peer out into the darkness, at the rain-streaked windows that faintly rattled in their frames.

"Damn." The curse slipped out of her, and she would say it another thousand times if it worked to rid herself of the guilt and embarrassment that threatened to overwhelm her.

She had kissed him.

Why had she kissed him?

Oh, but she knew the answer to that. Because she had wanted to. Because she had wanted to for the last dozen years. Since the day she had met him and he had looked at her as though she was a person in her own right and not merely the wife of the new vicar, quiet and subservient and nothing more.

She stood with her arms crossed over her chest, hands gripping her shoulders. When she trusted herself to breathe again, she slid her hands down over her breasts, down and down towards that persistent ache in her lower abdomen.

What had she thought she would achieve in coming here, to Langford? Yes, she had wanted to help Zora. Yes, her earnings would help to finance the running of the school and provide the poorer village girls with better materials for their education. But she had always known, deep down, that she had also come here to be near him. As though she was an infatuated fifteen-year-old and not a graying, barren widow in her fifth decade.

She undressed slowly, her fingers still trembling as she fought with buttons and ties and the last of the pins still clinging to her hair. Her bed was cold, but she tossed and turned until the sheets were warm beneath her legs. She ended up on her side, her feet drawn up beneath the hem of her nightgown, her hands tugging at the corner of her pillow while she watched the shifting glow of the dying coals in the fireplace.

If she slept at all, it would be a miracle. And so her thoughts drifted to Mr. Halberd — not particularly difficult, as they had hardly taken a moment to abandon him — wondering if he was still awake or if he had already gone to bed, if he had been able to dismiss her aberrant behavior from his mind without any difficulty.

But what if...

What if he sent her away? What if he had been offended by her misstep and told her to leave? To go back to Mrs. Cochran's, back to her former life, or the faint shadow of a life it had been. She could claim she had drunk too much wine at dinner, that she'd been disoriented when he'd woken her up suddenly in the nursery. But he might not take to keeping someone in his employ who took to kissing him in the same room in which his child slumbered.

No, she would not sleep. Her fate seemed to be dangling over her, a sword tethered to the ceiling while Mr. Halberd's hands gripped the shears.

In the morning, when she saw him — if she saw him — she would apologize. Perhaps he would be lenient with her. Perhaps he saw her as nothing more than a silly woman, sad and alone and...

But he hadn't pushed her away.

When she had kissed him, he'd given no sign of offense. He had not reared back or cried out, appalled at her advance. And she could still hear his soft moan, the way it had vibrated through her, down to her very core.

Julia closed her eyes. Her hands released their grip on the pillow and moved inward, towards her breasts. She paused there, wondering if she should. Her husband had been adamant that to touch oneself in pursuit of pleasure was a sin. Even when they had lain together, when he had been on top of her, inside of her, she had done nothing to help herself towards satisfaction. Neither did he, for that matter.

Her fingers danced over her nipples, light brushes through the plain cotton of her nightgown. And then a bolder touch, her thumb sliding over and over again until first one nipple tightened and then the other. She relaxed her legs, letting them stretch down towards the foot of the bed while her other hand gathered up her hem, while she sought out the pulsing heat between her thighs.

It was Mr. Halberd she thought of, as her fingertips slid through the wetness there.

Alexander...

Because like this, in the quiet of her own room, she could use his Christian name, pretend they were familiar enough with one another for her to do so. And so it became his hands weighing the heaviness of her breasts, his fingers slipping inside her. First one, then two...

It didn't take long. She cried out, burying her face in the pillow as she did so, as her hips jolted beneath her touch. The shame over what she had done would come soon enough. It always did, no matter that Frederick had been gone for five years, that she had never believed an act that could bring people pleasure without harming anyone else could be wrong. But first, she would allow herself to enjoy the ripples of pleasure as they moved through her. Before she fully came back to herself and remembered that she was alone in her bed, and that she had been alone in her bed every night since her husband had died.

"I'm not sorry," she said, her voice a quiet thing beneath the sounds of the wind and the rain continuing their battle outside.

Eight

Julia did not see Mr. Halberd the next morning. Mrs. Holland informed them before breakfast that a tree had fallen during the storm, landing on the roof of one of his tenant's farmhouses. Mr. Halberd had ridden out at dawn to help with the removal and subsequent repair. The housekeeper claimed no knowledge of when he might return, and conveyed this lack of knowledge in tones that worked as a warning to Julia that the comings and goings of Mr. Halberd were no concern of a mere governess.

After breakfast, Julia and Zora attended church. Julia went every week, shuffling into one of the rear pews, hardly speaking to anyone beyond a few rote pleasantries and a handful of nods. She went because it was expected of her, because she was the widow of the former vicar and so it would have been more remarkable for her to absent herself than to do her shuffling and mumbled 'how-do-you-dos' every week without any real intention behind them.

But today, Julia could not succeed in hiding herself with her very presence. She had made no great announcement of her removal from Mrs. Cochran's to Langford, but Barrow-in-Ashton was a small town, and so word traveled with more speed than if she had put the news in a passel of letters and sent them out to everyone she knew.

She was aware of the glances as she walked up the main aisle with Zora beside her, the whispers poorly hidden behind gloves and bonnets and handkerchiefs. It had been some time since she'd last found herself a popular topic of gossip in the town. Her years of failed attempts at motherhood, of keeping to herself inside the vicarage and all of the talk it produced had already inured her against most of what anyone could say. Yet here she was, introducing herself as a new topic to be run like grist through the mill. The former vicar's wife, brought down in the world by her husband's untimely death, now lowered further to the status of paid employee in order to survive in this world.

A world designed for her failure, Julia thought, with no small amount of bitterness, and followed Zora into the Halberd's pew at the front of the church.

The service was fine if immemorable. Julia had few dealings with the new vicar and his family (though it seemed a bit of a disservice to refer to him as new when he had been in residence at the vicarage since only a short while after Frederick had died) and felt him to be more self-serving and pedantic than she cared for. In other words, very much like most men who dedicated themselves to the Church of England whom she had come across in her lifetime.

As soon as the last words of the closing prayer were sent heavenwards, the congregation let out a collective sigh of relief and made their way out of the church and into the middling wind and drizzle that lingered in the wake of the previous night's storm. Julia took Zora home, set her up in the nursery with a small meal and a seat beside the basket that held her kitten, newly-dubbed Ellen, now that the furry creature had been fully weaned from its mother.

Julia gathered up her things — paper, paints, brushes, and several other items — and left for the schoolhouse while Isadora plied her new darling with minced bites of chicken and warm saucers of cream. She chose to walk to school as the rain had stopped and slivers of clear sky were visible between the rows of clouds marching from one end of the sky to the other. The girls wouldn't be along for another hour, and so Julia spent the quiet time building up a small fire in the stove and sweeping away any cobwebs that had collected in the corners while she'd been away.

Today, they would create art. She set up a bowl of flowers to paint or sketch as they wished, bright blooms taken from the hothouse at Langford. No doubt she should have asked permission before helping herself to Mr. Halberd's flowers, but she'd had no desire to speak with Mrs. Holland about it. Julia suspected the housekeeper wouldn't want to go out of her way to help the poor girls of the town with their education. And as for asking Mr. Halberd himself...

She would see him tonight, she supposed. Possibly at dinner or afterwards. And she would have to speak to him, or wait for him to speak to her, as she didn't doubt he would have something to say.

She tried not to think about what a fool she'd been the previous night, allowing her physical attraction to him to rule her behavior. Perhaps if she was a couple of decades younger she could have excused herself as impassioned. But she was older now, with a husband dead and buried. There wasn't supposed to be any passion left for people her age. Especially not for poor widows, or insignificant governesses.

For the rest of the afternoon she was able to distract herself from her thoughts with teaching. The girls arrived, straggling in one or two at a time, excited as they always were to be out and away from their families, to have this brief moment of attention set aside just for them.

The art and the flowers were a surprise, and Julia took the time to relish their appreciation of the blooms as she didn't know if there would ever be a repetition of such an event. The girls settled down with barely-constrained chatter, pleased with the fine paper and paints and charcoal already arranged for them.

To begin with, Julia gave them no further instructions than to paint. To draw. To bring to life, to the best of their abilities, the bowl of flowers set out in the shifting daylight that poured through the small windows. As they worked, she paced around the room, observing their progress and doling out little tips and tricks to better show color, shadow, and perspective.

The results were... expected. Julia had not anticipated much in the way of skill, if she was to be honest. These were not girls who spent their days decorating bonnets or learning the steps of a quadrille. Their young hands already bore the calluses of hard work, their skin red and raw from the harsh soap used for cleaning and laundry, dirt beneath their fingernails and scrapes on their knuckles from planting and digging and cooking. There would be little more expected from them than to marry, bear children, and continue to wash and to scrub and to cook until the end of their lives.

But Julia wanted them to have these moments of magic, to try to capture them and hold them in their memories. Life would be hard for them, no doubt for their future husbands and children, too. But it couldn't be all darkness and toil and suffering. Julia learned that, after the loss of her first child. Her grief had dragged her to such depths she thought she might never see the light again. It was then she began seeking out shards of beauty among the mundanities. The warmth of sunlight on her back. The smell of woodsmoke curling up from a freshly-built fire. An act of kindness from another person, given to her without anticipation of anything in return. Little jewels of survival.

At the end of the lesson, Julia allowed the girls to take their work home with them if they wished. Some eagerly agreed, while others quietly admitted they had no desire to see anything to happen to it, what with siblings and animals and limited space at home. Instead, they offered their art as a present to their teacher, and took a flower with them, tucked into their hair or pinched between their fingers.

Julia gathered up the mess of paints and brushes and pencils while the fire died down. Any and every little chore to delay her return to Langford and the possibility of seeing Mr. Halberd again.

Of course, she would have to see him again at some point. Unless he went so far as to dismiss her from her position by letter or through a message delivered — with no small amount of exultation — by Mrs. Holland. To pack up her things, to return to Mrs. Cochran's house, to abandon her attempt of reaching for something more after less than a week instilled in his house as a governess.

She could try somewhere else, she reasoned. Advertise for a position in another household, somewhere away from Langford, away from Barrow-in-Ashton, away from the gossip and the shadow of her former life tainting every corner of her current existence. But she feared she was already too old to begin again. She still suspected the offer of employment from Mr. Halberd had only come about due to pity and their shared history, rather than because he truly thought her the best candidate for the job. Another such offer would be difficult to obtain. And so it would be Mrs. Cochran's again, or belittling herself further and begging for home and assistance from one of her sisters. No doubt at least one of them would offer to take her in; and then what would she be? The poor relation, tucked into a spare room, brought out for various holidays and fetes like a stiff, musty cap worn only on special occasions.

She finished packing things into her basket and took her bonnet down from its peg on the wall. Would she see Mr. Halberd when she returned to Langford? It was the waiting that was nearly unbearable, accompanied by the loss of control over her own future. Not that she had ever possessed much authority over her own fate. Even choosing to marry her husband had not really been a choice at all, but rather an acceptance of her loss of options.

She had been nearly thirty years old, with her younger sisters all married and moved away before her. Her father had been close to seventy at the time, and had nursed a weak heart for the previous decade. If he died, *when* he died, there would have been no place for Julia. Their mother was already gone, so it was either marry Mr. Frederick Benton or cast herself upon a relative like some piece of forgotten baggage.

Her bonnet tied tight beneath her chin, her shawl wrapped around her shoulders, she stepped out of the schoolhouse and into the waning afternoon light. She locked the door behind her, her basket jostling against her side before she turned and—

She didn't stumble. She was proud of herself for that much, at least.

Mr. Halberd walked towards her, his own steps slowing when he saw her. But he continued on as though it had been his intention to seek her out — and maybe it had — and so her heart decided to give her the stumble her feet could not.

"Mrs. Benton." He raised his hand to his hat as he approached her. He appeared to be all that was calm and composed, and not at all like someone who was about to tell her that she would have to leave Langford and seek out a position elsewhere. "I had wondered if I would run into you on your way home."

Home. She clung to that word. *Your home.* As though she belonged at Langford, as though he was not about to expel her from it.

"Um, good afternoon." She spoke a beat too late. She tried meeting his eyes, but her gaze flitted away too quick. There was warmth in her face, crawling up her neck until she thought her head might burst into flames if she didn't find a cold stream or an ice house in which to take up residence. "The fallen tree, on your tenant's home? Has it already been cleared away?"

"Yes." He sounded distracted. "And without as much damage to the roof as we feared."

"Good," she said, and swallowed.

Silence, then. Julia wished he would say whatever he had come to, because she could not imagine he had walked all the way out towards this end of the village for any other reason but to intercept her before she could return to Langford.

"Are those from the hothouse?"

She blinked and looked up at him. "I beg your pardon?"

He gestured towards the basket, where she had tucked what remained of the flowers and the paints and everything else she had brought with her to the schoolhouse. "The flowers. They look familiar, that's all."

"Oh, yes." She gulped over the anxiety that had grown like a burl in her throat. "I'm sorry. I should have asked permission to take them. It was an idea I had at the last minute, to bring along some flowers for my pupils. They painted today," she added, nudging the corners of the rolled up papers with her hand. "It's not something they're able to do very often. But with the weather changing so rapidly now, I thought it would be nice for them to have a bit of color in the schoolroom before everything fades completely into winter."

"An excellent thought," he said. "We probably have more flowers at Langford than we know what to do with. I'm glad to see them put to good use. My wife—" His jaw clenched, slicing off whatever he had been about to say. Julia stepped back, giving him a moment to decide whether or not he wished to continue. "She ordered fresh flowers in every room all through the year. Even when it was snowing outside, and there were icicles growing like stalactites along the edge of the house, she demanded her blooms." He tried to smile as he finished, but it faltered instead into a grimace.

"You're not upset then?" Julia blurted before she could stop herself. "That I took them without asking?"

He appeared genuinely perplexed at her question. "Should I be? Langford is your home now. Or at least I hope you'll view it as such. Anything you should need is always at your disposal. And as for the school—" He waved his hand at the building. "Do you have enough supplies for your students? Books, or...?"

She needed to move. The fact that he hadn't mentioned what had occurred between them the previous night made her wonder if it was his intention to pretend it had never happened at all. But was he doing it as a favor to her, to save her embarrassment? Or had it been such an inconsequential thing to him that it simply wasn't worth dredging up again? She shook her head in reply to her own questions and turned towards the road, Mr. Halberd falling into step beside her.

"I do plan on purchasing a few more things for them, yes." She switched her basket from one arm to the other as she drew her shawl tighter around her shoulders. The wind had picked up again as the last of the clouds scraped the sky clear, and the chill that came with it made her long for her bed and a fire and a very hot cup of tea. "Once I have a look at my budget—"

"Your budget?" Mr. Halberd shook his head. "Do you mean to pay for everything yourself?"

"Well... our current vicar claims there aren't enough funds to support the education of both the boys and the girls equally. He gives us leave to use a few things, but the slates and the primers... coal for the stove, paper and pencils, I pay for all of that myself whenever I can manage to set aside a little bit of money. I always..." She stopped speaking when she realized he was watching her as they walked, as if she was a rare bird ruffling her feathers beside him. "What? What is it?"

He gave his head a small jolt, as though she'd startled him from some other thought. "Who is the new vicar? Mr.—?"

"Parker," she reminded him. "He arrived after my husband—"

"Yes, right. Of course."

"—with his family. Mrs. Parker, and, um, three sons."

Mr. Halberd nodded. "I remember him, vaguely. Carries himself a bit like an ostrich, if I'm not mistaken."

Julia didn't know if she should laugh. She wanted to. It twitched at the corners of her mouth, but she tamped it down, instead biting at the inside of her lower lip until the urge diminished.

"Speak to Mrs. Holland," he went on, as though he hadn't compared the vicar to an oversized fowl. "When you request anything for Zora, please add whatever you might need for your other pupils as well."

"Oh," she said. And then, "Oh!" once his intentions became clear. "I couldn't ask you to do that, Mr. Halberd."

"Which is why I'm doing it. And you shouldn't have to ask."

They walked on a ways, neither of them speaking. Julia took to shifting her basket about on her arm, for no other reason than because she was restless and needed some task to occupy the nervousness in her limbs.

The memory of the kiss hovered in the air over her head, a thing to which neither of them would allude. It made Julia aware of precisely how much distance there was between them, how tightly Mr. Halberd held his hands clasped behind his back, and how shallow his breaths were with each cloud of vapor to escape his mouth as he exhaled.

"Mr. Halberd." She put his name into the air without any clear idea of what she wanted to say next. But he spoke her name in return and held out his hand, his palm turned upwards.

"Allow me." He gestured towards the basket. "I'll consider myself the worst sort of gentleman if I make you carry that all the way back to Langford."

She didn't want to give it to him at first. It was a strange sort of independence that came over her from time to time, a reluctance to immediately accept help from others, even small, polite acts of generosity and kindness. She wasn't certain if it stemmed from a distrust that others could wish to do something nice for her without expecting anything in return, or if she was simply stubborn and determined to do everything in her own way, even to her detriment.

But the truth of the moment was that the basket was heavy and her arm ached with the weight of it, and if Mr. Halberd wished to take the burden of it from her for a little while, then she could think of no reason to reject his help.

"Thank you," she said, and handed it to him.

He ducked his head, a small sound of reproach coming from the back of his throat. "I should have made the offer sooner."

"No, don't trouble yourself over it. And I hope you will not see me as some wilting lady who cannot carry a—"

"Mrs. Benton." His steps slowed, but he did not stop walking entirely. He looked at her again from under the brim of his hat, his brow furrowed and his mouth turned down at the corners in an expression of self-recrimination. And it was an expression that looked all too comfortable on his face. "I should have reached out to you sooner. Offered you this place as Zora's governess months... years ago. I should have made certain you were not suffering unduly after the death of your husband. It was shameful of me to appear so unconcerned."

Julia clasped her hands in front of her. Without the basket she was forced to find some other way to hide her fidgeting. "You had your own fair share of grief to deal with, along with a young child to raise. Believe me when I say you didn't owe me anything, neither your care nor your attention. And I did not expect it. We both muddled through everything as well as we could."

He looked out towards the horizon, where the sun was already making its descent. "I regret allowing myself to become so mired in my own concerns, Mrs. Benton. I will try to do better from here forward."

She could say nothing more to that. It was a lesson she needed to take to heart as well. How easy was it to obsess over one's own problems to such an extent that the rest of the world and its various difficulties seemed to cease their existence? But she wasn't the only woman who had ever suffered disappointment in marriage. She was not the only woman who had ever lost a husband and children. And she was still there, with her strength and an endurance that would not allow her to settle quietly into her dotage.

And now she had Zora to look after, as well. A fine distraction from her own problems. More than a distraction, she had to admit. The girl had a lively, inquisitive mind, and yet the poor child trailed her own shadows behind her.

"Mr. Halberd," she ventured to speak again once they were in view of Langford, because if she didn't attempt it now, she might never again work up the courage to speak what was on her mind. "There is something Zora told me, a bit of gossip she claims to have overheard from the servants." She took a deep breath, one meant to fortify her for the rest of what she needed to say, but instead it caused her words to stagnate in her lungs.

"Yes?" Mr. Halberd moved closer to her as they turned off the main road and stepped onto the lane leading towards the house. "What is it?"

Julia licked her lips. It did little to help, as her tongue felt like sandpaper. "Zora seems to believe... I mean, that is..." She stopped walking. Her arms at her sides, her hands curled into fists, she shut her eyes and spoke all the rest of it in a rush. "She does not believe you're her natural father."

Mr. Halberd turned to face her, his back towards Langford and the hill behind him. She watched him, waiting for shock or anger or at least a mild amount of surprise to register in his features. Instead, he remained frustratingly stoic.

"I-I wanted to say something, before Zora mentioned it to you or the rumor found its way—"

"It's not a rumor."

Julia opened her mouth to speak, thought better of it, and closed it again. His words rang in her ears, over and again as though the truth of them might change with enough repetitions. But there was sincerity in his face. And pain, of the like she had never seen in him before.

"Zora is not my daughter." He set her basket on the ground, then pulled his hat off his head and pushed his fingers through his hair, making it stand out at odd angles. Julia resisted the urge to reach out and smooth those errant strands back into place. "Anna was not... She was not faithful during our marriage. I had hoped Zora would never hear of it. In fact, it was partly what took us to London for a while, wanting to put a distance between us and any tales she might hear of..." He fussed with the brim of his hat, his fingers working with enough strength Julia worried he would tear the thing to pieces. "There had already been enough talk while my wife was still alive. And I could... I could only hope it would fade away after she died. But if Zora's heard of it, then I suppose it was wishful thinking on my part." He looked at her, his expression suddenly concerned. "You never heard any of it, before my daughter mentioned this to you?'

"No, never." Most likely because she had been too ill with each pregnancy to keep up with the gossip that trickled through the village, because she'd had no desire to titter over the trials and tribulations of others while her own body struggled to hold onto a life it would inevitably lose.

He appeared relieved at that. "Well." He returned his hat to his head. "I'm sorry Zora has already been exposed to it. I was probably a fool to think I could hide her from the truth forever. These sorts of things always have a way of slinking out into the daylight. But I'll remind Mrs. Holland to keep a better eye on the servants, make certain there is no gossiping, at least where my daughter might be able to overhear." He took a step towards her. "Did she seem upset by the knowledge? I would hate for any memories she may still have of her mother to be tainted because of it."

Julia hid her astonishment. How could he care more about what Zora thought of her mother than how she might feel regarding the fact that Mr. Halberd was not her father? "She, um... didn't appear particularly troubled by the possibility. Though if it is something she's suspected for some time..."

Mr. Halberd nodded. "I'll have to speak with her at some point. You can imagine it's not a conversation I will have any pleasure in. But if the rumors are going to continue, I suppose the truth is our best weapon against them."

"Do you know who her father is?" As soon as Julia said it, she knew she had gone too far. She shook her head, taking a step back and even putting up a hand in warning that Mr. Halberd should disregard her question. "I'm sorry, I should not have... I'm sorry. It's none of my concern."

But he waved away her panic. "It's all right. I've no worry the man will want anything to do with her, though if she ever asks, I'm not sure what answer I will give." He bent down and retrieved her basket from the ground, his fingers picking idly at the handle in a show of the same restlessness she'd fought to overcome only a few minutes before. "I would never cast her off," he went on, his voice lower than before. "She is my daughter, regardless of..."

"Yes," Julia said, when he trailed off and did not finish. "Of course."

"She will have my name. She will have her dowry, everything she would ever need. The rumors and the gossip... Well, I will protect her from those, too, as much as I can. Or perhaps her status alone will be enough to shield her from the worst of it. Scandal always seems to weigh heavier on those who have no power to oppose it."

Did he realize, Julia wondered, what a singular man he was? She could well imagine her own husband's reaction if she had carried on an affair with someone else, or if there had been a child from the relationship. He would've thrown her out like so much refuse, she and the child both. "You must strive to set a godly example," he had so often said to her, in myriad variations of the phrase. "I cannot abide those who flaunt the rule of the Lord and shape it to suit their own will."

"Your daughter is fortunate to have you," Julia said as they resumed their progress towards Langford.

"And you, Mrs. Benton." He smiled. A small grin, but enough to slough away some of the darkness from their previous conversation. "Zora will do well, I think, with you here to guide her."

Nine

⁓

Mrs. Decatur arrived on Monday morning, complete with a small retinue of employees carrying bolts of fabric and lace along with yards of ribbons. She was not from Barrow-in-Ashton, as their village was neither populated nor sophisticated enough to boast the presence of a dressmaker among its inhabitants. But her fame was known well enough throughout the county, and perhaps a few other towns beyond. Julia had never dealt with her personally, as she had always taken to sewing her own clothes. But to own a gown made by Mrs. Decatur was considered a symbol of wealth and status to the citizens of their quiet village, and Julia wondered if it was a display of Mr. Halberd's care and attention towards Zora that he would have her brought in for the making of Zora's clothes.

Julia hadn't known the dressmaker was to be coming that day, no word of the visit coming from either Mr. Halberd or Mrs. Holland beforehand. But her and Zora's presence was requested in the sitting room after breakfast, and so they trooped there hand in hand, Julia chivvying her charge along when she had a tendency to loiter in front of the tapestries and paintings if permitted.

The sitting room was not a space Julia had visited before. It was airy and bright, all done up in whites and yellows and with a certain something that marked it as a room set aside primarily for the former Mrs. Halberd's use.

"Ah, and this must be Mrs. Benton and Miss Halberd?"

The dressmaker approached them upon their arrival. She was older, her fair hair mostly changed over to gray beneath the edges of her cap. Her clothing was impeccable, a gown of shot silk in a deep green that carried pockets of black in its shadows. Julia was suddenly aware of the state of her own clothing, and smoothed her hands down the front of her skirt, all the while wondering if the other ladies in the room could see where she had repaired a tear in the hem, where she had turned up the sleeves or fixed a frayed collar.

"Mr. Halberd has decided his daughter is in need of a new wardrobe," Mrs. Holland said after the perfunctory introductions had taken place. "There will be no need for anything spectacular, no party gowns or the like for her yet. But it would be preferred if she has styles befitting her rank, the quality of her parentage and the like."

Mrs. Decatur snapped her fingers and one of her assistants bustled over with her hands full of sketches and fashion plates. "Something like these?" She offered one of the drawings to Julia, ignoring Mrs. Holland entirely.

Julia saw the tightening in the housekeeper's jaw at the slight, and realized Mr. Halberd must have instructed Mrs. Decatur to deal with her directly. She cleared her throat and looked down at the sketch in her hand. It was a lovely picture, of a lovely girl with lovely curls in her hair and lovely slippers on her feet. It was also not at all a reflection of the sort of child Zora was, unless the gowns in question would also be infused with the power to completely alter a person's character once the garment was slipped over their head.

"Something simpler, I think." Julia looked through the rest of the drawings. "This one would do very well." She indicated a plain muslin gown, with a simple amount of trim at the hem and hardly any piping to be seen.

"And pockets," Zora interjected, as she flipped through a few of the pictures herself. "I like to have pockets for when I find a shell or a rock I particularly like. And they have to be deep, not tiny little things I can barely fit my fingers into."

"Is that possible?" Julia handed the drawings back to Mrs. Decatur. "I would not wish to give you more work than is necessary."

"Oh, it would not be difficult at all! Such minor alterations are what I delight in, making each gown special to every wearer. And, of course, Mr. Halberd's first instruction was to make the two of you happy, so if Miss Halberd wishes for pockets, then pockets she shall have!"

Beside her, Mrs. Holland made a soft sound of disagreement in her throat. Julia chose to ignore it.

"And what materials do you have with greater durability? Miss Halberd spends a large portion of time out of doors, and anything too delicate might not hold up to lasting wear."

Bolts of fabric were produced, a rainbow of colors laid out before Julia and Zora for their perusal. Zora gravitated towards the more vibrant shades, jewel tones and a blue dotted with yellow flowers that looked like a summer sky wrought in cotton and embroidery.

"She also doesn't need much in the way of ruffles and lace," Julia went on as Zora plucked up the corner of a deep indigo wool and rubbed it against her cheek. "I fear it will only catch on things while she plays."

"Perhaps," Mrs. Holland stepped forward, tossing out that one word like an anchor from a ship. "We should consider outfitting Miss Halberd with a wardrobe that will serve an aspirational purpose. Dress her in the styles she should be wearing. That is, for a child with such prospects as she can claim."

Julia breathed in slowly and then out again. This was not the first time Julia had endured Mrs. Holland referring to Zora in terms that made her seem more like a manufactured thing than a breathing, feeling person. "And if she wishes to lay claim to those prospects at a future date, then I will be more than willing to guide her in that direction. But as her current interests have more to do with climbing trees and acting out imaginary sword fights, I believe a simple, well-made gown should suffice."

"If Mrs. Halberd was here," Mrs. Holland pressed on. "I'm not certain she would wish to see her daughter left to run loose like a common hoyden."

Zora tugged on Julia's sleeve "What's a hoyden?"

Julia smiled down at the girl. "Er... someone with a surfeit of energy."

"Oh." Zora screwed up her face in thought. "I like that."

"Unfortunately," Julia said, and returned her attention to Mrs. Holland. "Mrs. Halberd is not here. And so Mr. Halberd has placed his trust in me to make such decisions from here forward. "Without the frills," she said to Mrs. Decatur. "And no silks or anything that will crease too easily."

They set about measuring Zora, choosing out fabric and trim, and deciding on precisely how many pieces she would need. Julia thought the visit was nearly over when Mrs. Decatur turned to her and asked, "Now what sort of wardrobe do you require, Mrs. Benton? Mr. Halberd was vague as to specifics and said I should leave the matter entirely up to you."

"What do I...?" Julia closed her mouth with a snap. She remembered Mr. Halberd mentioning his wish to provide new clothing for her, but she had not believed he would follow through with it. "Um, I don't think that's necessary. Or I could simply choose out some fabric and—"

But Mrs. Decatur shook her head, her eyes almost mischievous. "Mr. Halberd was very clear that you were to have three new gowns, made by me, and your only input is to be in what styles and fabrics you would prefer."

Julia couldn't help but glance at Mrs. Holland, who stood off to one side examining a sample of printed muslin. This wasn't the time to barrel into a discussion about her reluctance to accept a gift from Mr. Halberd. And hadn't the housekeeper already claimed that Zora should dress according to her station? Shouldn't it also mean that Julia herself should present herself as a suitable governess for her?

"Very well." She turned her attention back towards Mrs. Decatur. "Three gowns, then. I shouldn't need anything extravagant," she added, stifling a chuckle. "And I would like fabric for some new shifts, a chemise, but I shall purchase that myself." If she was to have a salary now, she could spare at least a few coins for some new material.

"Everything is to be paid for by Mr. Halberd," Mrs. Decatur stressed again. "But if you wish to discuss the bill with him afterwards, that is entirely up to you, Mrs. Benton."

Julia could not find the energy within herself to fight such a small, seemingly inconsequential battle. And so she allowed herself to be measured before she looked again through the dressmaker's samples of fabric and various patterns, before she gave herself a brief reprieve from the stress of counting pennies and mending another tear. She gave herself to the joy of having new things cut and stitched and measured for no one else but her.

Frederick, when he had been alive, had always touted the benefits of economy, of running a household on a stringent budget. And so Julia had never purchased a new gown for herself, had only occasionally splurged on the material for one. More often than not, she had simply madeover her old wardrobe again and again, had re-trimmed bonnets and stitched up gloves until she feared they consisted of little more than new seams and repairs.

She had spent years telling herself that to want new things, to loiter over shop display windows and periodicals that had made their way up from London, was to tread the dangerous line of greed and avarice. To waste her time pining for things she could not have. Should not have.

And yet it had always been there, in the tenor of her husband's sermons, in the cadence of his prayers, that perhaps the reason behind Julia's deficiencies — as he referred to them — as a wife and mother were due to some spiritual failing on her part. If only she had saved more, prayed more, been more humble...

But, no. She wouldn't let her thoughts spiral down that tortuous path again. For the last five years she'd fought to escape the pernicious notion that she had somehow been to blame for her inability to bear children, that it had all been due to a fault in her own character. But she wouldn't permit herself to think that way anymore. For her own well-being, she could not.

* * *

After Mrs. Decatur and her assistants departed, Julia took Zora outside. They still had their regular lessons to do, and they had lost a morning to measurements and patterns and far too many types of lace. But the sky was clear and the wind was low, and so all thoughts of math and geography tumbled out of their heads in favor of enjoying the beauty of the day while it was available to them.

And Zora needed the exercise. She had been close to bouncing off the walls like a shuttlecock while it had been Julia's turn to be measured, and so a race to the stream was proposed, one which ended with Zora as the clear victor and Julia clutching her side and wondering why she had thought running at full speed would be a good idea for the ten seconds she had managed it.

By the time Julia made it to the stream, Zora was already on her knees in the grass, picking out rocks from the water's edge and turning them over in her hands. "Why are these so smooth while others are so jagged?"

Julia flumped down beside her charge, tipping her head back

so that the weak light of the sun warmed the top of her head. While she regained her breath and the steady beating of her heart, she explained the slow process of erosion, which led to a discussion of different types of rocks and how they were formed, when led to a discussion of fossils, which led to Julia laying a hand on Zora's arm to prevent her from fetching a spade and bucket in order to dig up an expanse of lawn in search of a primitive tool or relic left-over from an earlier age.

"Oh, look!" Zora straightened up with Julia's fingers still clutching her sleeve. "There's Papa!"

Julia turned her head. There, indeed, striding down the slope from the house was Mr. Halberd, clad in his greatcoat and boots, looking as though he'd just dropped out of his saddle to find them. "Well met, ladies." He nodded towards the both of them in greeting. "Are lessons already concluded for the day?"

"Lessons have been postponed until tomorrow." Julia pulled herself up onto her knees while she made certain her skirt hadn't hiked itself up somewhere it should not have been. "We had a visit from Mrs. Decatur this morning, and I thought Zora was in need of some time out of doors after a morning of being measured and fitted like a doll."

"I'm to have five new gowns," Zora announced in solemn tones. "As long as they don't make me itch, I think I shall like them very much."

"A testament to Mrs. Decatur's skills, if she can produce such a miraculous garment." He crouched down beside Zora on the bank of the stream. "And what have you been looking at here?"

"Mrs. Benton has been telling me about fossils," Zora said, while gathering up a collection of what she deemed to be interesting rocks in order to hoard them in her lap. "I want to find one, but she says I shouldn't go about digging up the yard or else Farnsworth will be cross with me."

"Yes, he might," he said, referring to Langford's head gardener. "But I do recall a trip to the shore when I was a boy... Weymouth, I believe it was. I found a rather large collection of ammonite fossils tucked away in a small cove. If I have a look around, I might be able to find one or two of them that survived my childhood years."

"What are ammonites?" came Zora's expected question. And so Mr. Halberd began an impromptu lesson about the origins of marine fossils, while Julia looked up at the position of the sun in the sky and realized it was time they returned inside for their midday meal.

But as she opened her mouth to catch Zora's attention, she noticed Mr. Halberd and his daughter with their heads close together. He had abandoned his hat on the ground while he bent over to show her a piece of quartz he'd found at the edge of the stream. It was a moment containing just the two of them, a father and his child, his attention fixed on her while her curious senses lapped up every nugget of information he had to share.

A small flare of anger erupted within her, directed at the late Mrs. Halberd. In her unfaithfulness, she had deprived him of a child of his own. But the anger dissipated as quickly as it had sparked to life when she realized... it did not seem to matter. They needed one another, Zora and her father, despite the lack of blood tying them together. There was love between them, in every word and every glance. And it was enough. It was more than enough, the bond they shared. It did not matter, his wife's indiscretions, because there sat a family before Julia, a perfect portrait of shared affection.

"Ah, I suspect your governess is more than ready to see you returned to her care," Mr. Halberd said when he noticed Julia still seated behind them. "We certainly wouldn't wish to have her upset with us because I've kept you from the rest of her itinerary for your day."

Julia stood, biting back a groan at having been seated on the ground for so long. "I was worried it was rather us keeping *you* from some greater task."

Mr. Halberd glanced around him, as though searching idly for something of interest on the horizon. When his gaze settled on her again, he raised one shoulder in a small shrug. "Is there a greater task than this, Mrs. Benton?"

She looked at Zora, still poring over her rocks, pausing to hold one of them up to the sun to better watch it shine or sparkle or reveal its secrets. "If there is," she said quietly. "I've yet to discover it."

Mr. Halberd prodded his daughter to collect her rocks and get to her feet, while Julia collected the shawl and bonnet Zora had tossed to the ground the moment she'd arrived at the side of the stream.

"Oh, Mrs. Benton. You've—"

Mr. Halberd was still on one knee, his right hand extended towards her. She followed the line of his sight and saw a damp clump of grass clinging to the side of her skirt, tangled with a few soft clots of dirt she'd picked up from the ground.

"Let me," she said, before she realized her hands were full of Zora's things.

"Here," he said. And then he hesitated, his fingers crooked an inch from the folds of her skirt.

"Go ahead. It's all right." But she held her breath, waiting.

He brushed the grass away with slow, careful movements, his knuckles scraping over her gown. She felt the pressure of his touch against her thigh, the heat of him soaking through the layers of fabric between them like water.

But it was only a touch. A few blades of grass and some dirt scattered to the ground and that was all. He stood up beside her, turning his hat in his hands once, twice, before he put it on again.

"I won't return until late tonight, possibly not until morning. There is a meeting with several of the local magistrates. Nothing serious, but they do like to listen to the sound of their own voices for far longer than should be allowed. If the meeting runs too late, I'll stay the night at the nearest inn, but..." He shook his head.

"Regardless, I hope to dine with you and Zora tomorrow? Breakfast, perhaps? I shall see you then."

With a nod and a tip of his hat, he left them to cut across the lawn towards the house. Julia dragged her attention away from him and held out Zora's shawl, letting the girl pile more rocks into it in order to more easily carry them back to the house. "Inside now, before you've collected all the rocks from the stream and there's nothing left for the water to burble over." And she cupped the girl's elbow and nudged her along when she would've lingered, studying her rocks until the sun set and darkness marched across the lawn.

Ten

The rest of the day passed in quiet comfort, Julia and Zora settling in the library with a tray of food. Zora ate too much cheese and busied her hands with a game of solitaire while Julia read to her from a book — rescued from a dusty bottom shelf — titled "The Geology of the Outer Hebrides". Evening came on before either of them noticed it, but the days were swiftly growing shorter and the servants moved through the house lighting candles and stoking up fires as the windows darkened.

At bedtime, Zora asked for stories about Julia's childhood.

"My... what?" Julia was caught off guard as she tucked the edge of the blanket around Zora's shoulders.

"What sort of house did you live in?" Zora went on. "Was it a large house? Was it as big as Langford?"

Julia smiled. "Not as large as Langford, no. But... we were not poor, either. We each had our own room, and as I was the eldest—"

"You have brothers and sisters?"

"Sisters," Julia corrected her. "Two younger sisters. And there was also my parents' room, and another we kept free for guests."

"Do you still visit?" Zora asked, and squirmed her arms free of the blanket to begin twisting the edge of it between her fingers.

"No." A frisson of sadness swept through Julia with such swiftness she almost couldn't blink away the tears in time. "When my father passed away, the property passed down to a cousin of ours. But my sisters are both married, with homes and children of their own."

"Oh." Zora kept tugging at the blanket, plucking at a thread until Julia had to gently smooth her hand away before she could unravel the stitching. "But you see them often?"

"I do not," Julia confessed.

What she failed to confess was how many invitations from her sisters she had rejected during her marriage. Frederick had never approved of her leaving the vicarage for any extended period of time, that it would not look well for his wife to always be away visiting instead of seeing to the role of his wife and helper. And then it had become easy to pen those excuses when she had become ill with her first pregnancy, and the next, and the next after that.

Soon enough, the invitations arrived with less frequency, until they failed to come at all. And what desire did Julia have to see them again, to show herself as inadequate? The near-spinster sister who had married out of desperation, who had come out of her marriage less than a decade later as a widow and with too many lost children to her name.

"But they are busy with their families," Julia stressed. "Running their own households now. And perhaps I will visit them someday, when the timing better suits everyone." She didn't want it to be a lie, and yet it tasted like one, bitter in the back of her throat before she spoke again. "Now, shall we hear more about our coal-hearted dragon? I'm sure he wouldn't wish to be forgotten."

Julia added new chapters to the tale until her throat was hoarse, until Zora fell asleep with her head on her shoulder, a thin line of drool threading from the corner of her mouth. It was late, she realized, as she removed herself from the bed and glanced at the clock. If she was lazier, she'd be tempted to sink down onto the bed beside Zora and spend the rest of the night there. But there was already an ache forming in her shoulders from how she had propped herself against the headboard, and her undergarments had begun to shift and threatened to become uncomfortable if she didn't take them off soon.

She lit a candle from Zora's lamp before putting it out, giving her a light with which to return to her room. The hall was cold in comparison to the warmth of the nursery, and she wished for a shawl or blanket for the few steps that took her to her room. As she placed her hand on the knob, her foot kicked against something hard on the floor, and she stepped back to see what it was.

A small parcel, she realized, as she bent down to pick it up. Carefully wrapped in a slip of newspaper that began to unfold itself as she held it up to the light.

Juggling the candle and the parcel, she slipped into her room so she could open it with better light and the freedom of more than one hand. A small rock tumbled into her palm, and she turned it over, clearly defined ridges and curves etched deeply into its surface.

It was a fossil. An ammonite.

There was a note as well. She picked it up from amid the folds of newspaper and opened it, her eyes squinting in the low light and the fatigue that hung over her vision like a veil.

I did not wish to startle you a second time, it began.

This is for Zora, a memento from my childhood. I hope she will like it.

Alexander

She slid her thumb across the page, underlining his name. He was home, then. He must have come upstairs while she had been putting Zora to bed, but hadn't wanted to disturb them.

"Alexander." She exhaled the name on a sigh. She returned to

Zora's room, placed the fossil on her bed, just beside her pillow, and swept a few dark hairs from the girl's cheek.

It was there, beneath the flickering light of the candle she held, that Julia was again struck by something familiar in Zora's face. She thought of the painting hanging in the parlor, Mr. and Mrs. Halberd looking down upon the room in all their beautiful splendor. She saw Mrs. Halberd in Zora's face, stamped and set like a seal into soft wax. But it was the peripheral things, the edges and angles of her features that made Julia pause. Unfortunately, it was like grasping at a fading memory, like running her hands through a thread of morning mist and wondering why her fingers still came away empty.

She left the nursery again, intent on returning to her own room. But she hesitated in the hall, her desire to slide into her own bed and sleep brushed away by the knowledge that Mr. Halberd was home. She didn't know what to do with the information, only that she wanted to hold onto it, hoarding it like a piece of treasure. Because she would not seek him out. No matter that she thought of it, and that a dozen different outcomes spiraled out from the very idea.

She chewed at the corner of her mouth until it hurt. There would be no decent sleep for her tonight. Books would be a requirement. And maybe...

No, she didn't know where the wine was kept. But a drink would be more than welcome to smudge the edges of her thoughts and perhaps prevent her from doing something foolish. Or...

... or it might fuel the foolishness into an action that might become all too regrettable.

Julia turned herself around in the middle of the hall, as though she had somehow lost her way right outside of her room. Then she stopped, her gaze fixed on the dark blot of shadow that was the entrance to the servants stairs at the far end of the hall.

Food, on the other hand, would not be responsible for any regrettable choices, at least apart from a touch of indigestion.

Still clutching her candle by the copper ring of its holder, she worked her down to the kitchen area. The rooms below were quiet and empty for the night, the servants having already gone to bed in order to be up early for another day of work. She didn't know her way around the kitchen as well as she would have liked, unsure of where the bread and cheese and jars of things would be kept in a larger house such as this. But she found the larder after a few minutes of poking around in the darker corners. The shelves were piled high with eggs and butter, tucked in beside half-eaten pies and tarts that would still taste good cold.

She fetched a plate and picked out an assortment of food, bits of cheese and half of a hand pie stuffed with onions and potatoes and pears. There were also scones with dried cherries and cinnamon and-

She stopped herself there, before she could attempt to drag half the contents of the larder back up to her room. Balancing the plate in one hand and her candle in the other, she left the kitchen and headed back towards the servants' stairs. The light of another candle halted her progress. Julia blinked at the approaching glow, tucking the edge of her plate against her waist as Mrs. Holland blocked her path forward.

"Mrs. Benton." The housekeeper carried a small oil lamp in one hand and clutched her shawl tight about her shoulders with the other.

"Oh, forgive me, Mrs. Holland. I didn't realize anyone was still awake."

The housekeeper's gaze dipped to the plate Julia held and returned to her face. There was judgment there, somewhere in the wavering shadows that passed over Mrs. Holland's features. But whether it was because the woman didn't think Julia should have been pilfering from the larder, or that she shouldn't be carrying the food back up to her room, or that she shouldn't have put cherry scones and a wedge of Stilton on the same plate, she neither knew nor cared.

"I always walk through the house once more before bed," Mrs. Holland explained, answering a question Julia hadn't bothered to ask. "To check the state of the windows and make certain all the doors are bolted and secure. I hope I did not startle you."

"No, not at all," Julia said. Because what else was she expected to say? She stood there, clutching her plate, feeling like a child caught in the middle of an indiscretion. "Um, if you'll excuse me..."

"I know you think me officious," Mrs. Holland said, just as Julia would have stepped around her and continued on her way. "But I hold this house and its inhabitants in very high esteem. As you should as well," she added, and switched her lamp from one hand to the other, blinding Julia all over again. "In a few years, Miss Halberd will be the most eligible lady in this county. If her father has her best interests at heart, he may even send her to London for a season. And allowing her to run around in the dirt, to climb trees and play with toy soldiers and behave with no more decorum than a common farm boy is no way to see her raised. If you—"

"I am sorry you do not care for the way I instruct Zora," Julia interrupted, mostly out of concern that Mrs. Holland would never cease her criticisms if she didn't put a stop to it. "But she is startlingly intelligent, and at the moment she has no interest in becoming a proper lady touring around the ballrooms or drawing rooms or any other room of London society. And Mr. Halberd seems to have no complaint with the current course of her upbringing."

Mrs. Holland made a sound with her tongue and her teeth that sounded like a hundred unsavory words crashing against the back of her molars. "Mr. Halberd is a man. He does not know what is best—"

"Mr. Halberd is her father." Julia spoke louder than intended, her voice reverberating off the walls around them.

And... oh. Something in Mrs. Holland's face at that moment. If Julia had been asked to describe it to someone else, she would have failed. The change was too subtle, little more than a smudge of movement in the corner of her vision. But it was there, and Julia knew. Julia knew that Mrs. Holland knew.

About Zora. About her parentage. About-

"Her name is Isadora," Mrs. Holland said, voice so tight it could have been plucked like a harp string. "It was her grandmother's name, and it was Mrs. Halberd's dearest wish to honor her own mother in such a way. And for you to twist it with that absurd sobriquet..."

"It is what she wants to be called." Julia felt as though she was pointing out something as simple as the sky above them and the earth below.

"She is a child. She doesn't know what she wants. If her mother was still alive—"

"But she is not." Julia drew in a slow, shaking breath. A late-night snack was all she had wanted, and here she stood, arguing with Mrs. Holland about nicknames and what a dead woman may or may not have wanted for her child. "God rest her soul," she said, and stepped around the housekeeper and went up the stairs.

She did not understand Mrs. Holland's clear disapproval of her. Was it because she had stepped down from gentlewoman to servant in taking on the position as Zora's governess? Or was it due to the freedom Julia gave the child in her learning, allowing her to climb trees and read upside-down and march back to the house with her skirt and stockings splattered in mud?

Or did the dislike begin further back? She had never been a sociable creature in the first place, and years of suffering and grief had only made her retreat from the public further. Frederick had married her with expectations of her helping to organize events and the cleaning and decorating of the church and to simply be a visible part of village life in Barrow-in-Ashton. But Julia had failed at all of those things, never winning close friends or confidantes throughout her time at the vicarage. And so she had gone to Mrs. Cochran's because there had been no other offer of help for her in the immediate vicinity, no neighbors or parishioners rushing forward to offer meals or a home or assistance.

While Frederick had been alive, her sole contribution to the village had been her work at the school, teaching the poorer girls and young women of the parish. She suspected it had only been allowed to her because of how well her husband was esteemed and respected, and not because anyone with a modicum of power wished to see the daughters of local farmers and laborers taught about things beyond the boundaries of their village. Even Frederick had voiced his concern at educating the lower classes, that it was not their place to learn more than what was appointed to them.

"Their safety is in their ignorance," he had told her. "Let better, more learned men know what is best for them. A little knowledge is a dangerous thing, and will only harm them in the end."

No wonder Mrs. Holland did not like her. No wonder the other inhabitants of Barrow-in-Ashton didn't bring her cakes and tea, or come to have a chat with her, or trade recipes and gossip about the latest fashions. And yet Mr. Halberd had still sought her out, had trusted her with his daughter's care. Perhaps his time away in London had left him unaware of her place in the village's hierarchy of middle-aged ladies. Or perhaps...

... perhaps he simply didn't care.

She hesitated then, halfway up the stairs. She knew she should continue on to her room. She should slip into her nightgown and curl up on the bed with her feet tucked beneath her while she read and ate until exhaustion took her. To want more than that was too much. She had already gone too far the other night, kissing Mr. Halberd. As though she had any right to do so. No doubt he hadn't brought up the matter in order to save her embarrassment. But if she was to seek him out again...

No. She wouldn't even think of it. Up to the top of the stairs, and she paused again. One way would take her past the nursery and to her own bedroom. The other would take her towards Mr. Halberd's quarters, or where she believed them to be. Better for her not to know which room belonged to him, or else the temptation would be too great to walk up to his door, to knock and find out if he would let her in.

But her moment of indecision cost her. The light appeared off to the left, out of the corner of her eye. A longer glance and she saw the distinct glint of another candle, of Mr. Halberd making his way to his own room from the direction of the main staircase.

If she moved now, she knew it would draw his attention towards her. So she stood still, only turning slightly to the right to better shield the light from her candle. But she heard his steps, watched as his own candle grew in brightness as he approached her.

"Mrs. Benton? Is something wrong?"

She turned to face him. "No, I... I couldn't sleep, that's all."

His gaze darted towards her plate, and she thought she heard a soft chuckle from deep within his chest. "I'm glad I'm not the only one who contemplated a late excursion to the kitchen before turning in for the night."

She held up her plate for his perusal. "Do you want to take something?"

He looked at her.

Did she imagine the warmth there, in his eyes? Or was it merely the glow from his candle creating a reflection of something that didn't exist?

"Yes." And that was all he said.

She wished that one word meant more than it did. But he reached out and picked up a scone, and she held her breath as he brought it to his mouth and took a bite.

"Well, goodnight, Mr. Halberd." She said it in a rush, her voice still hanging in the air as she hurried the rest of the way to her room, as she stepped inside and shut the door behind her.

A part of her wanted him to follow her, to knock and prevent the evening from already coming to an end. But she stood with her back against the door, her hands trembling with their burden of the candle and the plate as she listened for his receding footsteps in the hall.

She had become a fool, she realized, imagining that every glance from him, every word held some deeper feeling than it did. It was because she wanted him to want her, but she suspected her desire for him was so strong it had begun to color his every look and action towards her.

Because — God, yes — she wanted him. She had wanted him since that first day she'd met him twelve years before. Her lust for him had weighed on her conscience for every remaining day of her marriage. And it had been lust, strong enough to make her think of him when Frederick climbed atop her in the night, to make her seek out ways to find pleasure for herself when she was alone, when the nights were dark and her thoughts inevitably wound their way back to every memory she kept of him.

And there, as expected, was the guilt. That she had committed adultery in her own heart, that she had coveted another woman's husband. Yet here she was, all these years later, living in his home, caring for his child. Or his wife's child, if what he had told her about his wife's penchant for infidelity was true.

Maybe she had no moral standing to think ill of Mrs. Halberd for breaking her marriage vows, when Julia had abandoned them every day in spirit. Perhaps her husband's insinuations had been correct, that she had failed, and that her failure had kept her from having the family she had so craved.

She banged the back of her head against the door, the pain reverberating through her skull. She was too tired to give leave to tears tonight. Indeed, she'd spent so many throughout the years of her marriage she wondered at her having any left to spare.

"Damn." Because it felt good to say it, that little morsel of vulgarity working to release some of the hurt inside of her. "Damn it all," she said, those words propelling her across the room, towards her bed and the cold, quiet night that awaited her.

Eleven

J ulia's lungs burned. The morning air was cold and dry, scraping in and out of her chest with every breath. There was daylight to the east, though the sun had yet to crest over the horizon. Above her rolled a silent line of clouds, lending an extra dose of chill to the air. She flexed her fingers inside her woolen mittens, her knuckles aching despite the heaviness of the yarn. But the cold helped to banish the restlessness she'd battled with all night, and a little bit of pain in her joints was worth the clarity of mind that came with it.

She couldn't see the house anymore. It sat somewhere behind her, up and behind the rise and the small wooded area that now lay between them. She breathed in again, long and deep, the cold filling her up as though it was solid, and exhaled with a droop of her shoulders.

This felt like the first time she had been able to breathe properly in days. Her sleep the previous night had been nothing short of abysmal, and she wondered if she would've done better to abstain from trying to rest at all and instead accepted her sleepless fate. But after too many hours of tossing and turning and fighting with the blankets on her bed, she dressed in the same gown she'd worn the previous day, dug out all of her warmest and most woolen accessories, and escaped outside for a walk while only a faint glimmer of dawn lit up part of the sky.

She had begun at a brisk pace, striding across the lawn to combat the pre-dawn cold. Her boots scuffed through the frost that coated everything, the dying grass crunching beneath her soles. She had considered walking along the road, towards the village and the more traveled lanes there, but decided she'd rather not encounter anyone along the way. She wanted to be alone, with her own thoughts, with the great open sky above her and the cold, solid ground beneath her feet.

She halted beneath the trees, long enough to blow a breath into her curled hands and warm them up inside her mittens. She would have to return to the house soon, as Zora had a tendency to rise early, but there was a part of her that wanted nothing more than to wander around outside for the entirety of the day and not go back until darkness fell.

It wasn't that she wanted to run away, or — dare she even think it — return to the life she had before, at Mrs. Cochran's. She was happy here at Langford, and spending her days teaching Zora coupled with her weekly lessons at the schoolhouse made her feel as though she was finally accomplishing something with her life.

Except that being so near Mr. Halberd so many thoughts she had believed she'd already conquered. It wasn't until she arrived here that she realized the years following Frederick's death had been nothing more than the gray shadow of an already pitiful existence. And now she was faced with all of the guilt and passion and grief that she had hidden away for so long.

For here was Mr. Halberd, who had lost his wife, just as she had lost her husband. And here was Zora, a motherless child, yet loved and adored by a man who knew he wasn't her father. And there she was, Mrs. Julia Benton, a woman who had married out of desperation rather than for adoration, who had spent seven years of her life praying for her broken body to give her a living child, and all while her husband drew further and further away from her because of her deficits.

Julia swallowed, hard. A pinprick of ice landed on her cheek, and she looked around, surprised to see a few soft, white flakes floating down beneath the mostly bare branches of the trees. As a child, she had loved the snow. The crispness of it, the soft whump of sound it made when walking across a pristine layer for the first time. The snowballs and snowmen and seeking out the perfect hill for sledding.

Now it made her think of slick roads and the tumbling of a carriage down the side of a bank, snuffing out two lives at once as the flakes drifted down from the sky.

She crossed her arms over her chest, gripping her shoulders as though she was about to break apart at the seams. Her pulse pounded in her ears as a stillness came over the area, the falling snow seeming to catch all the ambient sounds from the air and pull them towards the ground. She assumed it was why she didn't hear the hoofbeats right away, muffled by the thin layer of white already accumulating everywhere.

She knew it would be Mr. Halberd, not because of any gift of intuition on her part, but only because she doubted many other people aside from himself would be riding across his property this early in the morning. Her spine straightened as he approached, her arms dropping back to her sides as she lifted her chin. He stopped several yards away, sliding out of the saddle as flecks of snow sparkled on his hat and coat.

"Mr. Halberd." She spoke first, her voice sounding all at once too loud and too quiet with the trees and the snow surrounding them. It felt as though she was shut in all alone with him, despite the fact they were outside, without any walls or borders closing them in.

And still, he said nothing. He looked tired. Probably as tired as she looked, though she hadn't even bothered to glance in the mirror while getting dressed. But she knew she was in a state, clad in yesterday's gown, her hair straggling over her shoulder in a braid that had endured several hours of tossing and turning. And there would be shadows under her eyes, along with a grayness to her pallor she always sported when she hadn't slept well.

He walked towards her, while his horse dipped its head and nosed at the clumps of grass sticking out above the snowfall. Only a few steps, and then he stopped with several paces still left between them.

He hadn't shaved yet. A mixture of gray and black peppered his cheeks and jaw, highlighting the streaks of shadow on his face. She wanted to pull off her mittens and run her naked fingers across those bristles, wanted to feel the scrape of them against her cheeks, her lips, her—

"Tell me," he said, his voice little more than a gruff whisper. "Was it a mistake?"

She blinked at him, confused. "Was what...?"

"When you kissed me." He spoke the words as if he couldn't bring himself to believe them. "But when you said nothing, when you pretended as if it had never happened, I wondered if it had only been the wine, or that you were still half-asleep and took me for someone else."

"Someone else?" Did he think she regularly went around large, dark houses kissing brooding gentlemen in the middle of the night?

"Your..." He glanced down at his hands, flexing and stretching inside of his gloves. "I thought perhaps you mistook me for your husband."

"Oh." She saw it then, a touch of hurt in his eyes, and she wondered that she could've been the one to put it there. "No, I... I would never have..." *kissed my husband,* she nearly said. Because Frederick had always been appalled by overt signs of affection; holding hands, kissing, the mere brush of fingertips across his arm as she walked past. Physical touch was to be confined to the marriage bed, and even then only for the procreation of children. "No, I knew it was you," she said instead, and left it at that.

Relief, that was what she saw on his face, clearing some of the tension from his brow, from the pinched corners of his mouth.

But still, she feared the worst. "I'm sorry." Her hands fluttered in front of her. "I didn't know what I was thinking. I should never have... I'm sorry. I will understand if you want me to leave my place as Zora's governess."

"Leave?" He stared at her, baffled. "Why would I ask you to leave?"

"Because I..." Because she had done something she wanted, rather than push her desires deep down inside of herself, hidden away like a secret treasure that would never be uncovered.

"Julia," he said. Her name. And he took several steps forward, until he was close enough for her to feel the warmth of his breath on her face. "I want you to kiss me again."

She barely let him finish. She reached up and gripped the collar of his greatcoat, pulling him down until his mouth met hers. There was still a fear inside of her, that he would step back, that he would push her away, but he didn't. And she thanked God for that.

His lips...

They were soft. A stark contrast to the rough bristles of his beard, to the nip of his teeth at the corner of her mouth. She drew him towards her until there was no space left between them, until she could feel the thud of his own heartbeat against her chest. And then she tasted him, her tongue touching his, all that was shy and tentative. Until his arms wrapped around her and his hips pressed against hers, igniting a wicked warmth between her legs that stripped away the last of her fears.

And what had her fears been? That he would not want her. That his kindness towards her had only ever been fueled by pity. That he did not see her as she wished to be seen: as a woman, as a woman worth more than what she could provide as a wife and a mother and a housekeeper.

She released his collar, but only to strip off her mittens, letting them fall to the ground as she slid her hands around his neck, her fingers delving into the ends of his hair. His hair and skin were wet with melting snow, but she only felt the heat of him, warming her through better than if she had been standing in front of a roaring fire.

"Julia." He broke off their kiss to look into her face. His gloved thumb came up to stroke her cheek, the stitching of the leather rough on her skin, making her shiver. "I may call you that now?"

"Yes." It was better than hearing her married name on his lips, of being reminded of her husband while standing in another man's arms. She brought her hand around to graze her knuckles across his unshaven jaw, reveling in the feel of it. "Alexander."

Something passed through him, a shiver almost like ecstasy. "Say it again, please."

She smiled. "Alexander."

"I think you could order me to do anything you like, and I would happily agree, as long as you say my name like that."

Oh, if she could have such power over him... but perhaps she did. She licked her lips, and she noticed how closely he watched her as she did so. "Kiss me," she said. "Alexander."

He did. He kissed her with a fierceness that made her hands grip his hair, knocking his hat off his head. She bit at his tongue, drawing it deeper into her mouth. He reacted by pressing his hips more firmly against hers, by groaning in the back of his throat.

But it wasn't enough. She wanted more of him, all of him. Twelve years of stifling her attraction to him, of battling the guilt that overwhelmed her each time she conjured him up in her thoughts. And now here he was, touching her, kissing her, as though for at least some portion of that dozen years, he had thought of her, too.

"I need to go back," she said, her breathing quick as she rested her forehead against his shoulder. "Zora will be up soon. She often wakes early, and she'll be excited to see the snow."

"You're wonderful with her, you know." His hands still roamed over her, one settling on her lower back while the other moved along the side of her ribs, his thumb just brushing beneath the curve of her breast. "I was worried that—"

She tipped her head back when he suddenly stopped speaking. The snow was falling heavy enough that above them the sky was a soft swirl of drifting white. "What?"

Alexander shook his head. "Nothing. Simply thinking out loud."

She kissed him again, first a light kiss to the side of his jaw and then another to the corner of his mouth, where a faint line suddenly etched itself into his skin.

"Do you want me to return to the house with you?" He took a slow step away from her.

The cold slipped in between them immediately. She had to stop herself from going back to him, from sliding her arms beneath his coat, from dragging her onto the ground beneath them. "No, it's not far. You can return to whatever it was you were going to do."

"I rode out to find you," he said, and touched the tip of his finger to her chin. "I saw you, when I looked out my bedroom window this morning. There you were, cutting across the lawn like a determined thing." He bent down and plucked up his hat from the ground, giving it a shake to remove the light dusting of snow that had already fallen on it. "I will see the two of you at breakfast then. It will have to be Mrs. Benton again, won't it?"

Ah, of course it would. They couldn't call one another by their Christian names in front of the servants, in front of Zora. And all at once, she felt something shift between them. She was going to join him in his bed, and soon. Or she would bring him to hers. And they would not be married. They would not even be engaged. But she would do it, and joyfully.

She departed first, shaking out her wet mittens and stuffing her hands back into them as she walked. The snow blanketed the ground with only the tips of the grass still poking through. But it had already begun to slow, the breeze picking up again to push away the wintry clouds overhead.

Inside, the house had sprung to life during her short absence. Julia found a fresh fire blazing in her room, while the laundry she'd left on the floor had disappeared and her bed had been remade. She changed out of her cold, wet clothes, warming her bare arms and legs in front of the fire for several minutes before she donned clean stockings and gown and brushed out her damp hair. By the time she was fully dressed and took herself to the nursery, Zora was already awake and pressed against the window, gazing out at the white landscape with unfettered wonder.

"Can we play today? I want to make a snowman!" she chattered excitedly as Julia helped her to dress and tidy her room.

"I'm not sure there's enough snow to build an entire person. But yes, we can go outside. Not until you've finished yesterday's fractions, however. And not until after breakfast. An hour in the cold and you'll be trembling with hunger."

Breakfast was to be had in the dining room. Julia walked downstairs with Zora, the latter continuing to talk about the snow and if it was cold enough for the stream to ice over and how long it would all last if the sun came out later that afternoon.

Zora's steady stream of dialogue helped to distract Julia from the fact that they were joining Mr. Halberd for breakfast. He was already seated at the table when they entered, his clothes crisp and dry and his hair displaying only a slight dampness at the ends, causing it to curl around his collar and on the very top of his head.

He stood when they entered. Zora ran ahead to ask him if he'd seen the snow and whether or not he agreed with Julia about how much of it would be needed for the creation of a family of snowpeople.

"I'm afraid I have to agree with Mrs. Benton." His gaze

skipped over Zora's head to settle on Julia. A light in his eye, a spark like fire that made her cheeks flush. Apart from that, there was nothing in his expression to betray what had occured between them only an hour before. "And I wish I could stay home with you today to witness the answer to your question myself, but I've business out by the Paxton's property today, to do with their proposed drainage project. But I promise to be back in time for dinner with you. Both of you," he added, stealing another glance at Julia. "And perhaps you may even grant me the privilege of reading a story to you at bedtime?"

"Mrs. Benton has been telling me a story about a dragon," Zora said as her father pulled out two chairs for her and Julia. "And he has a heart made of coal, but every time he breathes fire he burns up a little bit of his heart. Which means he has to be careful during a fight, or he might use himself up entirely."

Mr. Halberd's eyes climbed high on his forehead. "Is that from a storybook? I'm afraid I've never heard that one before."

"No," Julia said, while she subtly scooted her chair nearer to the table. "It's merely something I made up. We started it the first night I was here, and every few days I add a little more to the telling. Unfortunately, I never really know what will happen next until I sit down and begin speaking. But I believe it adds to the adventure that way. Or at least I hope it does."

"Then maybe I will simply be a part of the audience for your story," he said, as one of the maids brought over pots of coffee and hot chocolate for them to choose between.

"You could help her tell it!" Zora bounced in her chair, nearly leaping up to grab a bun and some butter before Julia placed a hand on her arm and passed the plate into her reach. "Sometimes I'll tell her that the dragon should have barbs on its tail, or that the day should be cloudy rather than sunny, and she always makes the changes. I think it's fun that way, telling a story all together."

Julia kept her head down while she buttered Zora's roll, then spooned on a healthy portion of orange preserves. "Please don't tip your cup," she reminded Zora as she nearly sloshed half of her hot chocolate over the rim.

She filled her own plate then, with a selection of buns and jams and far more butter than she should've allowed herself. She reached out to return the butter knife to the dish before she could be tempted to take more, when a whisper of something her husband had once said to her wafted past her ear. That she shouldn't eat more than was necessary, that years of attempting to have a child had filled out her figure without her having done anything to encourage it. But then she recalled how that comment had made her feel, that yet another part of her was defective, her body taking on the shape of a woman ready and willing to bear children without her being able to enjoy any of the benefits of it.

She picked up the knife again, scraped up a large dollop of butter, and smeared it across the top of her bun.

"Mrs. Benton said that I need to work on my fractions before I can go outside," Zora said after she'd finished her first bun and half of her hot chocolate. "What do you think, Papa? I think we can finish my fractions after we've gone out and come back in again."

Her voice was all sweetness, and Julia had to bite her lips at the child's attempt to circumvent her rule and apply to her father instead.

Mr. Halberd sipped his coffee, his expression serious. "If Mrs. Benton believes it correct for you to finish your lessons before play, then I will agree with her judgment on the matter."

"Thank you, Mr. Halberd." Julia wiped her mouth with a napkin, but her gaze leapt over Zora's head to meet his. Still, she thought, he gave little away. A small quirk of his mouth, a flare of his nostrils, and Julia felt heat pool between her legs at the warmth in that glance. And then he looked at his daughter again, his features transforming as he cleared his throat and picked up a crust of toast from his plate. Kindness and love were what she saw then, though with an edge of command underlying it all, enough to make him appear almost daunting at first glance.

It was part of what had sparked her interest in him all those years ago, that mingling of hard and soft in both his behavior and his face. She remembered...

Seven years ago? No, it must have been eight. After church on Sunday, the first Julia had attended after debilitating morning sickness that had resulted in her losing another child. She had still been weak and tired, even trembling if she stayed on her feet for too long. But Frederick had wanted her to be there, claiming that the townspeople were beginning to talk, that her prolonged absences did not reflect well on either of them or their position in the parish.

It had been warm that day, unseasonably so. Julia had stepped out of the church and into the sun, perspiration immediately forming under her arms and across her brow. There had been the usual trade of greetings and meaningless pleasantries, a few pointed glances at her flat abdomen which would have carried a more telltale rounding if she had still been with child.

The dizziness came on quickly. One moment, she had been fine. The next, a blackness flooded the edges of her vision, and her legs turned to jelly beneath her. She reached out — for something, for anything — all while knowing she was going to fall, and it was only the hard stonework of the path outside of the church to catch her.

But she hadn't fallen. Arms came around her, holding her up before she could collapse.

"I have you," he said. Mr. Halberd said. Alexander. Because of course it had been him. He carried her back inside of the church, into the coolness and the shade, the sunlight coming through the stained glass windows in jeweled tones that set the dust in the air on fire.

He made her sit, made her bend forward until her head was nearly on her knees, made her breathe while the grayness pulled back from her sight and the sludge of her thoughts began to flow again. And all with his hand drawing soft circles on her upper back, his fingertips occasionally brushing across the damp skin above her collar. When she could raise her head again without fearing a relapse, it was to see him on his knees before her, his head bare and his eyes wide and worried.

"Can you stand?" he had asked her, his voice low. And yet how it echoed against the high, arched ceiling of the nave.

She shook her head. She had felt this way before, and she knew it would be several more minutes before she could trust her legs to support her. "I'm sorry." The apology tumbled out as if by rote. Because she was so accustomed to apologizing, for begging absolution from those around her for all she continually did wrong.

"What on earth for?" He looked genuinely perplexed.

"Because..." But she couldn't finish. A few of the other ladies must have finally noticed her absence outside, and they bustled into the church with the determination of hens, fretting and fluttering around her, offering her smelling salts and gently pushing Mr. Halberd out of the way until he picked up his hat and slowly backed away from her.

When she could stand again, she returned outside at a slower pace, her hand hovering near the outer wall of the church in case she would need it for support. The sun was still too bright, the air too warm, but one of the ladies offered to walk her back to the vicarage if needed. Julia looked for her husband, and she found him standing off to one side, speaking with Mrs. Halberd about the planning for the summer fete. He told her later that he hadn't noticed what had happened, had been oblivious to her plight. So of course she began to think that she had overreacted, that she hadn't been as unwell as she had thought.

"It's very trying to have you so ill all of the time," Frederick had said later that evening, when the incident had passed into the realm of things she might have only imagined. "It doesn't look well for you to demand so much of others' goodwill."

Julia closed her eyes. When she opened them again, she was in the dining room at Langford, with Zora at her side sipping choco late with loud slurping noises. Julia couldn't bring herself to admonish her for it. "Half a page of fractions from the book and then you may go outside to play. But that means another full page when you come back in again."

Zora beamed, chocolate and buttered crumbs clinging to her upper lip. "I'll do two pages if you help to make a snowman," she bargained, still grinning.

"Agreed," Julia said, and accepted the second cup of chocolate Mr. Halberd offered to her.

Twelve

The snow was nearly gone by the time Julia and Zora returned inside for their midday meal, only a few slashes of white still lingering on the shadowed portions of the lawn. They stripped out of their wet outer garments and huddled beside the fire in the nursery, Zora sitting cross-legged with her kitten in her lap while she ate apples and cheese and a few leftover buns from breakfast.

Julia sat beside her, her legs curled up beneath her skirt, her cheeks warmed by the fire and her stomach assuaged by too many apples and bites of melted cheese. Instead of a kitten, which she would have much preferred, she had Zora's page of fractions that still needed to be tended to, as well as a list of French verbs that would have to be memorized tomorrow. It had been a lovely morning, and spending the afternoon in the warm, quiet nursery should have been soothing to her soul. Instead, she was restless, despite the amount of energy she'd expended outside. Her thoughts continually strayed to Mr. Halberd, to when she would see him again, to when-

A knock at the door dragged her back to the present. Julia levered herself up from the floor and answered, only to find Mrs.

Holland standing there with a small stack of boxes and parcels in her arms.

"A delivery, for you," was all the housekeeper said.

Julia gestured her into the room, helping her with half the boxes as they laid them out on the table. "What is it?" she asked as she fussed with the knotted twine wrapped around the top box.

"They're from McKinley's," Mrs. Holland told her, which left Julia with as many questions as before, as a parcel from McKinley's could be anything from a pair of stockings to a book about the amphibians of Australia.

Julia raised the lid off the first box and found herself staring down at an assortment of paints and paintbrushes. "Oh," was all she could think to say before opening the next box, this one filled with fine quality paper. The next was a collection of charcoals and pencils and pastels, while the final one held a stack of new slates and chalk. "This is much more than I will need for Zora."

"Mr. Halberd informed me that he ordered items for the school, as well." Mr. Holland brushed her hands down the front of her skirt, as though there was dirt on her hands that needed to be wiped away. "There are also some books, but those will be coming all the way from London if I'm not mistaken."

Julia ran her fingers over the bristles of the paintbrushes. They were excellent quality, finer than anything she had ever owned or used. And Mr. Halberd had purchased them for the school, for the daughters of farmers, for girls who would never have access to such expensive materials otherwise.

"Quite a waste, really."

Julia replaced the lid on the box of brushes and moved to do the same with the others. "How so?" she asked Mrs. Holland without looking up from her task.

The housekeeper sighed. "It is not wise to hire girls who can read and write. Not only does it give them ideas above their station, but it tempts them towards prying into matters that have nothing to do with them."

"I see." Julia swallowed down another dozen words she wanted to say but stopped them before they could leap off her tongue.

"You give these girls too much credit, Mrs. Benton. They are not people who are capable of thinking for themselves, of making wise choices if left to their own devices. They require guidance and hard work. Without work, they become idle and find their way into mischief."

"And is that not an argument for them to be taught?" Julia closed up the last box and looked at Mrs. Holland. "To be educated? So they will know better and be able to make wise and informed decisions towards their own lives?"

Mrs. Holland shook her head, her lips drawn into a thin line. "There is a place for them, and nothing more. Mark my words—"

"I'd rather leave them unmarked. Thank you, Mrs. Holland." There was no point in wasting breath on further argument. Julia had heard the same comments from some of the villagers when she had first begun teaching, that the children of farmers and common laborers — especially their daughters — should not be taught. That they were fit for employment that would never require them to know their letters, marriage and the bearing of children, and nothing more.

"And here, you think your unconventional upbringing of Miss Halberd will serve her well," Mrs. Holland continued, even as Julia walked to the nursery door and opened it for her. "But you'll turn her into something no man will want for a wife. And then what will there be for her?"

Julia turned to face the housekeeper. She knew that she shouldn't, that she should ignore Mrs. Holland and allow her to continue nurturing her horrible ideas, as people like her — at least in Julia's experience — would never change their opinion on such matters, even should the world itself shudder to a halt and begin spinning in the opposite direction. But she turned, and she clasped her hands before her, and she drew in a breath that fueled her next words like the blast of a bellows across the coals of a hot fire.

"What will there be for her? Anything she wants, I assume. Zora is fortunate to have enough settled on her that she'll have no need to marry for money or security, if that is not her wish. She may grow up to be a writer, or a historian, or perhaps she will indeed marry and have ten children while painting pictures of far-off places, if that is what she so desires. It is all I want for her, what her father wants for her, the ability to choose the life best suited for her wants and needs."

Mrs. Holland began to walk out of the nursery, but she stopped in the doorway, pausing long enough for her gaze to sweep over Julia, eyes narrowed as though appraising her with some new insight. "You are not her mother, Mrs. Benton. You will never be her mother."

So there it was, the reason for Mrs. Holland's dislike of her. She believed that Julia had come to Langford in order to take Mrs. Halberd's place, either as Zora's caretaker, or perhaps even more.

"Good afternoon, Mrs. Holland. I need to return to Zora." And she shut the nursery door in the housekeeper's face.

Julia turned around and saw Zora still seated beside the fire, teasing her kitten with a feather on a string.

"Maybe I will be a housekeeper when I grow up," Zora announced without raising her head, her fingers still making the string dance. "But a nice one, rather than someone who goes around being horrid all the time."

"We'll see," Julia said, and bit back a grin.

* * *

Mr. Halberd joined them for dinner, just as he promised. But instead of gathering together in the dining room, with all the fanfare that came with it, he arrived in the nursery as the maid came up with their tray. A simple meal, a venison stew with crusty bread on the side, and perfect for the room's cozy atmosphere.

They took their seats around the small table, Julia hiding her amusement at how incongruous Mr. Halberd appeared sitting in a chair that was several inches too short for him, spooning stew into a bowl that sat a few inches too low in front of him. And all while Zora regaled him with stories from their morning spent outside in the snow, in-between bites of grave-soaked bread and pauses long enough for her to lick the butter from her fingers.

"Use a napkin." Julia pressed the cloth to her charge, only for it to slip off Zora's lap and onto the floor, quickly forgotten.

Julia watched Mr. Halberd interact with his daughter, her attention catching on the crinkling of his eyes at the corners, at the bright gleam of his smile when Zora said something that brought up a laugh from deep within his chest. The love in his face shone brighter than any other lamp or flame in the room, and she could only hope that Zora would someday know how fortunate she was to be so thoroughly adored by another person, how rare and beautiful a thing that was.

After dinner, Mr. Halberd took the tray down to the kitchen to allow Zora her privacy while she washed and changed into her nightgown. When he returned, they spent an hour playing cards on the floor, Zora defeating him soundly four times before her father gave up and Julia declared it time for bed.

"Is Papa going to read to me tonight?"

Julia looked at Mr. Halberd. He appeared caught out, his eyes widening as she held out the book to him, a volume of Robin Hood tales and ballads. "Your audience awaits," she said, and switched places with him on the side of the bed.

Julia thought she might slip out of the nursery once he began reading and retire to her own room for the rest of the evening. A slight headache throbbed at her temples, and being outside in the snow that morning had left with her a chilled ache in her joints that only several hours of uninterrupted slumber would cure. But the moment he turned to the first page, the moment he began to read, she could not think of being anywhere else.

His voice was a rich thing. She knew this already, but it grew deeper as he read, insinuating itself among the words on the page, lifting them up and into the air like sparks drifting from a fire. She did not sit, but instead retreated back into the shadows, leaning against the door as she listened to him. Each line was like a spell woven, some ancient magic awakened, and she thought she might no longer belong to herself the more he read, the more pages he turned.

The silence came suddenly. Zora had fallen asleep a quarter of an hour before, her head lolling off the edge of the pillow. Mr. Halberd closed the book, setting it on his lap before he shifted his daughter's head back onto the pillow and brushed a few strands of hair from her cheek. Julia stepped forward again and relieved him of the book, slipping it back into its place on the shelf. When she turned around again, he had already begun putting out the lights in the room, leaving only the glow of the fire to illuminate their path to the door.

"Thank you," Julia said as soon as they were out in the hall, the door to the nursery clicked shut behind them. "Have you often read to her before?"

He shook his head, the candle he'd brought with him from the nursery smudging his features into broad swathes of gold and shadow. "Not enough. Not nearly enough. Zora was her mother's child when my wife was still alive, and then after she passed away it was... difficult."

She wanted to reach out to him. To place her hand on his arm, to give him some small amount of comfort she wasn't sure how best to express it in words. Instead, her fingers fluttered at her side and she took a step back from him. "I should..." she began, as though she had more to say. But she tipped her head towards the door of her own room and shuffled back again.

"Julia," he said. Low enough that his voice cracked on the final sound.

There were a dozen reasons why she should not even contemplate it. They were not married. He was her employer. His child was in her care. It was wrong. It was a sin. It was a sin. It was a sin. And yet she didn't move when he ate up the distance between them in one long stride. She made no protest when his hand came up to her face, his knuckles gliding along the side of her jaw.

"I don't want to be alone tonight."

Her lips parted on a small gasp. As if it was an invitation, he slid his thumb beneath the curve of her lower lip, stroking slowly back and forth. Until she closed her eyes. Until she stopped breathing.

It was too much, that simple caress. When she looked at him again, he had moved closer to her. And she knew that whatever he wanted, she wanted it, too.

"My room?" he asked.

She nodded once. In that moment, she would have agreed to going with him to his room, to her own room, to letting him lift up her skirts and push her back against the wall right where they stood.

He took her hand, his fingers lacing with hers as he led her down the hall. Julia had never set foot in his bedroom before, had only walked past the door a few times on her way to the main staircase. He released her hand long enough to open the door, and stepped back to allow her to go in first.

It wasn't completely dark. There was light from the fire casting the room in soft oranges and red, and there was still the candle in his hand, which he set aside on a small writing desk as soon as he had followed her inside and closed the door behind them. She noticed the bed first, of course. All dark and curtained, and set up on a kind of dais like something she would expect to see from the days of Henry VIII or Elizabethan rule. It made her wonder how many people had stood here before her, how many men and women over the last two centuries had gazed upon that bed in anticipation of what was to come.

Mr. Halberd—

No, she couldn't continue to call him that, at least not to

herself. Not anymore. Alexander came around to stand in front of her. He didn't touch her, though his hands twitched restlessly at his sides, his fingers tapping against his thigh before the movement ceased and he drew in a breath.

"Tell me what you want."

Her gaze flew up to his face. She thought he had looked calm at first, and she couldn't even begin to fathom how he could manage such a show of composure when she was burning up inside. But when she looked closer, she saw the tension in his jaw, in his shoulders, the flare of his nostrils as he waited for her to respond.

"What *I* want?" It seemed an absurd question. When, in all of her life, had anyone taken the time to ask what she wanted, what she desired? "I-I don't know."

He didn't smile. She thought he might, but he didn't. Instead, he licked his lips, and she watched that subtle movement of his tongue as though her very existence depended on it. "It wasn't an exaggeration this morning, when I said you could tell me to do anything and I would do it. So here I stand, asking you—no, begging you—to tell me what you want of me."

She remembered he'd said that. That if she said his name...

"Alexander."

He inhaled. As if called to attention, with a slight push back of his shoulders and a lift of his chin, waiting for her.

"I want..." *Anything*, he had said. "I want you to undress."

Her throat nearly closed up as soon as she said it, and she panicked over whether or not she could draw the words back into her mouth before he could hear them. Oh, God above. What would he think of her?

"Undress," he repeated, and nodded solemnly. "For clarification, do you mean you, or myself?"

She was sure the heat flooding her cheeks could warm the entire household for the rest of the month. "You. I want you to undress. To take off your clothes." Her throat threatened to catch again, but she pressed forward. "All of them."

Would he laugh at her? Surely he would laugh at her. She had never said such things to her husband during all of their marriage, and he had never invited it. Throughout their years together, their relations had never been anything more than... perfunctory. Something expected of them for the procreation of children and nothing more. A duty to be performed, without any superfluous emotions such as passion or desire or want ever being involved.

But she had imagined how it was supposed to be, how it could have been. Except that all too often those imaginings had replaced her husband with the face and figure of someone else. The man who currently stood before her, the one whose hands reached up to unfasten the top buttons of his waistcoat.

One by one, she watched the buttons wink in the light as they moved beneath his fingers. He shrugged out of the waistcoat and tackled his neckcloth next, making quick work of its knot before he unwound it from beneath his collar and let the long strip of fabric fall to the floor. His shirt would be next. He grabbed the fabric at his waist, tugging the hem of it out from his trousers as—

"No."

Alexander's arms went still.

"Your boots next, and then your trousers."

He released the fabric of his shirt. He glanced over his shoulder, as though he had momentarily forgotten the layout of his own room. There was a chair near the fire and he sat down in it, dragging off his boots and stockings one at a time before he stood again and began undoing the falls of his trousers.

Julia watched him. Goodness, a war could have broken out on the front lawn and she would not have been able to look away from his hands. And then his legs were bare, and he paused, waiting for her to tell him what to do next.

His shirt came down nearly to the middle of his thighs. Thighs that bore more muscle than her imagination had been able to concoct. And his hips...

"Your shirt," she said. She met his gaze, and the hunger in his eyes fueled the ache between her legs. "Take it off."

Julia couldn't recall how many times she had seen Frederick naked. Seven years of marriage to her husband, and everything between them had been in the dark, beneath blankets and dressing gowns, leaving behind the implication that nudity was a shameful thing, that there was no pleasure to be had in seeing another person as God had made them.

She looked at Alexander as though she was dying of thirst and his body was a cool drink of water brought to her parched lips. He wasn't built like an Adonis, like a piece of art carved from marble meant to last for ages. But there was leanness and there was muscle, and there was a pride in the way he stood before her, unashamed of what nearly five decades of life had wrought in his figure.

She wished she could feel as bold as him.

Her gaze roamed over him, over his shoulders and his chest, skimming across his abdomen and following the trail of dark hair that led her to...

Well.

She was not a simpering virgin. Despite the rarity of seeing her former husband fully unclothed, she knew a man's body, how its various bits and pieces looked and functioned. So she wasn't surprised by what she saw. And yet her blush wouldn't abate, and she forced herself to breathe slowly, to keep herself from becoming mired in the question of just what she was supposed to do with him now that she had him there in front of her, naked and prepared to fulfill her every whim.

A few steps forward and she was near enough to touch him. Her hand trembled as she raised it and placed her palm flat against his chest. His heart thudded a furious tattoo behind his ribs. Was he as nervous as she was? He had been without a wife for as long as she had been without a husband, but she also knew that men were often at greater liberty to satisfy their needs than women. Perhaps he had taken a lover at some point. Perhaps...

A slide of her fingers down the center of his chest, over his abdomen, down further until she brushed against him. His... manhood? That was what her mother had called it, when she'd taken her aside and given her an awkward and useless pre-marriage talk about what would be expected from her in the bedroom with her husband. But Julia had hated that word and she still hated it now.

He inhaled sharply as she touched him, as she lightly wrapped her fingers around him. She had never touched her husband like this. Once, she had tried, and he had pulled away from her in apparent disgust. As though a wife should never show any sign of wanting more intimacy than was minimally required.

"What do you call it?" The question sounded silly to her own ears, but she dragged her fingertips along the length of him, drawing out a low moan from him as if she had caused him pain.

"Christ," he muttered, his head falling back. "Did your husband never—"

"There are a great many things my husband never did or told me." She stroked him again and watched his eyes close, watched his lips part and his breath catch. "Alexander, what do you call it? This," she said, and stroked him again.

"My cock," he said. "Dear God, if you keep doing that..."

She pulled her hand away, suddenly ashamed. Had she gone too far? She had wanted to touch him. As soon as she saw him, that part of him, large and tipped upwards, she had wanted to wrap her fingers around him and— "I'm sorry." She shook her head. "I'm sorry. I shouldn't have done that. Please forgive me."

His eyes fluttered open. He looked at her, confusion pulling down his eyebrows. "Why are you apologizing? God in Heaven, I thought I was going to come right there."

She didn't know what he meant. In lieu of explaining himself, he took her hand and guided it back to him. "When you do this," he said, his voice a rough rasp across her cheek. "I fear I may break apart before I can repay you in kind."

143

Ah. That she understood. His hand fell away from hers as she slid her own down his length, but he stopped her again before she could go any further.

"No, not yet. Please," he added. "I've waited too long for this. I don't want to rush."

She didn't want to rush, either. They had the entire night before them yet, and there she stood, fully clothed, even a spot of gravy leftover from dinner still streaked on her sleeve. And then what he had said played over again in her head, as if she was only hearing it for the first time. "What do you mean you've waited too long?"

He brought his hand up to cup the side of her face, his thumb brushing along the edge of her cheekbone. "I would be lying if I said I hadn't thought of you over these last few years. And even... before."

"Before?" She tilted her head into his touch, but she watched his face, the clouding of his gaze as he seemed to slip away from her.

"My wife was not faithful to me in action, Julia. And I... I was not faithful to her in spirit." He kissed her forehead, then tipped up her chin to look at her, his gaze so intent the rest of the room drew back into a haze of nonexistence. "Perhaps it was wrong of me, to look elsewhere. Perhaps it did nothing but further drive a wedge between us. But if you think ill of me for wanting you while I was married to another woman, I won't blame you if you choose to turn around and leave me here."

Never in her wildest daydreams had Julia imagined there might have been something more to his kindness to her throughout all the years she'd known him. But that he had wanted her? That he had desired her while they had both been married to other people? No, she could hardly wrap her head around the realization.

"Why did you never...?" Oh, but she already knew the answer to that. Because if she had known how he had felt all those years ago, she might not have been able to claim fidelity to her husband during their ill-fated marriage. She might have been tempted to do more than simply dream of Alexander after her husband had rolled away from her in their bed at night.

"Enough," she said. To him. To herself. Before she pressed herself against him, her hands on his bare shoulders, sliding around his neck as she pulled his head down and kissed him.

Thirteen

~~

J ulia had no concept of time, of anything else in the world progressing beyond the four walls of Alexander's bedroom. She did not kiss him sweetly or delicately, but instead with her fingers pushing into his hair, with her lips parting his before their tongues met and her body arched against his.

His arms moved around her, his fingers blindly seeking out the buttons at the back of her gown. She startled at the realization of what he was doing, and she tried to pull away from his hands and out from the circle of his embrace at the same time. "No," she said, and broke their kiss. Her hands slid down from his head, her palms flat against his chest. She didn't push him away, but she held him there, placing that infinitesimal amount of space between them.

"I'm sorry." His own hands fell back to his sides. "What is it? What's wrong?"

Now that they'd come to it, she wasn't sure how to say it out loud without feeling like a fool. But she didn't want to undress in front of him. She didn't want him to see her body, the marks on her skin from the times she was with child, the heaviness of her belly and bosom, all of the evidence that she simply wasn't a young woman anymore. Perhaps it wasn't fair of her to tell him to take off

146

his clothes when she couldn't bring herself to remove her own, but the shame Frederick had instilled in her while he'd been alive... Well, it lingered. How he had never cared to see her naked, how he had advised her to eat less when her hips and waist had begun to thicken. How she had stopped checking her reflection in the mirror for fear she would find some new fault he would eventually point out to her.

She sighed. "I don't... I don't want to undress for you. Not yet."

He nodded. No complaints, no arguments. Just a simple acquiescence to her wishes. "But, may I...?" He reached for her, but waited for her to step toward him rather than close the distance himself. When she went to him, his hands grasped her above the waist, his thumbs beneath her breasts.

She buried her face in his shoulder as his caresses moved upwards, his thumbs gliding over her nipples, hard enough for her to feel it through the fabric still between them. Before Julia could stop herself, her tongue slipped out to taste him, the salt and sweat of his skin, the warmth of him even fully undressed as he was.

And then he was down on his knees in front of her, his hands sliding over her hips, her legs, before they delved beneath the hem of her gown.

"What are you doing?" The question tumbled out of her, while her hands wavered in the air before they found their way to his shoulders for balance.

He gave her no reply. His answer was to show her what he was doing, what he intended to do.

His hands skimmed over her calves, up and over her knees, and then above the line of her stockings to the bare skin of her thighs. She knew, even before he arrived there, where he was working towards.

"Julia," he said, and he looked up at her, eyes glinting in the firelight. "If you want me to stop at any moment, let me know and I will."

She nodded quickly, while her fingers dug deep into the muscles of his shoulders.

A soft brush of his thumb across her slit, and she gasped. It was how she touched herself, in her most private moments. Yet there he was, on his knees before her, drawing the same bliss from her she had only ever achieved with the work of her own hands.

And he didn't stop. Again and again, his fingers moved over her, until he slid one of them inside of her, and she sobbed with the pleasure of it.

She couldn't let go of his shoulders, even as he drew up the front of her skirt, even as he leaned forward and his mouth took over from the ministrations of his fingers. Another moment and then his tongue was teasing her there, thrusting inside of her, and her hands found their way into his hair, holding on for dear life while everything fell apart around her.

Her legs threatened to give out beneath her, but Alexander caught her, scooping her up and carrying her over to the bed. If she had been in any mind to protest at his help, she would have, that stubborn independent streak fighting for dominance. But instead she allowed herself to revel in his care of her, the way he gently laid her on the bed, as though she was incredibly precious. The way he stretched out naked beside her, the light from the fire at his back, casting him in silhouette.

"You're stealing all the heat from the fire," she teased him, while his hand slid up and down the length of her arm.

"I am the one without any clothes on." He grinned, and in that moment he both looked his age and yet somehow younger, the last several years stripped away from his features.

Between the aftermath of what he'd done to her and the calming touch of his hand stroking her arm, a languor swept over which she did not think she could defeat. The warmth and the golden darkness of the room, the presence of Alexander beside her all made her feel so safe that she could hardly keep her eyes open. "I'm sorry," she said, embarrassed that she couldn't stay awake,

148

that she had an overwhelming desire to let him wrap his arms around her and hold her until she...

Her eyes blinked open. It was dark above her, all around her. Goodness, she must have fallen asleep. For a moment, she thought she was in her own room, that she had tucked Zora in for the night and gone to bed and nothing else had occurred. But she knew, in that way even a mind and body fogged with sleep will always know, the room was not her own.

Alexander.

Julia rolled onto her side from her back. He was beside her in the bed, one arm flung over her waist, sound asleep. At some point he must have dragged a blanket over the two of them to keep from getting chilled. Because the fire had burned down, and as her eyes adjusted she noticed the faint, cool glow of moonlight from the windows. A clear night, then. And most likely cold.

Another shift and she tucked herself closer to him. A brush of her fingertips across his chest told her that he was still naked, or at least from the waist up. Should she wake him? She didn't want to, didn't want to spoil the moment; the peace and perfection of having him beside her, with his arm holding her close.

She thought back over what he had said before, his admittance that he had wanted her even while they had both been married to other people. All those years...

She didn't want to tell herself they were wasted years. But it still hurt, how the both of them had suffered with their spouses — she with a husband who had never loved her, Alexander with a wife who had turned to another man and left him with a child to raise that was not his own — when they could have had so much more.

No. No, she wouldn't think like that. Been unfaithful to their partners? Of course not. Julia had dealt with enough guilt at the mere thought of Alexander while her husband had still been alive, dragging her down like a weight around her neck. She could not have lived with herself if she had ever acted on her desire for him.

But the fact that five whole years had passed since the accident that ended both their marriages made her wonder why.

Why hadn't he said anything to her before now?

Maybe he'd feared his own feelings wouldn't have been reciprocated. Maybe that was why he had begun with asking her to care for Zora, as a way to bring her closer to him before he had the courage to make his true feelings known.

Julia sighed and closed her eyes. She had no idea what time it was. Late, of course. And also probably early. What time did the servants come through to rebuild the fires? She didn't want to be discovered sleeping in Alexander's bed, but neither did she want to leave and shuffle back to her room in the middle of the night. Surprisingly, she felt no shame over what they had done — or what he had done to her — but servants had a tendency to gossip, and if they had already spoken about Mrs. Halberd's... extramarital adventures where her daughter could hear, Julia didn't need a night spent in Alexander's bed to be used as more grist for their scandal mill.

She moved again. As reluctant as she had been to undress in front of him, several hours of sleeping in her gown and stays and stockings made her now rethink her previous shyness. She wouldn't be able to go back to sleep like this, with her buttons digging into her spine and something else around the area of her rib cage shifted down to where it wasn't supposed to be.

Slowly, carefully, she sat up and extricated herself from the weight of Alexander's arm without waking him. A low sound came from his throat as he rolled onto his back, the blanket slipping down to his waist with a brush of his arm. She looked at him, at the outline of his shoulders, his upper arms, his chest...

No. She shouldn't wake him, shouldn't bother him now. Instead, she reached down and slipped off her shoes, letting them fall off the edge of the bed with a dull thud onto the rug below. Twisting her own arms behind her back, she managed to undo the top few buttons of her gown, enough that she could breathe more easily and adjust the part of her underclothes that had moved out of place.

"There." She rolled her shoulders inside her loosened sleeves and began taking her pins out of her hair, or at least the ones that hadn't already fallen out while she'd been asleep. There was a tangle at the back she would have to work out with a comb in the morning, but she worked the worst of it out with her fingers, the heavy waves of her hair falling over her shoulders and down to her hips.

"Julia."

She gasped and looked down. Alexander's eyes gleamed at her in the darkness, picking out the pale moonlight and reflecting it back to her.

"Oh." She gathered up what she could find of her pins and set them on the nightstand beside her. "I didn't mean to wake you. I'm sorry."

"Don't apologize." His voice was low. Husky. "This is better than sleep."

"This?" She glanced down at herself, at the bed around them, as though there was something of great interest tucked into the shadows she hadn't yet noticed.

"Seeing you," he explained. "In the dark." He reached out and curled a lock of her hair around his fingers. "I've dreamed about what you would look like, with your hair down like this."

Julia had always loved her hair. Frederick had often expounded on how vanity and pride was a sin, so she had always kept it pinned tight in a simple knot at the back of her head, never taking the time for elaborate braids or twists or curls that would show off its beauty. But despite the vacillations of her health, her hair had always remained thick and shiny, always with a soft wave through it that ended with a slight curl at the tips. It wasn't much, she thought, but it was something that made her blush with pleasure as Alexander brought a lock of it to his lips.

"What time is it?"

He pulled himself up onto his elbows, the blanket skirting lower around his hips. "I'm not sure. I'd say..." He glanced at the windows, at the cold remains of the fire. "Around two, perhaps three o'clock?"

She swallowed. "I shouldn't stay here. If someone comes in..." She left the rest of it hanging in the air between them. If one of the servants was to arrive to light the morning fire, and found her in bed with the master of the house, no doubt the tale of it would spread like a poison through the lower floors. The governess who became a mistress only a short while after moving into the house, as though that had been her very intention from the beginning.

Alexander opened his mouth as if to speak, then closed it again with a shake of his head. "You must do what you think is best."

"I'm thinking of Zora," she said. The child already had a shadow of ignominy hanging over her head thanks to her mother's infidelity. Julia had no desire to add to the darkness with rumors of her own behavior.

"I know you are." And Alexander brushed his fingers across the tops of her knuckles.

She began to turn, to swing her legs over the edge of the bed, but something stopped her. Nothing Alexander said or did, but a tightening in her own abdomen, a resolve brought on by nothing more than a reluctance to scuttle back to her room like a church mouse when it seemed as though the night had only begun a short while before.

She moved back to where she had been. Her hands fidgeted with the collar of her gown until she worked up the courage to push the fabric down, baring her shoulders and the tops of her breasts to the chill air.

To anyone else, it might have been nothing. Many women, infinitely more fashionable than she ever claimed to be, often wore gowns revealing vast portions of upper arms and neck and chest. But she had been nothing more than the wife of a vicar in a small village, and now a widow and a governess. She was not the sort to put herself on display, to call more attention to herself than was permitted.

Alexander breathing. It was a sharp huff of sound, not quite a gasp but enough to draw a line beneath the moment. He reached up and brushed her hair back from her shoulder, then slid the tip of his finger along her neckline. When he came to the hollow between her breasts, he hooked his finger over the fabric and tugged down gently, until the bodice dragged lower and her chest...

With a deft turn of his wrist, he slipped his fingers beneath her left breast and lifted it free of the gown. "God in Heaven." His words sounded like a prayer, though the look in his eyes was anything but virtuous. Onto his side, he moved closer as he stroked his thumb across her bare nipple, as he cupped the heavy weight of her breast in his hand.

Julia wanted to close her eyes, wanted to let her head loll back as the sensations from the tip of her breast shot like a dart to the growing heat between her legs. But she couldn't bring herself to look away. She wanted to watch him as he touched her, to see what it looked like when someone brought pleasure to another person.

She thought it would be entirely one-sided, that every sweep of his thumb, every light pinch of his fingers was purely for her benefit and no one else. But she could see the shift of the blanket as his cock twitched to life, could not deny the lust in his eyes as his gaze drank in the heavy curve of her breast.

Without thinking about what she was doing, she leaned forward, towards him. His lips replaced his hand on her breast, his kisses light at first before he drew the nipple into his mouth, teasing it with the heat of his tongue, with a gentle graze of his teeth. Julia hissed at that mixture of pain and desire as it lanced through her. "More," she said, the word a mere whisper of sound. But Alexander heard her, and he nipped her again, hard enough that she grasped his head between her hands, holding him there until she could dare to breathe again.

He reached up and fumbled blindly with her bodice, yanking

at the collar until her other breast was exposed. Taking one of her hands, he guided it to her chest, pressing her palm against her flesh, urging her to touch herself. She hesitated at first, embarrassed to behave that way in front of him. But she wanted to do it, wanted to feel the brush and slide of her own fingers while he was there, while he was watching her.

Something changed then, a frantic energy taking over the both of them. His mouth abandoned her breast in order to trail kisses up and along the length of her throat, the bristles of his unshaven jaw scraping at the sensitive skin beneath her ear. Her skirt...

They both grabbed for it at once, but she worked quicker, while he shoved the last corner of blanket aside that still lay between them. He tipped her back and climbed over her, a shadow prowling across her vision, a darkness made of heat and palpable desire. She spread her legs wide, the chill air of the bedroom cool on her bare thighs, above the line of her stockings. But there he was, like fire in corporeal form, his knees bracketing her hips, not a tremble from his arms as he held himself perfectly still above her.

"Yes?" He was right there, the tip of him just nudging her entrance, and even that light touch was enough to make her hips jolt.

"Yes," she said. "Yes, Alexander. Please!"

Slowly... Dear God, he moved so slowly to begin with. Only an inch or so at first, the sheer size of him stretching her, making her hold her breath as he pushed inside. He was larger than her husband. She hated to think of it at such a moment, but it caught her off guard, the little sparks of sensation it sent through her, something she had never felt in all her years with Frederick.

"Are you all right?" He paused, and she could hear the constraint in his voice, that he was holding back, waiting for her assurance that he had not hurt her.

She nodded tightly. Her hands found their way to his shoulders, gripping him until her knuckles turned white, until her nails dug into his skin. And then she lifted her hips, urging him to keep going, to finish what they had started.

A sound rumbled out of him, not quite a purr and not quite a growl, before he slid the rest of the way into her. There was a moment then, when he stayed there, his hips flush with her own, their bodies fully joined. It was an irrevocable change in that instant, the realization that there would be no going back after this. That Julia would not ever want to.

Alexander pulled back and thrust into her again. Still slow, excruciatingly slow, as though he was afraid of harming her, of frightening her. But his reservations seemed to disappear quickly, and soon Julia's hands slid down to the middle of his back, her fingers gripping the slickness of his perspiring skin, the flex and pull of the muscles there.

Dear God, it was almost too much. All of her years of imaginings hadn't prepared her for this, for how it felt to have him inside of her, filling her up with every thrust of his hips. She wanted to make it last, but she could already feel that telltale wave of... something roiling up through her, spreading up and outward like a fever about to break.

She cried out before she could stop it, loud enough that anyone awake in the house at such an early hour would have heard her. But she couldn't think, could only clutch at Alexander as the aftershocks pulsed through her. Meanwhile, he thrust into her once... twice more, before he suddenly pulled out of her, his eyes shut tight as a hoarse cry scraped its way from the back of his throat. And then he collapsed beside her, his seed spilling onto the discarded blanket from before.

It took Julia a minute to catch her breath, to trust her eyes and her ears and her other senses to fall back into working order. She brushed the back of her hand across her brow, sweeping away her tangled hair along with a sheen of sweat that had accumulated on her face. Between her legs, she still throbbed. As though she had already had enough, and yet she still wanted more. But her gaze strayed to the blanket, the corner of which he used to wipe himself clean before he balled it up and tossed it onto the floor. Her mouth was dry as a desert, and she dragged her voice up from where it had gone to hide away in her lungs.

"Why did you do that?" She nodded her head towards the blanket. It wasn't an accusation. She understood what he had done, and why he had most likely done it. No doubt he thought he was helping her, saving her by withdrawing just before he could finish inside of her.

He stood up and crossed the room, passing through the shafts of moonlight that stretched through the windows. He gave himself a more thorough washing at the basin on its stand, then brought over a damp cloth for her use, as well.

As he strode back to the bed, she took a moment to appreciate the beauty of him. He was such a perfect mingling of hard lines and gentleness, and she blushed anew at the thought of having the liberty to touch and admire him, at having every right to do so.

The bed creaked beneath his weight. She let her legs fall open as he wiped her clean, taking such care that she couldn't prevent the burn of tears from forming at the corners of her eyes. "Why did I... what?" he asked, after tossing the used linen onto the blanket already on the floor.

She sighed. She was no good at speaking about such matters. Her mother had never encouraged questions about the marriage bed, and attempting to speak with Frederick about anything more personal than how one preferred their tea was regarded as equal to breaking one of the Lord's commandments. "Why did you stop?" She cleared her throat and plucked nervously at the edge of a pillow. "Why did you pull out and... spill yourself on the blanket instead?"

He drew back from her a little. "Forgive me, but I thought... Well, at the last minute I realized you might not wish to worry about finding yourself with child. And I would never want to force the condition on you, if it wasn't what you wanted, what you were ready for. I didn't want you to regret it or blame me for not thinking of you in time. So I thought—"

She reached out and placed her hand on his arm. He appeared sincerely flustered, but she didn't want him to worry about such a thing in the future when she could tell him the truth about it now.

"I can't," she said. As simple as that.

"You...?"

And yet it wasn't as simple as that. Of course it wasn't. "I can't have children."

There should have been more to her confession than the quiet statement of those four words. They should have rang through the air with the resonance of a death knell, anything more meaningful than the soft tremble of her ragged voice.

"You already know enough of it, I'm sure. Village gossip and my... absences. I was always so ill when I was pregnant. My younger sister wrote to me with assurances that it was good to be so unwell, that it meant the baby was more likely to be healthy. That my body was doing what it should." She pulled her hands into her lap, her fingers pulling at one another as though she could transfer the pain of the memories into each pinch and pull of her fingertips. "But after my last... loss," she said, wincing at the word, hating how weak it sounded. "The physician gave his opinion that I would never be able to conceive again."

"I see." He rubbed his hand against his cheek. "But perhaps—"

"Alexander, I've not bled for six years." She spread out her hands on her lap, before she could dislocate her knuckles by tugging on them too hard. "I'm done. My body is... it's finished. That is, if it had ever truly begun in the first place."

She told herself she wouldn't cry, even as he reached out and pulled her towards him, gathering her into his arms and wiping the tears from her cheeks with a sweep of his thumb.

"No," she said, shaking her head. But she pressed her face into the curve of his neck, listening to the thrum of his pulse against her ear until her breathing slowed. "It's fine. I'm fine." Such lies, the largest she had uttered in years. Because it wasn't fine. It had never been fine. For years, it had been the one thing pulling her through the quiet misery of her marriage to Frederick, that one day she might be able to bear a living child, someone she could pour all of her love towards, someone who would love her in return. And yet her body had failed her over and again, and all while her husband became more and more distant, and all because of her inability to perform the single task for which he had told her women had been created.

Alexander kissed her forehead and then her cheek. He said nothing, simply allowed her to cry onto his shoulder while he rubbed her back and brushed her hair back from her face. After several minutes, he reached for the edge of another blanket at the foot of the bed and wrapped it around them, creating a cocoon of safety and warmth in the middle of his chilled bedroom.

It was a remarkable thing, how good it felt to be held by another person. Neither of them needed to speak, and she didn't want them to. Just the sound of his steady breathing, his heartbeat beneath the palm of her hand was enough. "Thank you," she whispered, and pressed her lips to his shoulder.

His arms tightened around her, and the warmth of his breath settled on the top of her head as he pulled her down onto the bed with him.

Julia wouldn't go back to sleep, she told herself. Even as her eyes closed and her own heartbeat slowed inside her chest. But if she did, she wouldn't blame herself for it in the least.

Fourteen

Julia awoke at dawn. Alexander's bedroom was still cold, proof that no one had yet come to clean out the previous day's ashes and light a new fire. She slipped out from his embrace, careful not to disturb him, careful to tuck the blanket around him again as he'd never woken up again to dress during the night. Quickly, her hands still fumbling with tiredness, she gathered up her shoes and crept back to her own room on the balls of her feet.

She heard and saw no one during her brief dash down the hall. Once inside her bedroom again, she noticed it bore the quiet chill of a space that had been empty for the entire night. It also meant no one had visited her room yet either, and so she allowed herself to hope that no knowledge of her time spent with Alexander would make its way down to the floors below.

While the first light of day lit up the windows behind her curtains, she stripped out of her gown and stockings and hurriedly washed herself with the cold water and soap leftover from the day before. Her skin broken out in a crop of goosebumps, she dragged clean clothes from her wardrobe and dressed, all while ignoring the faint soreness between her legs that served as a constant reminder of what she had done only a few hours before.

And what had she done? Her fingers paused in combing out the tangles from her hair. She had spent the night with a man she had desired for the last twelve years. She harbored no regrets over it. Rather, she wished she was still in his bed with him, reveling in the warmth of his body, the gentleness of his touch, the ineffable kindness of him in his treatment of her.

Immediately, her mind went to when they might next be alone together. Tonight, perhaps? And would this now become the routine of her nights, slipping into his room under the cover of darkness and then sneaking back to her own before the servants awoke?

It all seemed so clandestine, so illicit. A laugh threatened to burble out of her at the thought of it. She, Mrs. Julia Benton, former wife and now widow of the vicar of Barrow-in-Ashton, carrying on an illicit affair with a man to whom she was not married. Goodness, no. Scandal was not for someone like her. Even if word was to get out, who would believe it? She could hardly bring herself to believe it, despite the fact she still bore the evidence of Alexander's nips and bites on her skin. If anyone expected Alexander to fall in love or marry again, they would no doubt anticipate his choice to be someone like his previous wife, a sparkling ornament of beauty and charm, and certainly not a woman who had spent seven years proving over and again that she could not have children.

Because they would expect Alexander to want to have another child. A son, of course. To carry on the family name and lay claim to any inheritance pinned upon his masculine shoulders. Though with the rumors of Zora's parentage, the village probably supposed he would be happy enough with any child — boy or girl — as long as it was truly his.

Julia placed her hands over her abdomen. She could never give him that. But was it even what he wanted? His wife had been gone for five years. If he had been in any kind of a hurry to marry again and father more children, she supposed he would have done it already. But, no. He'd returned from London without a wife, without any prospects or plans of a future increase to his family. Instead, he had sought her out to be his daughter's governess, and now she was...

What? His lover? His mistress? Surely Frederick would have been able to produce a more colorful selection of words, something along the lines of whore or harlot. But Julia didn't care. For once in her life, she did not care what her husband would have thought of her behavior. For when had Frederick ever cared about what she did, except in how it reflected on him?

Julia finished dressing, braiding her hair and pinning it around her head like a coronet before she wrapped a shawl around her shoulders and walked down to the library. The house was still caught in the peaceful boundary between night and day, but she could hear the faint clatter of pots from the kitchen as breakfast was prepared, and the light step of maids traveling upstairs to light the various fires of the house.

The library was cold, but she didn't mind as it helped to clear her head and keep her mind alert. The next hour disappeared as she searched through the vast shelves for books on ancient history, mythology, birds and beasts, and mathematics. There was little to be found of French or Latin, though she did find a book of German hymns and a volume of Italian poetry with accompanying illustrations that would not have been proper for Zora's eyes.

Armed with a stack of books for later perusal, she returned to her own room to leave them there before heading over to the nursery to check on Zora. The girl was already awake and sitting on the end of her bed, curled up in her nightgown with Ellen the kitten cradled in her lap.

"And how did she find her way up here?" Julia asked as she opened the nursery curtains and flicked at a thread of frost that had formed on the window.

Zora ducked her head as she trailed a piece of knotted string over her legs for the kitten to chase. "I thought she might be lonely, so I brought her up from the kitchen for someone to play with."

"Oh, of course." Julia wasn't about to tell her to return the kitten to the kitchen. No doubt the animal would soon be doing all of its sleeping in the nursery, in between roaming the corridors and shadows of the house for mice and other easy prey. "Come along. Time to get dressed and start the day."

The sun shining outside the windows promised fine enough weather for a short walk outside before settling inside again for breakfast and the day's lessons. They bundled up in cats and scarves and thick, woolen mittens, then began a leisurely trudge against the frost-gilded lawns. Zora stopped frequently to study the crystals of ice along the edges of the fallen leaves, and the trail of her footsteps behind her, and the feathering of clouds across the bright blue sky. And all while asking questions about how frost formed and why the days grew so short in the winter and if there were really places in the world where the sun did not shine for days or even weeks at a time.

The questions — and answers, courtesy of Julia's beleaguered mind — continued through breakfast, though Zora became more subdued at the beginning of her lessons due to the fact she was supposed to sit and read quietly about the geography of New South Wales. Julia settled down with an assortment of stockings — her own and Zora's — that needed mending, smiling to herself at how many snags and tears there were in the knees of Zora's, and wondering if she should not simply begin affixing knee pads to all of the girl's clothing in the future to save herself the extra work.

A knock at the nursery door interrupted the quiet. Julia had barely finished saying "Come in," before Mrs. Holland entered with one of the maids behind her, the latter carrying several parcels in her arms.

"A delivery for Miss Halberd," Mrs. Holland said in lieu of a greeting. "And for you as well, Mrs. Benton."

Julia set aside her sewing and went to the table where the maid deposited the packages. "From Mrs. Decatur?" She read over the card tucked among the neat strands of ribbon tying everything together. "Already?"

Mrs. Holland plucked out the card and opened it. "It seems she had a few ready-made items available, and with a few alterations to suit your measurements decided to send them on early. As a first installment, she calls it."

"Well, then." Julia opened the top package, displaying a swathe of fabric that when unfolded revealed a new gown for Zora. It was a simple day dress, nothing remarkable, but rendered with extraordinary skill and so beautiful in its tailoring and details that Julia gained a healthy measure of respect for Mrs. Decatur's — and her employees' — skills.

"Oooh," Zora pronounced with the same amount of awe reserved for a colorful caterpillar or a particularly sparkly rock discovered at the bottom of the streambed. "May I try it on?"

"To see if it fits?" Julia held it out to her. "Of course."

Julia helped her undress and dress again, stepping back as Zora twirled around and smoothed her hands down the front of the patterned fabric. "Do you like it? I like it. I think Papa will like it, too."

"I believe he will, yes." Though Julia didn't doubt Zora could come shuffling into the house caked in mud from head to toe and her father would still see her as one of the most beautiful creatures to inhabit the earth.

"Now let's see yours!" Zora dove for the other parcel, opening it up and pulling out a gown of pale green with a pattern of light pink flowers and pink and white braid along the high waist.

Now it was Julia's turn to feel overwhelmed, though she did her best not to show it. "It's rather vibrant," she said, running her fingers along the fine braiding. It also didn't look like the sort of gown a governess should wear. It was too well made. Too bright. Too brilliant at drawing attention towards it, along with the person wearing it. "I shall have to save it for a special occasion."

"You should wear it to dinner tonight. That way the both of us can show off our new gowns to Papa. I'm sure he'll want to see them."

"Hmm, well." Julia folded the gown over her arm and smiled at Zora. "We'll see." It was a reply meant to placate her for the moment, but she feared the girl might not be so easily distracted. "Now let me take this to my room and put it away before it becomes all creases and lines," she said, and swiftly made her escape. In her own room, she laid out the dress on her bed, wondering at how such a lovely garment had made its way into her possession.

When she had first learned that Alexander wanted them fitted out with new gowns, she had grudgingly allowed it as a part of her earnings, as a way for her to appear as a more suitable caregiver to one of the most respected landowners in the county. But now that she'd spent the night with him, now that she knew he not only desired her but had for some time, everything had shifted. The gown had become something of a gift, one shared between lovers. Even looking at it now made her think about being with him, how it would feel for him to caress her breasts above the braiding, to skim his hand beneath the flowered skirt and trail his fingers upwards until—

A quick knock on the door and Zora popped into the room. She was already clad again in her old, stained dress and pinafore from the morning. "Are you coming back, Mrs. Benton? I thought we were going to construct Viking longships out of paper and float them in some water. Is there still time to do that?"

Julia turned her back on her bed and the gown and followed Zora out of the room. The rest of the day fell into its usual, comfortable routine, or at least as much of a routine as could be shaped around Zora's frequently changing interests and brief flashes of obsessive attention. They ate a small meal together, then took their poorly constructed boats outside to dip and bob and ultimately crash into the rocks along the bank of the stream. The remainder of the afternoon was spent sketching in the library, both of them attempting to draw portraits of one another. The drawing took them until dinner, when they returned upstairs to wash the marks of pencil from their fingers and change their clothes.

Zora chattered happily about wearing her new gown, while Julia fought an internal struggle over the decision about whether or not to wear her own. She wanted to wear it. It was the finest piece of clothing she had ever owned, but looking at it now made her doubt her own ability to carry it off. The cut of it was far younger and fashionable than she believed suited her figure, a figure that was more round and soft than most considered something that should be put on display. And the last thing she needed was to put herself forward as a bit of mutton in the garb of a lamb.

"Damn it all," she muttered under her breath, and began tackling the buttons of her gown in order to change.

She took care dressing for dinner. She told herself it was due to the new gown, that she thought she should honor the fineness of it by bringing the rest of herself up to match its quality. But she knew it was because this would be her first encounter with Alexander since the previous night. Mrs. Holland had already informed them they were expected to dine downstairs, that Mr. Halberd (as he was still referred to everywhere but in Julia's thoughts and when she was alone with him) intended to return in time for dinner after spending the day examining the new drainage project on the western edge of the property. So she would see him again, would be expected to converse and behave with him as though nothing had happened, nothing had changed.

She gave herself a final glance in the mirror. Her hands trembled as she fixed a pin in her hair, as she adjusted the small cross at the end of its chain around her neck. Jewelry was a rare accessory for her, the cross and a simple coral necklace the only two pieces she owned. She had let her sister's share most of their mother's jewelry between them upon her death, as Frederick had frowned upon the flaunting of jewels by a vicar's wife. And so her few treasures had remained locked away, the lid of her small jewelry box gathering dust as it sat on its shelf.

No, no. Julia closed her eyes and blew out a breath, blowing away the memories along with it. It wouldn't do to dwell on such things. She was here now, clad in a new gown and wearing a necklace that had been a gift to her when she had still been a young, unmarried woman. And so it almost felt like a new beginning. A reminder that her life had not ceased to matter with the dissolution of her role as a wife and potential mother.

They went downstairs to the dining room, Zora practically skipping along while twisting a narrow strip of lace that trimmed her collar. "You'll pick it to pieces if you don't leave it alone," Julia admonished her. "It will be nothing but tatters and rags to show to your father, and then there might not be any more new gowns if you're not to take care of them."

Zora smiled at the lack of threat in Julia's words, then reached out and took her hand as they arrived at the dining room.

Alexander was not there yet. A large fire blazed in the fireplace, and a single servant stood at attention in the shadows, waiting to be needed. The table was set, candles burning and flickering with the subtle drafts that moved through the house when it was windy outside. Julia approached the table, unsure if the proper etiquette was for them to remain standing and wait for the master of the house to arrive, or if they should simply seat themselves in case he was delayed in joining them.

"Ah, am I late?"

Zora spun around first. "Papa!" came her shout, before she sailed into her father's arms. "Look at my new dress! Do you see?" She stepped back and performed an admirable pirouette on her heel. "I like the color. And I was worried it would make me itch, but it doesn't!"

Alexander laughed. "Well, I'm pleased it's passed the itching test."

"Oh, but have you seen Mrs. Benton's gown?"

At those words, Julia took a small step forward. She had not looked at Alexander since he had come in, instead focusing her attention on Zora's constant flitting. But she raised her gaze to him, and found him watching her over his daughter's head. There was a light in his eyes, glowing deep and hot as an ember. Their secret, threading its way between them, speaking a hundred words about a hundred touches in that single glance.

"Mrs. Benton looks very well indeed." Was his voice rougher than it had been only a moment ago? "But then Mrs. Benton always looks well, no matter what she is wearing." He bent down and tapped the underside of Zora's chin with his knuckle. "As do you."

Zora beamed. Julia let out a slow exhale and looked away again. But she couldn't keep her attention diverted from him for long. As chairs were pulled out and everyone was seated, Julia studied him from behind a show of adjusting her skirt and unfolding her napkin.

He looked impeccable. Like her, he appeared to have taken greater care in his dress, his jaw bearing the closest shave she'd yet seen on him, while his neckcloth boasted a substantial amount of starch. But there was a restlessness to his movements, a nervous edge corrugating his behavior. His hands fiddled with his silverware, then busied themselves with aligning his plate with the edge of the table before he nearly knocked over his empty wine glass with a sweep of his arm.

Julia was seated near enough to him — he sat at the head of the table, with Zora and herself on either side — that she accidentally kicked his foot beneath the table. She mumbled a quick apology, but then he reached his hand beneath the tablecloth, his fingers seeking out hers where the other people in the room could not see.

"Will you read to me again tonight?" Zora asked when the

meal was almost finished, a dollop of cream from her trifle still clinging stubbornly to the corner of her mouth.

"No, not tonight, I'm afraid." Alexander finished what was left in his wine glass before he pushed aside his plate, his dessert only half-eaten. "I've an egregious amount of accounting to do that I've avoided for too many days. Which is why I will not have a second glass of wine and I will abstain from eating anymore of this delicious trifle, or else I won't have any kind of a head for numbers this evening."

"What does 'egregious' mean?" Zora blinked up at her father.

He leaned towards her. "It means an amount so large it should not be permitted by either man or God."

"In other words," Julia put in, "if you were to eat an egregious amount of trifle, you would no doubt end up with a stomach ache."

Zora made a face. "Hmm, I do like numbers, though." She paused to lick more cream from her spoon. "I like how they always make sense, no matter what. Maybe I can help you with the accounts someday. But not tonight," she added, shaking her head. "I'd much rather play with Ellen while Mrs. Benton tells me a story."

Alexander smiled. "Well, perhaps a few more years under Mrs. Benton's tutelage and you'll be able to help me with my accounts as often as you wish."

From anyone else, it might have been dismissed as a flippant offer made by a parent in order to placate their child. But from Alexander, there was sincerity in every word. And with Zora's ability with numbers, Julia did not doubt that she would be able to help her father with his ledgers and account books before another year or two had passed.

"And now I'm afraid I must abandon you to your own devices, ladies." Alexander pushed his chair back from the table and stood up, while Zora quickly scraped up the last bite of trifle from her plate and followed suit.

Julia moved to stand up as well, having finished eating several minutes before, and Alexander moved behind her to help pull out her chair. "Thank you," she said, and intended to step around him and take Zora to the drawing room for an evening of card games or other fun diversions until bedtime. But he caught her hand as she passed, and held it. It was a brief grasp, barely more than the sweep of his fingers against hers, their hands hidden between them. But it was enough to draw her attention upwards, her gaze skimming over his jaw, his lips, the heaviness of his eyelids.

"Julia." A whisper from those lips, her name spoken like a caress, like a promise.

And then they broke apart before their proximity could be noticed. Julia chivvied Zora out of the dining room while Alexander parted ways with them at the door, taking himself off to his study and his accounts for the rest of the evening.

The drawing room was warm and cozy, the fire built up high against the cold winds blowing against the outside of the house. Julia and Zora tucked themselves into overstuffed armchairs fitted out with too many cushions, their shoes kicked off and their feet — well, Zora's, at least — warmed by Ellen the kitten and her twitching tail. They played games of cards created from their own rules, and snacked on biscuits until the clock chimed eight and Julia announced it was time to go upstairs and prepare for bed.

"But I'm not at all tired!" was Zora's protest, even though she had been hiding yawns behind the back of her hand for the last quarter of an hour.

Julia gathered up their cards and swept as many biscuit crumbs as she could back onto the plate. "And you'll be exhausted in the morning if I give way and let you stay up any longer. No, I will not be thwarted. Upstairs, now!"

Zora fairly dragged herself up the stairs, Ellen cradled in her arms. The girl's head was nearly rolling off her shoulders by the time she made it to the nursery, and Julia helped her out of her dress and into her nightgown. Once teeth were cleaned and hair was brushed out and rebraided and the first, second, and third requests to use the water closet were granted, they settled in for storytime. Zora wiggled down beneath the blankets, while Ellen flexed her claws on the pillows and began licking the end of her tail with a loud, slurping sound. Julia was three minutes into her story when she looked up to see Zora already asleep, her lips still moving around some silent words she hadn't been given enough time to say.

"Very well." Julia put away her book and tucked Zora in before she took the candle from the nightstand to light her way back to her own room. And yet she had only taken three steps down the hall when she realized she didn't want to go to bed yet.

She stood a few paces from her door, her breath guttering the flame of her candle.

She wanted to be bold. So rarely had she made the move to take what she wanted, and so she hesitated, the thought of seven years of unhappiness with her husband wrapping around her ankles like a dragging weight, combined with another dozen years of wanting another man outside the realm of her marriage. A man who, at that moment, was only a single floor below her.

Her heel scraped on the floor as she turned away from her room and began walking towards the stairs. She was quiet, thankfully. Years spent drawing in on herself, of slowly diminishing into an unseen creature had gifted her with the talent of moving from place to place without making a great deal of sound. The downstairs halls were lit with candles in sconces along the wall, and so she blew out her own light and passed like a shade the rest of the way to Alexander's study.

A seam of light shone out from beneath the door. She raised her hand to knock, then thought better of it and simply opened the door instead.

Alexander sat behind his desk, his shoulders rounded forward, the fingers of his left hand pinched around a quill that was busy scratching out figures in a massive ledger. He'd removed his jacket and his waistcoat, and his neckcloth — so starched and pristine at dinner — sat in a crumpled heap on the corner of his desk. She took in all the little details of his appearance, his bare forearms where his sleeves had been rolled up, the open collar of his shirt, his hair tousled from where he must have pushed his fingers through again and again in frustration at the numbers before him, and stored them away like little keepsakes inside her mind.

He gave no sign that he'd seen or heard her enter, so Julia carefully closed the door behind her and stood with her back against it, simply enjoying the opportunity to watch him work undisturbed.

Another minute passed before he set down his quill and looked up. He jolted at the sight of her, and she smiled that she had been so well undetected.

"I'm sorry," she said quickly, and took a step away from the door. "I didn't mean to disturb you. Well..." She tangled her fingers together in front of her. "I suppose I did mean to disturb you. But I can leave again if you wish. Or if you'd rather—"

"No." He slammed the ledger shut. "Stay."

She set down her candle on the nearest shelf. Now that she was here, her heart pounding in her throat, she wasn't certain what to do. She had come here with a single goal, to see him, and she couldn't push her thoughts beyond that first achievement. Would he come around the desk to her, or should she go to him? What if he would rather be upstairs, in the comfort of his room? The practice of seduction, she belatedly realized, came with more variables than seemed necessary.

"Um," she said, a small sound escaping her before she cleared her throat and smoothed her hands down the front of her gown. "Does this door lock?"

He stood up, his chair creaking at the absence of his weight. "Yes, it does."

She fumbled with it for a moment, then a flick of her wrist, a click of the lock, and it was done.

"I wanted to thank you," she said, taking another step forward.

She looked at him and then glanced away again, her nerves getting the better of her. "For the gown, I mean. It's much lovelier than I anticipated, even though I'm not entirely sure it suits me."

"Julia."

He was going to protest, she knew it. Not about her being there, but about her thanks to him for the clothing, along with her wariness about how well it looked on her. So she raised her hand before he could speak, even as his mouth moved to form the first word of his speech. What she was about to say made her heart flutter inside her chest, a bird attempting to escape the bars of its cage. And if she let him interrupt her, allowed him to distract her from her purpose with lovely words that she would have better appreciated at any other moment, she would never be able to say the words currently dancing on the tip of her tongue.

"Alexander." And she drew in another breath, taking courage from the pronouncement of his name. "It's my turn."

His brow puckered in confusion. "Your turn?"

Another breath. If she hesitated any longer, she feared she would float upwards to the ceiling like a hot air balloon. "Tonight, I want you to undress me."

Did he have any idea how frightened she was at that moment? It didn't matter that they had already spent one night together. It didn't matter that she already knew how much he wanted her. Still, the irrational fear lingered in her mind that as soon as he saw her fully unclothed, as soon as he saw the pale stretch marks on her hips and abdomen, the looseness of the skin on her belly, the dimpled fat of her thighs, he would recoil. He would demand the lights to be put out and for her to cover herself again. Frederick had never shown any interest in seeing her naked, so why should he?

He walked around from behind the desk. She was still only a step away from the door, her arms locked straight at her sides, her hands clenched tight. He stopped in front of her, and her gaze leapt upwards long enough to see the rapid beat of his pulse at the base of his throat.

"Come here," he said, and held out his hand.

She took it and followed him over to the fire, the room substantially warmer there than when she had been standing by the door and the drafts that slipped in from beneath it.

"Turn around." His voice was gruff, as though it took all of his effort to force out those two words with some measure of control.

Her eyes closed and she sighed. She turned away from him, her shoulders holding onto her tension as she waited for him to touch her. A tortuous wait.

His fingers brushed across the nape of her neck first, so light it could have been a sweep of her own hair. And then he found the fastenings at the back of her gown, and she felt the steadier touch of his hands at her upper back. A curse slid out of him on a hissed breath when the gown wouldn't immediately cooperate.

"Don't tear it. It's new," she reminded him. And a nervous laugh bubbled at the back of her throat.

"I would rip this gown to shreds if you told me to." The warmth of his exhale against her skin, a touch of his lips between her shoulder blades, and he continued on with his undressing of her. "But then I would have to buy another for you just like it. And the cycle would continue over and over until I was a pauper, and all because of these infernal buttons." He kissed her again, right above the line of her stays. "Ah, Julia." A push of fabric, and he bared her shoulders. Another tug, and the bodice slipped down to her waist, her arms still caught in the sleeves.

A shimmy over her hips, and the rest of it slid down to the floor, a pool of green and flowers and spring at her feet.

She wasn't naked. Far from it. There was still her petticoat and her corset, her stockings and slippers, but even that first layer of fabric stripped away had felt like so much more than a bit of printed muslin.

Her chin tucked down to her chest, her breathing shallow, she turned around to face him. "It laces up the front," she said, indicating the corset. A simple thing she could take on and off without the need for a maid to help her. She didn't look at his face, didn't want to see his reaction yet. Instead, she took in only the sight of his hands as he undid the laces, his fingers working carefully with the delicate ties. And then the corset joined her gown on the floor, and it was only her petticoat left.

Fear...

It writhed around her, telling her to bed down and scoop up her discarded clothes, to hide her body from him. Instead, she raised her chin, and she watched him as he dragged the straps of her petticoat down her arms and stripped the last of her shielding away.

His gaze remained locked with hers, even as his hands came up to her breasts, taking in the weight of them, the fullness of them, as his thumbs stroked across her hardening nipples.

"Kiss me," she said, because she couldn't stand it anymore.

The first touch of his lips was tentative, as though she was made of spun sugar and any further pressure would break her. But she arched towards him, wanting more, wanting what she knew he had to give.

His hands slid around her waist, then down to her bottom, gripping her there and pulling her hips flush against his. And there was his cock, hard against her abdomen, more evidence than any words he could say that he desired her, fully clothed or not.

Because he hadn't run away at the sight of her. Her imperfect body, marked and creased like a book left out in the weather. Instead, his hands skimmed over those wide hips, his fingers dancing over the crinkled skin of her stomach before they went lower, disappearing into her curls, sliding through the wetness that had already accumulated between her legs.

"Christ, Julia. You're so..."

Alexander didn't finish what he was going to say. He didn't finish because her own hands went to the front of his trousers, her nervous fingers tripping over the buttons before she managed to reach inside and find him. He was ready for her, his cock hot and hard in her palm. She slid her thumb over the tip, and his head dropped against her shoulder as a shudder coursed through him.

"Don't," he said. Or growled, rather. "I'm already too far gone, and I want to make this last."

He bent forward and drew one of her nipples into his mouth, teasing it with the rough rasp of his tongue until Julia gasped and dragged his head to pay equal tribute to the other side. And all the while she fought with his trousers, pushing them down his hips and halfway down his legs, wanting to see every inch of him before every one of those inches was inside of her.

They found their way down to the floor, down onto the small pile of Julia's discarded clothing and the rug already there in front of the fire. Alexander broke away from her long enough to remove his boots and trousers, though Julia took the liberty of taking off his shirt, dragging it up and over his head while her hands moved over his chest, his shoulders, his back. She cried out when he stretched out on his back and pulled her on top of him, helping her to swing one leg over his hips so that she straddled him.

"What are you doing?" But she knew very well what he was doing, his cock pressing upwards between her legs, so insistent she couldn't help but squirm along it, a move that made her shiver in anticipation. She lifted her hips, her hand grasping him long enough to guide him inside of her. Slowly, slowly she descended on him, her breath coming out in short, sharp gasps as he filled her completely.

"Oh... oh, God." She couldn't move at first. She wasn't sure if she wanted to. Simply the feel of him inside of her, of her muscles jolting with sensation was enough to make her want to stay there for an indefinite amount of time. And then he moved, pushing his hips upwards, his hands on her waist helping her to find a rhythm with him.

"Do you like this?" he asked. His voice was taut, and she saw the shine of dazed pleasure in his eyes.

She nodded. She did more than like it. She felt glorious like this, on top of him, riding him slowly. Frederick had never—

No, she wouldn't think about Frederick at a time like this. Not when she had Alexander with her, beneath her, inside of her. She looked down at him and found him watching her in turn, his gaze a heated caress that slid over her figure. There was no revulsion there as his hands held the fullness of her hips, nor in the guttural moan that escaped him as he raised himself up enough to return his attention to her breasts.

"God, yes," she said, as he bit at her with his teeth. She loved when he teased that border between pleasure and pain, how all of her senses seemed to heighten because of it. Her eyes fluttered closed in ecstasy, and she held his head there, tangling her fingers in his hair as she began to spiral out of control.

He kissed her as she cried out, muffling her shout before she could alert the entire household to her presence in the study with him. And then he bit her lip, and she heard in the raggedness of his own breathing how close he was to the end.

"Can I..." And he hesitated, his breath hot on her neck. "I want to come inside of you."

"Yes," she told him. Because she trusted him. Because she had opened herself up to him and in return he had held her close, had offered her a kind of safety she had never known before.

There was something bittersweet about the moment, even amid the whirling pleasure of it all. That there was no chance of a child from this, that there never would be. It was something she had resigned herself to years before, but still... it hurt. Whether she even still wanted children of her own at her age, the fact that the path of motherhood was forever closed to her would never fully relinquish its sting.

Her arms wrapped around him, pulling him close. His heart pounded in his chest, his breathing ragged as he burrowed into her embrace, as though she were a cocoon in which he could find warmth and protection. She kissed his brow, her lips pressed to those creases in his skin where it seemed so many of his life's cares had taken up residence.

"I'm sorry," he said, when he was again capable of speech.

"For what?" They were still joined together, and though it felt deliciously wicked at the moment, she was certain the sensation would ebb all too quickly and they would find themselves flirting with discomfort.

He chuckled, then nuzzled the dip in her neck where her jaw met her ear. "You deserve better than the floor."

"Oh." She looked at the mess around them, her new gown in a wrinkled heap, his trousers and shirt, all of their underthings scattered about beneath their legs and feet. "We were a bit hasty, I suppose."

He kissed her jaw, then her ear, then brought his face around to catch her mouth. It was a slow, languorous kiss, one that renewed the ache between Julia's legs and stirred Alexander's cock back to life inside of her. "I've wanted you for twelve years," he said, bringing his hands up to her face to caress her cheeks and brush away the loose tendrils of hair that had escaped her pins. "I think we're allowed a bit of haste."

She returned his kiss, then tightened her hold on him as they rolled together so that she was on her back, his wadded shirt behind her head as a pillow. "The door is locked," she mentioned as a reminder. "And there are still many hours before morning. There's no need to rush."

He smiled down at her. A mischievous grin, one that made him look as though the last dozen years had never even existed. "Many hours," he repeated her words, and leaned down to drop a quick kiss to her lips before he pulled his hips back and slowly thrust into her again. "I believe I'm going to hold you to that."

Fifteen

The wind overnight gave way to rain in the morning. Zora sat at the window in the library, which boasted a wide sill she had converted into a seat with copious amounts of cushions, her nose pressed against the glass while her breath fogged up her view of a waterlogged lawn.

"How is your story coming along?" Julia sat nearer to the fire, her legs stretched out and her skirt tugged up to her calves to allow more of the heat to soak into her muscles. She was exhausted from the previous night, her hips and legs aching from the hours she'd spent with Alexander in his study. They had both retired to their own rooms after midnight, shuffling upstairs like children expecting to be caught doing something nefarious. And then Zora had woken up at a quarter past six in the morning, awake and alert and begging to take a walk around the house before the rain began.

"Not very well," the girl confessed, her paper and pencil sitting forgotten in her lap. "I wanted to give my heroine an adventure, but now it's raining in the story and she's trapped inside, unable to go out and search for dragons until the storms are gone."

"Hmm, quite the conundrum." Julia hid her smile as she sorted through a stack of old letters from her sisters. She considered writing to them again, to let them know about the recent changes in her life. It had been too many years since she had last written to them, but then there had never been anything she'd wanted to share. And they would have replied with requests for her to come and stay with one of them, and she'd had no wish to see them again when her life had been so shaped by failures. But now... Now, she realized that she missed them, that she had missed them ever since they had gone off to be married years and years before.

She also realized how much of a hold Frederick had maintained over her communications with them. He had always been the one to advise her not to visit them, nor to have them as guests when they offered. "The vicarage is too small to host anyone comfortably for an extended period of time," he had said. Or that the expense would be too much. Or that it would not look well for them to be always entertaining guests. Julia saw it now, how much her husband had controlled her, stifled her. How he had done everything in his power to keep her under his thumb while also showing so little concern for her health or happiness. And how much his own opinion of her had slowly worked to erode her opinion of herself.

But she would write to her sisters now, she thought. She wanted to hear about their children, about their husbands, about the latest dinner they attended and whether or not they would expand their gardens in the spring. Would they care that she had taken on employment as a governess? As the daughter of a gentleman, they might not wish for her to make a trade of her skills and knowledge for financial security. In the end, however, they most likely wished for her to be happy, to be appreciated, and here at Langford, with Zora and Alexander, she was. For the first time in a very long time.

"Perhaps your heroine simply needs an umbrella and a sturdy pair of boots," she told Zora, who was still glaring at her half-finished story.

Zora heaved a dramatic sigh, an act that left enough fog on the glass for her to run her fingers through. "She cannot have an umbrella *and* a sword."

"Well, then." Julia folded up her letters and began to sort them according to date. How about a blade hidden in the handle of the umbrella? Two birds with one stone?"

Zora set the tip of her pencil to her chin and sucked her cheeks in until she resembled a fish. "I like that," she said, her cheeks popping back to normal. "Do you think Papa will buy one for me if I ask him?"

"No." Rarely had Julia spoken that single word with more haste or assurance.

"But I would be careful! And he could teach me to fight, in case I'm ever challenged to a duel."

Julia shook her head. "I don't believe ladies are very often challenged to duels, to be honest. Fortunate or unfortunate as that may be to any future plans you have for your imagined weaponry."

Zora fell back onto a cushion with a huff of frustration. "Why is it that men can do all the fun and exciting things? It's really not fair."

"I wasn't aware that engaging in a fight to the death with another person fell into the category of fun activities." Julia shifted forward in the armchair, letting the hem of her skirt fall back to her ankles. She winced as she stood, her body still protesting her treatment of it over the last two nights. There was no denying she wasn't young anymore, that she could no longer leap out of bed in the morning without several cracks and ominous sounds vibrating from joints she wasn't even aware existed. But she wouldn't dare trade what she'd shared with Alexander this week for knees that didn't ache when it rained or a lower back that didn't chide her in the most vociferous of terms when she forgot to put a pillow between her legs while sleeping. "But you're right. It is generally men who are more acquainted with adventure."

"While we sit inside, waiting for it to stop raining."

"Right." Julia crossed the room to join Zora at the window.

The rain wasn't as heavy as it had been a few minutes before, and if she looked towards the horizon, the sky was lighter. "Don your best foul-weather clothing and we'll take a long walk together into town. The road shouldn't be too muddy if we keep out of the ruts, and I need some new thread and needles, as I somehow managed to misplace half of my sewing things when I came to Langford."

Twenty minutes later, they were off. Julia carried an umbrella large enough for the both of them if they walked close together, though the rain was light enough they probably wouldn't even need it on their return. But the road showed all the evidence of having endured several hours of heavy precipitation, a few of the ruts transformed into small canyons that still sported rivers of mud and waterfalls fashioned in miniature. But the air was warmer than it had been for several days, but not so fine that they could leave their coats and scarves at home.

They went to McKinley's Fine Tea and Other Goods first, where Julia purchased new thread and needles and a packet of barley candy for Zora. Mrs. Cutler's shop was next door, a small bakery that also boasted a few tables set up inside for customers who wished to sample a few delicacies on site. Zora pressed her face to the display window, her teeth gnawing at her bottom lip as her gaze lit on a tray of petit fours topped with marzipan flowers.

"Go on, then." Julia held open the bakery door. "Before they chase you off with a broom for smudging their window."

They picked the table nearest to the window, giving Zora a view of the main street outside. "I've never been here before," she said, picking at a thread on the edge of the tablecloth until Julia told her to put her hands in her lap. "Papa never brings me into town with him, though we went all sorts of places in London."

"I'm sure if he wasn't so busy with the running of Langford..." She let her words trail off, allowing Zora to finish them in her head however she might wish. What she didn't want to say was that perhaps her father chose to keep her at home, at Langford, rather than expose her to any talk or gossip she might happen to hear about her mother. "Now, sit up straight, and please keep your elbows off the edge of the table."

Mrs. Cutler approached them then, her eyes sparkling beneath the lace edge of her cap, hands fiddling with the edge of her apron before she smoothed it down and clasped her fingers before her. "Ah, Mrs. Benton! And Miss Halberd! What a pleasant surprise this is, and on such a dreary day, too. But look at you, child! You have grown into quite the young lady since I last saw you."

Zora narrowed her eyes, as though suspicious of anyone who would bring public attention to her dimensions.

"And Mrs. Benton, does this mean the rumors are true? Are you at Langford now? Oh, what a fine house that is," Mrs. Cutler continued, before Julia could reply. But that was Mrs. Cutler's way, to talk and talk without the necessity of others offering another side to the conversation. "And so well positioned over the village! I remember, when I was there for one of Mrs. Halberd's parties, and the view! Nothing like it in all of England. I even told my sister that in a letter, that there is nothing to compare with the view from Langford on a fine, clear day."

"Yes, it is very lovely there," Julia said, before Mrs. Cutler could begin speaking again. "And yes, I am Miss Halberd's governess now. Mr. Halberd offered the position to me, and I accepted."

"And how wonderful that is!" Mrs. Cutler clapped her hands together, her face still beaming. "We were all so worried, you know, when Mr. Halberd began spending more and more time in London after the death of—" She cleared her throat, her gaze darting to Zora and then back again. "Well, we wondered if we were going to lose him to London entirely! And what a shame that would have been, to see the house shut up or for someone else to come in and rent it. But what did you think of London, Miss Halberd?"

Zora wrinkled her nose. "It smelled bad."

Julia coughed into her shoulder, though Mrs. Cutler laughed out loud. "Doesn't it just? All that smoke and filth and the people!

It isn't right for so many people to live in one place, that's what my Edward says. But now you're back, and now there's Mrs. Benton to look after you. And... oh. I'm sure it has been so hard for you since Mr. Benton passed away," she said, clicking her tongue against the back of her teeth. "Such a fine, upstanding man, he was. Handsome and clever, and I don't mean to malign our Mr. Tewson. No, not at all. But he doesn't have the same gift with words as your husband did. A true man of God, was your Mr. Benton."

Julia smiled. It was all she could manage in the face of such praise towards her husband. That, or dig her nails into the tabletop and risk leaving permanent gouges in the woodwork.

"But I often wondered why you didn't go home to your family, rather than languish with Mrs. Cochran as you did. But I told Edward... Well, I mentioned to him how important it is to feel as though one has some independence, yes?"

"And I have the school on Sundays," Julia added, twisting the folds of her skirt in her lap.

"Oh, of course! Your little class! And how kind it was of Mr. Benton to allow you the organization of it. I'm sure that was such a comfort for you, to have a distraction during your... difficult times."

Ah, her difficult times, yes. Julia was tempted to inquire as to which 'difficult times' Mrs. Cutler referred. The label could have applied to her marriage as a whole, her inability to have children, the loss of her husband, or the financial straits that followed it. "The class has been wonderful. Though hopefully more for my pupils than for myself, of course."

Mrs. Cutler leaned forward a few inches, her expression open and sincere. "It's nice to show a bit of charity to the less fortunate. It is how your dear Mr. Benton always spoke, to think of others before we think of ourselves."

"Yes." Julia bit at the inside of her lower lip. "That is... something he said."

Mrs. Cutler straightened up, her smile broadening again. "Now, what will we have today, hmm?"

Julia ordered tea for herself and hot chocolate for Zora.

"Can we have biscuits or..." Her gaze darted towards a few of the confections in the display window.

"And a few of those little cakes for Miss Halberd," Julia added.

Mrs. Cutler's eldest daughter worked at the shop as well, and she brought their tea and chocolate to them while her mother filled a plate with a sampling of the delectable petit fours.

"For Miss Halberd," Mrs. Cutler said, with a smile and a wink to the girl as she set the plate on the table. "And I must say, it is an absolute wonder how much you resemble your dear mother. "Why, when you first set foot through the door, I almost thought Mrs. Halberd had come back to pay me a visit!" She laughed and tugged at one of Zora's limp curls. In response, Zora scooted her chair several inches towards the other side of the small table. "Oh, but she was such a beauty," Mrs. Cutler went on, seemingly oblivious of the silent rebuff. "And she was so good with all of her parties and fetes she organized every year, along with the charitable works she arranged with your husband," she added, glancing again towards Julia. "All of the little baskets and things she put together and delivered to the poor, and it was so good of her to take care of it all when you were too indisposed to manage it yourself."

Julia picked up her cup with a grip she feared might shatter the delicate porcelain of the handle. "Yes, she was—"

"It's really no wonder, then, why she was so adamant about recommending your husband as vicar when the post became vacant. They worked extraordinarily well together."

"She..." Julia returned her cup to its saucer with a faint clatter. "What?"

"Oh, yes! I remember it well. It was supposed to go to Mr. Pennyworth, as he was more senior and also a local gentleman, but Mrs. Halberd was stubborn as a mule about it! Declared she didn't know a finer candidate than Mr. Benton, though I suspect some of her partiality had to do with the two of them growing up together..."

"They grew up together?" Julia shook her head. "You must be mistaken. My husband made no claim of any acquaintance with her before he was offered the post. They were strangers, I'm sure of it."

Mrs. Cutler wiped her hands on her apron, while her gaze skimmed the rafters of the ceiling as though she was searching them for her own memories. "Well, I never heard Mrs. Halberd say it directly. But your husband was originally from Cornwall, was he not? A small place outside of Tregony, if I'm not mistaken?"

She was not mistaken. Frederick had indeed hailed from Cornwall, but was sent to be educated for the church under the tutelage of a Mr. Burney in Surrey, where Julia had met him. But he had never mentioned knowing Mrs. Halberd before being called to the post in Barrow-in-Ashton. In fact, she remembered the day they had met, when Mrs. Halberd and Alexander had come to greet them at the vicarage, there had been no word or sign of a previous acquaintance between them. "Yes, just a few miles east of Tregony," she managed to say, her mouth suddenly gone dry. "But Mrs. Halberd wasn't from Cornwall. She was from London."

"No, no. That's what she preferred people to believe, I think." And Mrs. Cutler wrinkled her nose at this little quirk in Mrs. Halberd's personality. "She did live with an aunt and uncle for some years, and it was with them she had her come out and everything! But, no. It was Mrs. Powell who said she hailed from Cornwall, not far from where your Mr. Benton came from. I suspect she didn't speak about it much as her family was not..." She glanced at Zora, fully engrossed in her cakes and hot chocolate, and hesitated. "Well, her father was a gentleman. But I heard tell their family had fallen on hard times, and so what a fine thing it must have been to end up as mistress of Langford!"

Julia nodded. She found it impossible to do more than that. So instead she took a sip of her tea, but the taste of it was suddenly too bitter and acrid on her tongue, and she set it down again with disgust.

At that moment, the bell over the door rang, announcing the arrival of another customer. Mrs. Cutler excused herself and Zora slurped down her hot chocolate while Julia sat with her fingers threaded together in her lap, her gaze focused on nothing in particular.

Surely Frederick would have told her if he had been acquainted with Mrs. Halberd before moving to Barrow-in-Ashton, especially if her influence had been so critical towards his having earned the post in the first place. What reason would there have been to keep it a secret? Unless he was acquiescing to Mrs. Halberd's wishes to keep her humble origins in the dark, so her past could not become fodder for gossip.

And of course, Mrs. Halberd may have grown up quite near to where her husband had been born and raised, but it did not necessarily mean they had known one another. Merely a coincidence, and nothing more. But as they departed Mrs. Cutler's shop and began the walk back to Langford, Julia had difficulty shaking off a disconcerting restlessness that invaded her limbs.

"I want to share my candy with Papa," Zora declared, clutching the small paper sack that contained her sweets. "Do you think we'll have dinner with him again tonight?"

"I don't know." Julia was distracted. A niggling worry burrowed its way into the foundation of her thoughts, but every time she tried to focus her full attention on it, it slipped away, as ephemeral as smoke between her fingers.

By the time they made it home, the clouds had broken apart and brilliant shafts of sunlight stretched down from the sky, illuminating the puddles and turning them to silver coins scattered across the drive.

"Wipe your feet," Julia remembered to say when they reached the door, even as she nearly tracked mud across the foyer with her own boots, such was the muddle of her thoughts. They went upstairs to change, their hems soaked and streaked with dirt, then settled together in the nursery. Zora scattered the pieces of a puzzle across the table while Julia read to her from a book about the flora and fauna of Scotland.

If someone was to ask Julia what she was reading, for her to recite a single word or idea of it back to them, she would not have succeeded. She read line after line in a flat monotone, her mind somewhere else, far from the moors and mountains of Scotland, instead reeling back through her memories and all the times she had seen her husband and Mrs. Halberd together.

Had there ever been a spark of something between them? The glint of a secret shared over quiet glances or a brief touch, the sort one would share with a friend? Or... perhaps more than a friend?

She closed her eyes, fighting the urge to laugh at such a suspicion. Of all the people to suspect of carrying on an affair with someone else, her husband was at the bottom of the list. His adherence to the tenets of the Bible had always been unparalleled. Never could she even imagine him committing the sin of adultery, not even in the privacy of his dreams. He, who had only ever been cold and passionless—

"Why did you stop reading?"

Julia opened her eyes. The book lay in her lap, forgotten. "Oh, um." She cleared her throat and tried to find her last place on the page. "I'm sorry. My mind must have wandered."

She began reading again, but a sudden hoarseness in her throat made her stop. She told herself that the walk in the damp air had been too much, that perhaps she'd unwittingly caught a chill and was in need of a hot cup of tea to clear the congestion from her head. But she knew the thickness in her voice had nothing to do with any walk in the rain.

"Come along," she said, and closed the book with a snap. "Let us find something else to do."

Sixteen

They sat together on Julia's bed, sorting through her trinkets. There was nothing like precious jewels or combs of silver and ivory, but instead little odds and ends that Julia had collected and saved through all the years of her life.

"What is this?" Zora asked over and over again, holding up each new item from the small wooden box Julia had taken down from the top shelf of her wardrobe. It didn't seem to matter that most of the items — a feather, the shell of a starling's egg, an empty vial of perfume with a carved soapstone stopper — needed no description. It was the stories Zora wanted, the accompanying tales of how Julia had acquired them and why she had chosen to hold onto them.

"And this?" Zora held up a small button between her thumb and forefinger.

"Oh." Julia held out her hand, and Zora dutifully dropped it into her palm. "I was at a party. A Christmas party, in fact. And... I found it on the floor. It must have popped off someone's waistcoat or gown. But I liked it, and so into the box it went."

That wasn't the entirety of the story, of course.

Julia had been a guest at the annual Christmas party at Langford. It was the only time she had felt well enough to attend, and so she and Frederick had dressed and prepared, Julia taking extra time with her hair, instead of simply pinning it to the back of her head in its usual bun. Mr. Benton had complained the entire time, claiming that balls and parties were frivolous and a waste of time that could be better spent doing something much more rewarding for one's immortal soul. But of course — of course, he always said — it was necessary for him to at least make an appearance at the event, insisting it would be impolite of him to refuse every invitation.

Alexander had been there, as expected. Mrs. Halberd was the hostess, and so she had seen to it that every inch of the great house was transformed into an exaggerated recreation of a woodland glen, complete with pine boughs and silver ribbons and enough candles to suffuse every room with the aroma of beeswax. Julia and Frederick took their turn through the receiving line, Mrs. Halberd glittering like a star as she complimented Frederick on his sermon from the previous week. Julia tried to push her shoulders back and straighten her spine, tried to appear as she thought the wife of the vicar should. But all the while her legs trembled beneath her and her jaw ached from the tension running through her bones.

"Good evening, Mrs. Benton."

Julia had smiled at Alexander. She remembered that, how her expression had felt as brittle as an autumn leaf. "Mr. Halberd," she said, her voice a taut thread of sound. "Th-thank you for inviting us. The house is lovely."

He nodded to her before the next guests in line moved them along. And then he spoke again, his words coming out in a low rush, as though he hadn't thought to say them until the very last moment. "It is good to see you, Mrs. Benton. Here, at Langford," he added, before they were ushered further into the house.

At dinner, Julia had eaten little and avoided the wine, the former to prevent Frederick from offering a criticism of her eating habits in public, and the latter to avoid feeling ill from the effects of the alcohol. But all through the meal, she had caught herself glancing at the upper end of the table, where Alexander sat. He had looked so much the portrait of a happy husband and father — Mrs. Halberd having given birth to Zora earlier that year — that it twisted in her abdomen, the pain that she would never be able to bring such contentment to her own household.

After dinner, the guests retired to the drawing room for games and music. Julia had taken herself off to one side, usurping a cushy armchair near the fire (and a tray of bite-sized cakes set out for anyone to pick from as they chose). Frederick had complained about the heat of the fire and so had settled in another part of the room, nearer to the piano where Mrs. Halberd was entertaining everyone with a selection of songs. But Julia didn't mind being alone, not really. A few people stopped to converse with her, but for the most part, she kept to herself beside the fire and the tray of cakes, able to watch everything without having to interact beyond her boundary of comfort.

Mrs. Halberd was in the middle of her final song when it happened. Alexander had been slowly making his way around the outer edges of the room, trading a few words with each guest and inquiring as to any needs they might have before moving on to the next group. And then he came over to the fire and Julia's chair.

There had been a smile on his face before he approached her, a few lines on his face carrying the laughter he'd shared with another guest. But it faded as he stepped into the circle of light cast by the fire, his expression suddenly guarded. "Mrs. Benton," he said, and nodded in greeting.

"Good evening, Mr. Halberd." He was all shadows and gold in the firelight, while the black of his jacket and waistcoat flowed over him like cloth cut from a puddle of ink.

"Are you well?"

At the time, she had not imagined his question to have carried any serious measure of concern, at least not more than he would feel for any other person in the room. And so she had given him the reply she would've offered to anyone else, something vague and mired in politeness and untruth.

"I am very well, thank you."

"And the fire..." He glanced at the blaze, sending up sparks as the logs shifted. "You're not overwarm here?"

"Oh, not at all. I'm often too cold, and so this is perfect."

"Are you still cold now?" There, his brow had creased in worry.

"No, I'm—"

"Because I can fetch a blanket if you—"

"Please, no." And she had smiled, because all of the fuss and bother was too much, more than she believed she needed or deserved. And Frederick would not have wanted her to make a spectacle of herself, to take too much of Alexander's attention away from the rest of his guests. "The only thing I shall want is to take a turn about the room when my feet begin to fall asleep. Aside from that, I'm fine."

He looked down at the floor, around her legs and behind the chair, until he bent down and pulled out a small, padded footrest. "Should you need it."

It was as he stood that there was the ping and strike of something hard landing on the floor. Julia saw it before he did, the bright shine of a button, and she reached down and picked it up before he even had a chance to notice it was missing.

"I think this belongs to you," she said, and held it out to him.

Rather than take it from her, he checked his sleeves and his jacket, then discovered the frayed threads of a missing button on his waistcoat. "Forgive me, it seems I am falling apart in your presence." He smiled, and Julia's abdomen had tightened at the sight. "Just keep it for now. No doubt I'll turn around and lose it again the moment you entrust it back to my care."

And so she had held onto it, thinking she might leave it on the table beside her for him to discover once all of the guests had departed and the house was once again his own. But instead, it found its way into her handkerchief, wrapped up snug and tucked into her sleeve.

"Is it gold?" Zora asked, poking at the button's shining surface while it sat in Julia's palm.

"Most likely not." Julia tipped it back into the box. "Possibly painted steel, or maybe silver. I'm not well-versed in precious metals, so I really couldn't say."

"My Mama used to wear gold and jewels all the time." And with that pronouncement, Zora slipped off the edge of the bed and dashed from the room.

"Zora!" Julia fit the lid back onto the trinket box and followed her charge. "Zora, where are you off to? You know you're not to run indoors!"

But Zora would not slow down. She trotted along in that determined way she had when she wasn't to be thwarted from her purpose, down the hall, past her father's room, around the corner, and further along until she came to a door at the very end of the corridor.

"Wait, no—" Julia managed to say, just as Zora opened the door and stepped inside.

It was a bright room, a circumstance helped along by the fact it was afternoon and they were on the westernmost side of the house. The walls and trim were painted in shades of white and a soft blue, like fine porcelain shaped into a bedroom. The curtains were made out of a sheer fabric, allowing light to stream in through the windows even though the draperies were all closed. Julia stopped in the doorway, her gaze skipping over the bed, the rich carpets, the delicate furnishings as pristine and free of dust as though they'd only been carried into the room the day before.

"These are some of Mama's jewels." Zora helped herself to a silver jewelry box set on top of the dressing table. "Some of her things have been put away for safekeeping, but there are few pieces left I like to come in and play with."

"Zora." Julia continued to hover on the threshold, uneasy

about setting foot in the former Mrs. Halberd's personal space. "I suspect you're not allowed to come in here whenever you please."

"Oh, no. I come in here all the time and no one cares. Look!" She pulled a silver comb out of the box and held it up for Julia's inspection. "Isn't it pretty? And there's one with pieces of coral in here, too. Do you know what coral is? I thought it was a stone, but Papa says it's not, that it was a living thing in the oceans. I wonder if he could take us to Brighton and we could see some there!"

"I doubt there's any coral in Brighton," Julia said, and took a tentative step into the room. "It prefers more southern waters, if I'm not mistaken."

"Oh." Zora furrowed her brow, clearly disappointed. "But I suppose that's what makes it special, that it's not from here originally."

Julia progressed further into the room. The carpets were thick and plush beneath her feet, like walking on freshly fallen snow. "Come along. I doubt your father would wish for you to be in here without his permission." She had no idea if what she said was true or not, but she didn't want to see Zora get into trouble for rifling through Mrs. Halberd's things. "Let's return to the nursery. We cannot avoid our French all day, you know."

Zora pulled a face as if she was about to protest, but she closed the lid of the jewelry box and walked past Julia and out of the room.

Out in the hall, Julia shut the door behind them and stood there for a moment, her fingers curled around the doorknob. She wondered why the room was still kept so beautifully, as though Mrs. Halberd had only gone for a brief excursion into town and was expected back at any time. Julia would've expected there to be dust cloths over everything, the carpets rolled up and stored away, the entire room perhaps put to some other use rather than continuing on as a shrine for a woman who had died five years before.

As they made their way back towards the nursery, they passed

Mrs. Holland as she came up the stairs, her arms laden with a stack of clean, pressed shirts.

"Mrs. Benton." The housekeeper paused at the top of the stairs. "I have a message for you from Mr. Halberd. He said that dinner is to be served in the drawing room this evening, and he hopes the two of you will be able to join him."

"The drawing room? Are you sure?"

Mrs. Holland's mouth thinned. "If you wish to interrogate him yourself, in order to ascertain whether or not I am telling the truth—"

"Oh, no. It's not that. It's only that we've never eaten in the drawing room before," she pointed out, before Mrs. Holland could take further offense.

"He says it is to be a special occasion."

Beside Julia, Zora bounced on the balls of her feet, her hand reaching out for hers.

"And what time is dinner to be served?" Julia asked, before Zora could begin pinging off the walls with excitement.

"Seven o'clock." The housekeeper's gaze darted past Julia, towards the end of the corridor and Mrs. Halberd's room. "A bit of advice, Mrs. Benton. It would be good not to let the child wander all around the house as she would wish, and I'm sure Mr. Halberd would prefer for you to set an example in the same manner."

Julia smiled. A small smile, one that acted as a barrier against the dozen other things she could have said to Mrs. Holland but wisely — in consideration of Zora's presence — chose not to. "Mr. Halberd was kind enough to give us leave to use any part of the house and grounds we needed for his daughter's education and care, apart from any room or space belonging to anyone currently living in the house," she added. "But I thank you for your concern. Though if you wish, you may go to Mr. Halberd himself and see what he says. In case I misheard him."

"That will not be necessary," Mrs. Holland said, her voice low.

They said nothing more to one another before parting ways, Mrs. Holland moving along with her stack of shirts and Julia shepherding Zora back to the nursery.

"Mrs. Benton?"

Julia closed the nursery door and walked over to check the state of the fire. "Yes?"

"Is it all right to not like someone?"

"What do you mean?"

"Well..." Zora scuffed her foot across the edge of the rug, flipping the corner over and back again. And again. "I know the Bible says we're to love one another, but it's not very easy to do. At least with some people."

"Some people." Julia prodded one of the logs in the fire, splitting it in half with a crackle of sparks and flame.

"What do you think? Do you like Mrs. Holland?"

"I'm sure it's not my place to say," Julia hedged, and returned the poker to its stand.

"That means you don't." Zora put her nose into the air, victorious. "But she always looks at me as though I've done something wrong, even when I haven't. Sometimes I wish Papa would send her away and hire someone else."

Julia turned from the fire and bent down to pick up a few puzzle pieces that had been left on the floor. "If your father hired her and is satisfied with her work, then—"

"Oh, no." Zora picked up the empty puzzle box and held it out for Julia to drop the pieces into. "Mrs. Holland came with Mama from London, when she and Papa married. I think she was her maid before that, and then Mama made her the housekeeper once they came to Langford."

"And where did you hear that?" Julia asked the question before she could stop herself. She didn't want to trade in gossip, but unfortunately it seemed to have become a day for it.

"From the servants, when I would overhear them talking to

each other." She leaned forward. "Most of them don't like Mrs. Holland, either."

"Perhaps you shouldn't listen to other people's conversations so much," Julia said, as gently as possible. Considering this wasn't the first instance when Zora had overheard something she shouldn't have, Julia worried it might soon develop into a bad habit. Both the listening and the gossiping.

"I suppose." Zora shrugged and put the puzzle box away. "I'd rather learn where we can find some cora than listen to silly old gossip, anyway."

Julia swept her hand over the girl's dark hair and finished the movement by plucking a piece of fuzz from the collar of her dress. "Agreed. So why don't we see what the library has to offer in the way of ocean creatures, hmm?"

* * *

Julia and Zora arrived in the drawing room promptly at seven o'clock. They were astonished to find most of the furniture cleared away and a large blanket spread out on the floor in front of the fire, complete with a large basket filled with food and a pitcher of lemonade set out beside several glasses.

"A picnic," Alexander announced in greeting, and in such a way as to make it seem completely natural to have a picnic dinner on the drawing room floor as frost crackled its way over the outside of the house.

Zora jumped and tumbled onto the blanket, ecstatic when she realized her kitten, Ellen, was already curled up on a corner of the heavy wool, clumsily cleaning a paw.

"What's the occasion?" Julia asked. "Or does there even need to be one?"

"There doesn't need to be one," he replied, and held out a hand to help her down onto one of the cushions that had been strategically placed on the blanket. "But I should admit that as it's my birthday today, something should be done to commemorate the date."

"Happy Birthday!" Zora bounced on her knees while clapping her hands. "But why didn't you tell us? I could have made a present for you."

"I don't need any presents," he assured her, and reached out to tweak the tip of her nose, making her giggle. "I'm happy enough with a roof over my head and a basket of our cook's finest comestibles. And fine company to go with it," he added, brushing a curl back from her shoulder before his gaze settled warmly on Julia.

"And Ellen!" Zora declared, holding up her kitten while it tried to claw its way up the length of her arm.

"And Ellen," he echoed, and helped to rescue the edge of a ruffle from one of the kitten's back paws.

Julia took on the task of emptying the basket of its contents, which included all manner of salads and sandwiches, and also a collection of jam tarts, their crusts so flaky they threatened to break apart with every brush of her fingers. At the other end of the blanket, Alexander crouched on his hands and knees, dancing his fingers along the floor as prey for the kitten to pounce on, all while Zora laughed and squealed with delight.

It was a beautiful moment. Julia watched it unfold, all while wondering how she had been fortunate enough to stumble into a situation that brought her such joy. She had more than prepared to whittle away the rest of her existence in her rented rooms from Mrs. Cochran, doing her best to avoid the society of townspeople who had never made her feel truly welcome for as long as she had lived among them. But here, at Langford, she'd found something she had feared was never truly meant for the likes of her. Happiness. Desire. Being wanted. Being needed.

There were times when she thought she might have to pinch herself, to discover if she was dreaming. Surely this new existence couldn't be hers, could it? After so many years of loss and grief combined with Frederick's steady lack of affection, she had begun to believe it was all she would ever have, all she deserved.

Was that what Frederick had done to her? Had seven years with him slowly eroded her into a creature unable to see herself as worthy of love? She tried to imagine what her marriage would have been like if Alexander had been her husband instead. Would he have made her feel unattractive? Would he have made her feel as though she had to earn his affection — or the affection of anyone — through the birth of a child?

For too long, she had thought she was the faulty piece in the whole of their marriage, that if only she had been more, done more, there could have been joy. All those years, wasted, believing that happiness was something only to be doled out to her when she had suffered for long enough.

"Oh! She's gone under the piano!"

Julia put down her lemonade and looked towards the corner of the room. Zora was already halfway beneath the piano, wedged between a stool and the wall as she reached out towards a curious — and oblivious — Ellen. Julia stood up quickly and moved the seat aside, while Alexander helped to reach beneath the piano, his longer arms making quick work of scooping up the kitten before she could venture beyond anyone's ability to catch her.

"Poor thing," Zora cooed as her father tipped the mewling kitten into her waiting arms. "Naughty girl!"

"She's only exploring," Julia reminded her. "Here, give her to me for a minute." Zora handed over the kitten and Julia sat down on the piano seat, settling the animal in her lap and petting her slowly until she began to purr. "After so much excitement, I suspect she is greatly in need of a rest."

Zora squeezed onto the seat beside her, her hands in her lap for all of a moment before they fidgeted their way towards the keys of the piano. She pressed one, which let out a low vibration of sound, but she snatched her hand away again as though waiting for a reprimand about touching the instrument without permission.

"Mrs. Holland said it isn't a toy," Zora said, her voice wary. Her fingers fluttered forward again, wanting to play another note. "She said it belonged to Mama and that it wasn't to be trifled with."

"No, it isn't a toy," Julia admitted. But instead of shaping the statement into a warning, she hoped it would ignite a spark of respect in Zora's heart, and hopefully one that wasn't underlined with fear. "But if you're careful..."

"Mrs. Holland says that Mama used to play all the time, that she never heard anyone with greater execution and taste. Is that true, Papa?"

Julia looked towards Alexander. After his help rescuing a wayward kitten, he had resumed his place on the blanket, this time lounging with one leg stretched out, the other bent and acting as a prop for his arm. "Your mother played very well, yes." His attention drifted down to the floor, his gaze seeming to focus on a frayed edge of the blanket. "Though she spent a great deal of time practicing, which had much to do with it."

"Do you play, Mrs. Benton?" Zora looked up at Julia, then reached out another tentative finger towards a black key.

"Yes, I play. Or I did. Though it's been some years since I took the trouble to practice." There had been a small pianoforte at the vicarage, old and always dreadfully out of tune, but Frederick had never considered it a priority to bring it into working order again.

"Can you play now?"

Julia laughed at Zora's insistence. "As I said, it's been several years. Too many years, more than likely."

"Something simple, then?" Zora's voice took on a pleading tone that Julia found difficult to resist, though it wasn't a good lesson for the girl to learn that should she only whine and beg for long enough, she would get her way. "Papa, please tell her to play for us! I've never heard anyone play the piano here before."

Alexander finished the small triangle of sandwich he'd been eating and brushed the crumbs from his hands. "I am not about to make Mrs. Benton do anything she does not wish to." His gaze caught Julia's, and there was a brief flash of heat in his eyes, a memory of how they had spent the last two nights together. "She has a mind and will of her own," he said to Zora, though his attention did not break from Julia. "And I would not want to see them diminished."

"Um." Julia cleared her throat and looked away as a flush of warmth flooded her cheeks. "If it hasn't been played at all recently, then I daresay it will sound terrible regardless of any deterioration of my skills." She adjusted her position on the seat, careful not to wake the sleeping kitten still curled into a ball of orange fur and pink toes in her lap. Her hands hovered over the keys as her mind swept back to all of the music lessons she'd had as a child, all of the hours she'd spent practicing and playing for her younger sisters while they giggled and trotted through their dancing steps on the parlor floor.

And then... she began to play.

She was slow, at first. Her fingers and wrists were stiff, and the piano had indeed been neglected, despite the regular dusting and polishing it had regularly received from the servants. She made one mistake, and then another, before she struck a key that made her wince at how out of tune it was. But she kept on, working her way through the tune at an awkward, plodding pace.

And it was amazing. Or at least it felt amazing to her. She had never been especially skilled at playing, but she had always enjoyed, had thrilled at the vibration of sound carried on the air by that little bit of pressure from her fingers. And all of it working together to create a melody that could evoke sadness or joy or any other emotion from its listener.

When she finished, she sat very still, waiting for the final note to fade out of the air. Zora began to clap, as enthusiastically as if she was in a concert hall filled with an audience standing up to share their adulation for her performance.

"Don't, please." She scooted back in her seat and picked up the still-sleeping kitten, returning it to Zora's care. "No doubt you heard how I cheated my way through half of it."

"You just need to practice more," Zora said, swinging her legs beneath her as she reached out again to gently touch one of the keys. "If you want, you can teach me, and then you'll get better while I learn."

"Sound logic," Julia said, biting back a laugh. "But you should learn to play an instrument, I suppose. Only if you truly wish to play, however. I would not want to force it upon you when you could apply your interest elsewhere."

Zora assured her that she wanted to learn, and Alexander promised to send word into town for someone to come to Langford and return the instrument to peak performance. After that, all three of them settled fully into their forgotten meal, the sandwiches and tarts disappearing rapidly as both Julia and Alexander amused Zora with humorous stories from their childhoods.

"Can Ellen sleep in my bed tonight?" The question came from Zora as Alexander packed the remains of their meal into the bottom of the basket and Julia shook all of the crumbs off the blanket.

"Well," was all Julia said, and looked towards Alexander.

"I see no reason why not." Alexander smiled at his daughter. "I had a spaniel when I was about your age. Followed me everywhere and would not spend a single night away from me without whining loud enough to keep the entire household awake. Micah, was his name," he added, his expression growing wistful. "He was a champion protector, and so I think Ellen should be allowed to prove her worth as your guardian."

"Or maybe I am to protect her," Zora announced with staggering resoluteness. Julia could almost picture the girl girding her loins and drawing a sword against anyone or anything that might pose a threat to the small, orange kitten.

"Off with you, then," Julia said, and finished folding up the blanket. "Grand Shieldmaiden of Langford. Will you still be requiring a story tonight?"

"Of course!" Zora furrowed her brow, as though the prospect of bedtime without an accompanying story was reprehensible and to be thoroughly frowned upon. "And Ellen will want one, too. I'm sure of it."

Alexander took the blanket from Julia as Zora left the drawing room with Ellen and skipped towards the stairs. Julia moved to follow her, but Alexander touched her arm, stopping her with that single brush of his fingertips.

"Thank you," he said.

"Me?" She looked around at the basket, at the blanket on his arm, the furniture all pushed to the sides of the room to make space for their picnic. "This was all your idea. And you should've mentioned to me that it was your birthday. I could've helped with the planning of everything and—"

But he shook his head before she could finish. "No, not with this. What I mean is... your coming here, and everything since." His hand wrapped around her wrist, his thumb stroking where her pulse pounded beneath her skin. "You've done something here, worked some sort of magic. With Zora, with..." He sighed. Despite the open door behind them, despite the fact that anyone might walk by and see them, he raised her hand to his lips and kissed the tips of her fingers. "For too many years I've felt like a vagabond, wandering through my own life in search of something I couldn't even put a name to. And now, finally, I think I've found it."

"Alexander." His name slipped from her lips, her throat thick with emotion. She would be happy, she realized, for things to remain as they already were, for him to give her no more than had already been offered. A home, a purpose in caring for Zora, his help with the school and supplies for her pupils. His affection and desire. She would be greedy for expecting more, wouldn't she? But there was something in his eyes, in his expression, in the very warmth of his fingers on her skin that told her he would not be content to keep their relationship as it was, a hidden and secret thing. And at that moment, she didn't believe she would be content with that, either.

"I want—" he said. But whatever the rest of his speech was, it was interrupted by Zora calling out, "Mrs. Benton! Are you coming?" from the stairs.

"I have to go." She had already lingered with him for too long. But she rose onto the balls of her feet and she kissed him quickly, her hand lifting to touch his cheek, to glide her fingers along his jaw and remind herself that he was real, and not merely a figment of a dream she'd held onto for the last decade. "Goodnight," she said, and rushed out of the drawing room to follow Zora up the stairs.

Seventeen

J ulia didn't sleep well. After putting Zora to bed — three stories, two for Zora and one for Ellen — she returned to her own room instead of giving in to the ache of desire between her legs and seeking out Alexander. She feared a third night of lovemaking would leave her too exhausted to fully attend to Zora's lessons in the morning. But instead of falling asleep, she tossed and turned in bed, dozing for only a few minutes at a time before waking again and listening for the incessant ticking of the clock.

It was before dawn when she staggered out of bed, dressing in the dark without even the aid of a candle. A glance out the window told her it would be cold, the clouds cleared away and the moon shining down like a lamp from the firmament. By the time she made it outside, the eastern sky was a pale gray, fringed with pink.

She pulled up her scarf over the lower half of her face, her breath coming out in blasts of pale steam through the crocheted wool. Everything seemed sharp and fragile, even the frosted grass crunching like broken glass beneath the soles of her walking boots as she crossed the lawn.

The woods laid like a smut of shadow on the horizon before

her, but she had no interest in walking beneath the bare branches of the trees this morning. Instead, she directed her steps towards the row of outer buildings that circled the rear of the main house like a crown. The stables were what drew her interest, the smell of the horses and fresh hay reaching her even through the muffler wrapped over her nose.

She didn't know why she had avoided the stables for so long. She'd told Zora about her love of horses the first day she'd arrived at Langford, but so far had avoided anything to do with them. It was a reluctance, she realized, to believe that anything here could truly be at her disposal. Because she was a servant, really. No matter her relationship with Alexander and how it might progress from here, at the moment, she was still an employee in the eyes of everyone around them. She could not picture herself calling for a horse to be saddled, as though she was mistress of the house and could send a footman or a stablehand to cater to her every whim.

Inside the building, it was warm enough that Julia could unwind the scarf from around her neck, pull off her knit cap, and tug the mittens off her hands. She was greeted by the soft shuffling of the horses moving about in their stalls, the scrape of hooves and the soft nicker of animals suddenly aware of her presence.

The pink light of dawn shone through the windows as she made her way along the stalls, her boots catching on the stray bits of straw that hadn't been swept away from an otherwise clean floor. She passed the ladder she had climbed that first day with Zora, when they'd gone up into the loft to see the kittens. She smiled at the memory, at how she could never have guessed at the time where that meeting with a lone child in the middle of the village would lead.

At the end of the building, in the last stall, she peered over the top of the door and saw a mare resting on the floor with her colt. Even in the muted light, she could discern the sleek black of their coats, the bright white star on the mare's forehead and the matching white on the tip of the colt's nose. There had never been such fine animals at home when she was a child, and she wondered how excited she would have been as a girl to simply pop into the stables and see these beautiful horses whenever she wished.

She wasn't sure how long she stood there, her arms folded on the top of the stall door and her chin resting on her hands. There was something almost hypnotic about being there, the absence of other people bustling about, while the pink light of the morning transformed into a golden thing, picking out the tiny bits of dust floating through the air and making them glimmer like fairies.

"Good morning, Julia."

She didn't look around right away. She had heard his approach, seen his shadow cross in front of the window before the first strike of his boots landed on the stable floor. It didn't feel like a surprise that Alexander had found her. That is, if he had even been looking for her. When she looked over at him, he appeared dressed and ready for an early morning ride on one of his horses.

"I didn't sleep well," she said, in place of a perfunctory good morning.

"Neither did I." He took off his hat and ran his hand through his hair, making himself look even more disheveled than before. "I missed you last night."

She had missed him, too. And what did that mean? That only a few hours away from him had left her miserable? She stepped back from the stall and turned to face him, her fingers tugging at a loose thread on one of her mittens. He looked irresistible to her at that moment, with his hair mussed and his jaw still sporting a shadow of the previous day's stubble. Her first instinct was to go to him, to feel the scrape of his beard across her cheek, to grab his hair and tug his head down so she could kiss him, so she could taste his tongue against hers.

But there was something heavy in the air between them, the unfinished edge of their last conversation impossible to ignore.

"I had an entire night to think about what to say to you, and yet now I stand here feeling like a fool." He rubbed his hand over his face, and Julia saw how tired he was then, the dark bruises of exhaustion beneath his eyes and the lines settling at the corners of his mouth. "When I asked you to come here, to Langford, I tried not to hope too much. I told myself you were here for Zora, that my own wants shouldn't interfere with that. I thought it would be enough, to have you near. Because I didn't know what your feelings were, and I was too afraid... too cowardly to make any sort of overture beyond sharing a simple tray of toast and cheese with you in front of a fire."

Julia blew out a breath slowly, willing herself to remain calm. There was a part of her that wanted to stop him before he could say anything else, to keep things as they were. Because she was afraid to want more, to reach for it and be denied. She had been denied so many things for so long that the act of settling for what she'd been given had also become an act of saving herself from future pain.

"Alexander—"

He held up his hand, his eyes fluttering closed. "Please allow me to finish before I lose the words all over again."

She bit down on her lips and clasped her hands in front of her.

"I want a partner in my life, Julia. I want a mother for Zora, someone who will love her and care for her, who won't seek to use her as a weapon." He winced at that, and she wondered what details he was leaving out for the admission to cause him that stab of pain. "I don't want to be forever hiding in the shadows with you, but..." And there, he took a step towards her. Only a step, leaving an ocean of space between them. "... if you're content with that, then I will be, too. Or if you'd rather I rush to London and fetch a special license for the two of us, I'll saddle up my horse this moment and be off. But what I want the most, what I'm certain I cannot live without, is you. Just you, and any way you'll let me have you."

It took her a moment to parse through his words and understand that he had made an offer of marriage to her. If she had been younger, if her life up to this point had traveled along a different path, she might have immediately leapt with excitement at his proposal.

But she had been married once already, and the more she looked back at those years, the more she realized how painful and miserable a time it had been for her. Even though she knew down to the very core of herself that Alexander was nothing like Frederick and never would be, the thought of being a wife again made her hesitate.

He would give her time, of course, if she wished. He would most likely give her anything it was within his power to give. And she wanted him in her life. She wanted Zora as well, and the prospect of being a mother to her filled Julia with an excitement that stole the breath from her lungs. But still, she couldn't say the words she knew he wanted to hear. So instead she walked up to him, laying her cheek on his shoulder while her hands slid inside of his coat and wrapped around him.

They stood like that for several minutes, simply holding onto one another while the light grew steadily brighter in the stables.

Alexander kissed the top of her head. "I take it this means I'm not rushing off to London this morning?"

She groaned and buried her face in his collar. "I'm sorry." She looked up at him as he tucked a loose tendril of hair behind her ear. "I know it's not what you want to hear, but... I need time. Not to think, but merely to accustom myself to the idea. Marriage is..."

"Frightening?"

"Yes."

"I know." And he kissed her forehead. "Believe me, I know. We've both been hurt, and one doesn't recover from such wounds quickly."

Her thoughts drifted towards Zora, the very person who had succeeded in bringing them together. A child without a mother and with an unknown father...

"You love her very much, don't you?"

He nodded without her having to mention who she was talking about. "My wife... She would try to use her to hurt me. I think she wanted me to resent Zora because she wasn't my own child, so she never allowed me to forget her infidelity. But I think Anna was unable to see beyond her own limitations for love and acceptance. She could only imagine what her own reaction would be in a similar situation, could only assume others would behave in the same manner."

"I'm sorry," she said again, blinking away a burning at the corners of her eyes. "I wish..."

"No, none of that." His thumbs swept the moisture from her cheeks, and then he kissed the tip of her nose, her lips. "I don't want anything to be different. I don't want to wish Zora away or alter anything that led us to where we are now."

She closed her eyes, allowing herself to revel in his embrace, the warmth of him beneath the heavy outer layer of his coat. And he was right. To change anything that had already happened would be to change who they were at that precise moment, and she could not bear the risk of such a loss.

But where *were* they now? She was Zora's governess, and he was the owner of Langford and the father of her charge. And they were lovers. As it stood, their relationship could never become public knowledge, or else the scandal of it would ruin not only her own reputation — something she little cared about, she had to admit — but had the potential to cast shame on Zora.

Marriage, Julia knew, would be the safest choice. The one that would allow her to be Zora's mother and Alexander's wife, to become mistress of Langford along with all of the privileges that came with such a position. Her school would very likely benefit from her rise in society, which would mean she could eventually do more for her students, and then...

Oh, but she didn't want to think about all of that. Not yet. So instead, she stretched up and pressed her lips to the side of his jaw, nipping at his unshaven skin. He let out a hiss and pulled her tighter against his chest.

"We should go back to the house," he said, as his own mouth grazed her temple. "It's early yet. Not everyone is awake. We could—"

"No." She brushed away his suggestion, not wanting to risk a servant catching them sneaking upstairs to one of the bedrooms or into his study. Her fingers found the buttons of his jacket, flicking them open to give her access to his waistcoat and shirt.

"Wait." He pulled her hands away, but only to turn and give a cursory glance over his shoulder to make certain they were alone. "But... here? Are you sure?"

They could have been standing on the lip of a volcano and she did not think she would be able to put off having him for as long as it would take to find a more suitable location. "Come," she said, and took his hand, pulling him towards the ladder. She thought they might climb up to the loft, where there was hay and a few extra blankets for the horses stashed away. But they didn't make it that far.

Alexander pushed her against the ladder, his hands reaching down to drag up her skirts while her legs parted in anticipation. She fought with the fastenings of his trousers, rushing as though there was a clock ticking away the seconds above their heads. And then he had the hem of her gown up to her thighs, and his fingers were there... already there, teasing her, sliding through her wetness before he dipped one of them inside.

"Alexander!" It startled her that she could be ready for him so quickly. Fiery passion, she had always assumed, was for the young. The young farmer's daughter caught under the spell of the handsome laborer hired to help with the harvest. The soldier yearning for the daughter of the local squire. But she'd fallen into the belief that she was too old for lust and wantonness. And yet there she stood, arching her back towards Alexander, reaching for his hips as he touched the tip of his cock between her legs and thrust hard and deep inside.

"Christ!" He growled against her neck, then hooked his hand beneath her right knee and hoisted her leg up until she wrapped it around his thighs.

She felt a sudden flash of fear that someone would walk in on them, that they would be discovered there by some sleepy-eyed stableboy come in to muck out the stalls for the morning. Her gaze darted frantically towards the stable door, but there was nothing, only the sunlight pouring in through the windows and the soft sounds of the horses stirring in their stalls.

So she allowed herself to enjoy the pleasure of the moment, the hard thrusts of Alexander's cock inside of her, filling her up until she could no longer catch her breath. It was so wonderfully wild, so elemental to love him like this; unable to keep their hands off one another, to deprive themselves of each other for no more than a few hours at a time.

And then that single word chimed loud in her thoughts, making her eyes flutter open.

Love.

There was no reason to argue with herself about it. She knew the truth, that what she felt for Alexander extended beyond the realm of sexual desire. But it was still a nascent thing, her love for him like a seed just planted, still vulnerable beneath a thin layer of soil.

But she loved him. And the realization rippled through her as she tipped her head back, seeking out his mouth for a kiss. His hand moved between them as her tongue tangled with his. His fingers found the tight, swollen bud at her center, caressing it in rhythm with his thrusts until she couldn't take anymore. Her release crashed over her, so quickly her legs buckled beneath her and Alexander had to wrap an arm around her waist to keep her from sliding into a boneless puddle on the floor.

Aftershocks of pleasure sparked through her like little fireworks as he cried out with his own release, finally cursing loudly before he leaned against her, panting heavily into the side of her neck.

"God in heaven, Julia," he rasped, and pressed a kiss to the sensitive spot beneath her ear. "You make me..."

"Yes." She agreed. To whatever he was going to say, she agreed. "Me, too."

She held onto him for another minute, until she could trust herself to let go without toppling over. A part of her didn't want to move, didn't want to return to the house and have the secret of what they'd shared weighing over her while she slipped back into the role of governess and forgotten widow.

But if she told him she loved him, if she married him...

She burrowed her face into his shoulder, breathing in the scent of him. The words were there, a confession balanced on the tip of her tongue. That she loved him. That she wanted to marry him and yet was afraid. That their affair deserved more than the clandestine treatment it had already received. That Zora needed a mother and Julia's heart ached to fully step into that role.

They stepped apart, each of them taking a minute to smooth down rumpled clothing, to fix hair and buttons and ties. As soon as they appeared somewhat presentable again, she found her mittens and hat on the floor and wound her scarf again around her neck.

"Will we see you at breakfast?" she managed to ask, her voice carrying a tremble that matched the one still shivering through her legs. Hopefully the walk back to the house would be enough to restore her equilibrium and disguise the fact she'd been ravished in the stable only a few minutes before.

"Not this morning, unfortunately." Alexander gave his coat another adjustment, then looked for his hat which had been abandoned on the floor near to where her own had been. "There are improvements that need to be made at some of the farms before winter fully sets in. Roofs that have begun to leak with all of the rain, and a chimney that collapsed with our last bout of wind. I need to make my rounds this morning and see exactly what needs to be done."

"Zora will be disappointed," she said. And so would she, but she didn't trust herself to say for fear that everything else she felt for him would come tumbling out on its heels.

"I'm in need of a new land agent," he said, setting his hat on his head. "The previous one retired last year, and I've been lax about finding a suitable replacement. When I do, I shouldn't be gone from the house as much, and I'll have more time to spend with her. But you can let Zora know that I should be home this evening. We can have dinner again tonight. A proper dinner," he added, smiling. "In the dining room. At the table."

"Perhaps the picnic needs to become a birthday tradition?" She stepped up to him and adjusted the collar of his coat, the folds of his neckcloth, everything that had been shifted out of place during their lovemaking.

He placed one hand over hers, stopping the fussing of her fingers over his heart. "The first of many new traditions, I hope."

She nodded. Her throat felt thick but her heart was full. But the happiness she felt was still fragile, and she worried that if she wasn't careful it might shatter like glass before her eyes. "I'll go and see to Zora, before she can come storming out of the house in search of us."

A quick kiss that turned into something more lingering, and Julia strode briskly away from the stables, across the lawn, shielding her eyes from the brilliant light of the sun that had already melted all of the frost beneath her swiftly moving feet.

Eighteen

Zora decided that she was interested in the human body later that morning. She began her inquiries at breakfast, asking about how the lungs knew when to draw in a breath and how hearts continued beating even when someone was sound asleep. This led to a discussion about various organs and digestion and myriad other topics that were most likely not appropriate for a period of time involving the consumption of food, until Julia finally declared a postponement of the subject until something could be found in the library to help answer all of their questions.

That was how they spent the morning, poring over an old edition of Hooke's Micrographia and drawing their own illustrations of various plants and insects they had seen around Langford, while Julia promised they would order more books concerning the human side of things.

After lunch, Zora went to the kitchen with Ellen — to fetch the kitten a saucer of cream and any leftovers that might be sitting about — and Julia took herself upstairs to make certain all of the paints and ink had been put away after their illustrative work that morning. It was while she was fitting everything back onto the shelf that she noticed the glint of something hidden behind a small stack of books. She reached into the shadow and retrieved the small silver comb that Zora had shown her the day before, the one from Mrs. Halberd's jewelry box.

"Oh, Zora." Julia sighed and turned the comb over in her hand.

The room at the end of the hall was unlocked, just as before. She opened the door with a feigned carelessness, as though stepping into the former Mrs. Halberd's bedroom did nothing to heighten her anxiety. But there was sweat on her palm as she turned the doorknob, and her heart skipped a beat as she crossed over the threshold.

The jewelry box was still on the dressing table where Zora had left it, still gleaming as though a maid had swept a duster across its surface only a few minutes before. She raised the lid and tucked the comb inside, nestling it on its bed of blue velvet along with the other sparkling trinkets. As she closed the lid, a sliver of white caught her eye, a slip of something like paper sticking out from behind the edge of the velvet.

Later, she would wonder why she didn't simply shut the lid and walk away. But the curious part of her strove for dominance, and she pinched the corner of paper, tugging at it until the entire bottom — a false bottom, as it made itself known — of the box lifted upwards. She hadn't noticed it before, how the inside of the box didn't match the overall size of it. Tucked underneath the layer of velvet was a thick stack of folded papers. Letters, she realized, stuffed together so tightly they moved as a single clump until she separated a few of them with a flick of her thumb.

She flipped one of them over, tilting it towards the light streaming through the window. The writing across the front was faded, and her eyes were fatigued from all of the drawing she had done with Zora that morning. But she saw the swoop and slant of the first few words, and her heart clenched inside her chest as though a hand had inserted itself behind her ribs and squeezed.

Julia knew it, her husband's handwriting.

She could still leave them there, unread. Stuff them back into the jewelry box, pretend she had seen nothing. Pretend that...

Unbidden, her hands began to flip through the letters. There were dozens in all, some more faded than others. And all of them written by her husband.

She blinked. She would have expected tears in her eyes, but instead it was astonishment that made her eyes feel dry and her throat close up as though she was suddenly parched.

They weren't hers to read. They had belonged to Mrs. Halberd, to her husband, she reminded herself. But neither of them were still counted among the living. So who was there to tell her that she was infringing on someone else's private thoughts when she was the nearest living relation to the person who had authored them in the first place?

She put the jewelry box back together and shifted it back to where it had been before she'd opened it. The letters she picked up, stacking them neatly again, pressing them together and tucking the bulk of them behind a fold in her skirt in the hope no one would see them clutched in her hand should someone catch her leaving Mrs. Halberd's room. She thought of Zora, still down in the kitchen with Ellen, and prayed the kitten would prove to be a distraction for a few more minutes, at least.

Her own room seemed dark in comparison to Mrs. Halberd's, situated on the other side of the house as it was. She shut the door behind her, standing against it as though she expected someone to break it down and accuse her of stealing from the former mistress of the house. By the time she crossed to the window, a feeling of sickness began to roil in her stomach. She was torn between wanting to read the letters still clutched in her hand or throwing the lot of them into the fireplace, to be burned into a smoking clot of ash.

Because she knew what the letters would say. Even as she

opened the first one, the paper as fragile as an autumn leaf between her fingers.

Dearest Anna...

She read every word. She knew her husband's handwriting well enough, had read enough copies of his sermons to skim across it quickly without having to pause and decipher any peculiarities of his penmanship. In her head, it was his voice reciting the words, lifting them from the page and flinging them at her feet like a gauntlet.

... until I see you...

... the pleasure of your touch, your kiss...

... I want to be inside you again...

... when we can be married...

She started at that. There was a date at the top, from over a dozen years earlier. Before she had married him and become Mrs. Benton, perhaps even before Mrs. Halberd had become Mrs. Halberd.

Quickly, she searched through the rest of the letters, trying to sort them into chronological order, though not all of them were dated. The most recent ones were less faded, less worn at the corners and creases, and she saved those for last. Like sliding a knife into the wound as slowly as possible.

... my tiresome wife...

... your fool of a husband...

... the earrings I gave you, the emeralds so striking against your complexion...

And she couldn't stop reading. Minutes ticked away, possibly an hour or more. She read on because she feared if she stopped, she would curl forward and be violently sick at her feet.

... our child...

... our daughter...

... Isadora...

"Mrs. Benton?" There was a light knock on the door before

Zora stuck her head into the bedroom. "Mrs. Benton, did you forget? We were going to take a walk this afternoon."

... our daughter...

Julia snatched up the letters scattered across the windowsill, holding them to her chest like she could staunch the bleeding with that flutter of pages. She didn't turn around. She found that she couldn't. Not yet, not yet.

"Um, give me a minute." Her voice sounded nothing like her own. "C-could you go and play in the nursery for a little while? Just a few minutes, at the most. I have a bit of a headache and I want to give it a chance to go away."

She heard Zora take a few steps into the room. Dear God, but Julia could not bear to look at her right then, not without losing the last thread of control she had over her emotions. "Should I fetch one of the maids? Mrs. Holland has some headache powder, and she can—"

"No, no." Julia waved an errant hand. "Only a few minutes rest, that's all I need. Put on your boots and find your gloves and... and I'll be right there."

"Very well." And there was the soft retreat of her footsteps, followed by the click of the door closing behind her.

Julia dropped to her knees. She didn't cry. It seemed unusual to her, that she couldn't even dredge up a single tear or a hitch in her breathing to mark this new knowledge pitched at her out of nowhere. But she stayed there on the floor, her fingers digging into the edge of the rug as she lowered her head, as her shoulders slumped and she tipped onto her side, as the room spun slowly around her.

Just a few minutes of rest, she thought. That was all she needed.

* * *

"Julia?"

She opened her eyes to darkness.

She was still on the floor, but even as she nurtured that thought, strong arms slipped beneath her and she was carried over to her bed.

"Alexander?" She still did not sound like herself. Beside her, Alexander lit a candle on the nightstand, and she winced at the sudden illumination.

It all came back to her in that moment: Mrs. Halberd's jewelry box, the hidden letters, her husband's looping scrawl. She jerked upright, scrabbling for the edge of the bed even as Alexander grasped both of her arms and held her still.

"Julia?" He peered directly into her face. "Julia, what happened? I returned home and Zora told me you weren't feeling well. When I knocked on the door, you didn't respond. Are you ill? Should I send for the doctor?"

"The letters…" She tried to wrench free of his hands, her only thought for the letters still over by the window, the letters that revealed everything about his wife's affair, about Zora's true parentage. She couldn't let Alexander see them. Yes, he had known his wife was unfaithful to him, but to have the details written out across the page, and in Frederick's own words…

Oh, she didn't want him to know. Not about her husband, not about Zora. It was too cruel, too cruel that the man for whom she could never bear a child had been father to the little girl now in her care.

"Julia, what letters? What are you talking about?"

She stopped struggling. The concern in his face nearly tore her heart open all over again. "The…" she began, but cut herself off. She wasn't ready to say it, the words sticking to the roof of her mouth like an acrid taste. "Where is Zora?"

"She's in the nursery. She's having her dinner. Why?"

… our daughter…

"The letters," she said, as though she would've endured any amount of pain in place of the one she was about to inflict upon him. "Over by the window, on the sill. I-I found them today, and..."

He went to the window and gathered up the letters, right where she had left them. She expected him to bring them over to her, but instead he stood with his back towards her, and she heard the slide of paper against paper as he shuffled through them.

He sighed. And with that rush of breath, she realized how very wrong about everything she had been. "I take it you've read them?" he asked, still not turning around.

Her fingers sought out the edge of the blankets, the edge of the mattress, anything to grab onto before the world tilted again and tipped her into uncharted waters. "Alexander?"

His shoulders dropped. When he finally turned around to face her, the shadows from the candlelight made him appear as though he'd aged a decade in as many seconds. "I'm sorry, Julia. I didn't want you to find out this way."

Her gaze dropped to the letters in his hands and back again to his face. Why didn't he look surprised? Where was the shock, the revulsion she had endured only a few hours ago? Why was he not cursing her husband for sleeping with his wife, for fathering the daughter that should have been his? "You knew."

He winced as though she'd crossed the room and slapped him. "I did, yes."

"For how long?" Surely not for years. Surely not when he'd asked her to come to Langford, to be Zora's governess. Because she didn't want to believe that he'd knowingly put her in charge of her husband's illegitimate child.

"Before my wife died..." And he paused there, slapping the letters against his thigh as he took two steps towards the bed. His gaze leapt over everything but her, and the halted sound of his breathing told her that he didn't want to say any part of what he was about to tell her. "Some months before she died," he began again. "We had a fight. We always fought, but this was..." He ran his free hand over the top of his head, then gripped the back of his neck, his shoulders rising up again as though in preparation for his next words. "I always knew that Zora wasn't my daughter. I knew from the moment Anna told me she was with child that I couldn't have been the father. And after Zora was born, she became more restless, more unhappy. Here, with me. It wasn't long after that she told me she was going to leave. That she would take Zora, and she would run off with..." Finally, his gaze darted towards her and held. There was agony in his eyes, and she could not tell if it was for the pain he'd already lived through, or the pain he was about to inflict on her.

"Go on," she said. There was no reason to continue dragging it out. She already knew the truth. The first blood had already been spilled. Now, it was just a matter of rubbing salt into the wound.

He began to pace across the room, though he didn't come any nearer to where she was on the bed. "I didn't know it was him, at first. Your husband. Not until... Oh, I think Zora was at least a year old when I found out. When she told me. That was when I discovered the history between them—"

"Cornwall," she blurted out, thinking back to what Mrs. Cutler had mentioned to her in the village. "They grew up together, didn't they?"

He looked at her strangely. "How did you know?"

"Village gossip," she admitted. "I only learned of it this week."

"Well." He started another round of pacing, both of his hands now gripping the stack of letters as if he could tear them to scraps with a turn of his wrist. "They wanted to marry, even then. Before they'd ever met either of us. But your husband was poor, and my wife was expected to marry well, to resurrect her family's fortunes. And a country vicar wouldn't do. So if they couldn't have one another under the law, they..." He cleared his throat. "They found a way to be together."

Julia buried her face in her hands. "She brought him here, then. As vicar."

"So they could be near one another," he said, confirming her words. "I don't know why I didn't suspect at first. I was too trusting, and they seemed to work hard at keeping everything secret. At least in the beginning. Even when I found out Anna had been unfaithful, I never would've thought..."

"No, of course not." Not Frederick. She never would have thought that about Frederick. Who had always been so pious and upstanding, who had been unerringly rigid in his views on what he believed the Bible categorized as sin. "Even when people hurt us, we too often bow our heads and try not to think the worst of them."

For seven years she'd tried not to think the worst of Frederick. Even as he had torn her down, as he made her believe she was not someone who could be loved, who could be desired, she had taken the burden of her marriage's faults upon herself.

And all that time, he had been having an affair.

"God, I was such a fool."

It was as though her husband had been two entirely separate individuals; the man to whom she'd been married, the one who railed against decadence and carnal desires from the pulpit, and also the man who kept a mistress and gave gifts of fine jewels to his lover. At home with her, he had always been cold and distant, prudish and ready to spit out shaming words at her if she dared to add too much lace to the edge of a gown or take too long styling her hair. And always — always — he had made her feel like a broken, cursed thing because of her inability to give birth to a healthy child.

Though none of her deficiencies had ever stopped him from crawling atop her in bed at night, like an animal rutting himself to release.

The man who had written those letters was a complete stranger to her. A man of passion, a man who gave gifts. A man unafraid to receive physical pleasure and eager to give it in return.

Which one had been the real Frederick Benton? Or had he

been all of them, only showing various sides of himself to whomever he chose?

"Why didn't you tell me?" She looked up at Alexander. He had ceased pacing at her question, his expression stricken. When he gave no immediate reply, she continued speaking, the words coming out like poison draining from a wound. "You asked me to come here, to be Zora's governess, and yet you knew that Frederick... that he... How could you do that? How could you ask me to come here and help raise my husband's child?"

She knew he was in pain, just as she was. It was there in every line of his face, every gray hair and every shadow edging his features. But he'd had years to let it erode into something dull and aching. For her, it was fresh and biting, making her want to lash out, to throw off some of the injury before it could settle into the marrow of her bones.

"Do you know what it was like to lose every child I tried to bear? When I would feel the pains come on and it was always too soon, and all I could think was that I had done something wrong, that I wasn't fit to be blessed with the... the crown of motherhood," she said, stealing one of Frederick's horrid phrases.

Alexander took a step towards her, but she put out a hand to stop him.

"No." She shook her head, her gaze pinning him in place. "You had years to tell me, to say something. But instead you ran off to London, hiding away from all of this, as though the world here should cease to turn in your absence. Did you think I would never find out? Did you think I was such a fool that—"

"Julia—"

"I'm not finished!" Her voice reverberated through the room. Alexander didn't take another step, nor did he give any indication of trying to interrupt her again. So she swung her legs over the side of the bed and she sat there, gripping the edge of the mattress as she leaned slightly forward, holding herself back from committing some act she couldn't even fathom. "I have every right to this anger. I have buried children who never took a single breath. I have etched their names on my heart and they sit there inside of me like scars. And I hate your wife," she spat, the venom in her voice burning through the air. "I hate her for so easily being able to do what I could not."

She stood up then. She wasn't worried about collapsing again. The worst of the shock had worn away, and now it was only rage flowing through her veins, pumping through her heart, filling her lungs to shape the words that flew out of her mouth. "Perhaps it's unchristian of me to feel so. Perhaps I should be more charitable, more forgiving, having been the wife of a vicar, a supposed man of God," she added, each syllable like the shot from a pistol. "But for seven years I lived with someone who tore me down piece by piece, only to have him turn around and use those blocks to build a stronger foundation for the woman he loved. The woman who wasn't me. Me, his stupid, useless wife. His wife!" she cried, her voice tearing at the back of her throat.

"And you!" She pointed a finger at him, her hand remarkably steady despite the fury frothing inside of her. "I know what you'll say. That you thought you were protecting me, shielding me from some great hurt. But — oh!" Her hands flew to her head, and she wished she could tear out her hair, or rend her clothes into rags, or wreak any kind of destruction on herself or something close to her. "All this time, I kept looking at Zora, seeing something in her face that seemed so familiar to me. I thought I was only imagining it. I thought..." Her arms fell back to her sides. "How could they do this to us? How could two people who claimed to love each other cause so much pain to those around them?"

"I don't know, Julia." Alexander sounded defeated, and she tried not to dwell on how many years he had spent nursing his own injuries, keeping everything secret so as not to bring harm to Zora by revealing her mother's transgressions. "And I loved her, or at least I thought I did." He shrugged, as if he was unable to provide a better explanation than that. "I cared for her in the beginning. I wouldn't have asked her to be my wife if I hadn't. And I thought..." He closed his eyes. "I thought my love might be enough even after I realized I had made a mistake, that she didn't... that she would never love me in return."

Julia wondered which was worse, to love someone as Alexander had, and be hurt by them when their love went unrequited? Or to enter into a marriage without any expectation of great affection, as she had with Frederick, and slowly lose herself beneath the onslaught of his disdain? "How did you find out about the affair? Did she simply look you in the eye and tell you?"

"I had always suspected she was carrying on with someone else. I didn't want to believe it at first, but you can only ignore the evidence for so long." He spoke as though every word caused him fresh pain, as though he was scraping the scabs off old wounds to tell her what she wished to know. "When she told me she was pregnant, I knew... Well, I know what's involved in the conceiving of a child, and seeing as how I hadn't been welcome in her bed for several months before that... Anyway, I had no idea she and Mr. Benton were lovers. When he first came here to Barrow-in-Ashton, when she so stubbornly fought for him to be given the post, she had claimed it was because their families had been old acquaintances in Cornwall, that she wished to repay them for a past kindness by giving him the living. For years, I watched them work together, and nothing untoward ever crossed my mind. But the entire time, she drifted away from me. Oh, in public she was always the perfect wife, made Langford shine like a jewel. But in private, I knew how much she despised me, and for the life of me I could never figure out what I had done wrong. Unfortunately, my only sin seemed to be that I wasn't... him."

Julia understood that sensation, that particular pain. That nothing he could have done would ever have been good enough.

"And then Zora was born." A blast of sound issued out of him, not quite a curse and not quite a laugh. "I was smitten from the moment I laid eyes on her. This tiny thing, helpless and pink and squalling. And I held her in my arms, and I loved her from the start. So, of course, Anna chose that moment to tell me about your husband, that he was Zora's father, that she had been in love with him for half her life. She was almost gleeful about it, like it gave her so much joy to inflict pain on someone else. On me."

He turned and began to pace again, but he only made it a few steps before he arrived at the fireplace. He reached out to the mantel with a grip so fierce Julia thought he might tear the wood free of the wall if he was so inclined. "But I didn't tell you. Because I cared about you. Because I was afraid to hurt you. Afraid of exactly this! I thought... Christ, Julia. I don't know what I thought."

She wanted to go to him. She wanted to shake him. She wanted to take every single one of her husband's letters and use them to light a fire that would burn through the rest of the night. And still she was angry, without even knowing for certain who was fueling the majority of her rage.

Her husband, she realized. The man who had married her because she was there, because she was convenient, and all so he could keep up the appearance of a holy man of God complete with a biddable wife and family — a family she was never able to provide — while quietly, secretly carrying on a years-long affair with another woman.

Except her husband was gone. And so was Mrs. Halberd. The only person left at whom to direct her ire was Alexander, and he'd been hurt just as much. But she couldn't let her anger dissipate. She didn't want to. It felt good to hold onto it after so many years of allowing her life's failures and disappointments to wash over her again and again, as though she was little more than a stone to be slowly worn down.

"It was not your decision to make, to choose whether or not I could handle the truth." She walked towards him, close enough to smell him, to feel the warmth emanating from him. To reach out and touch him, if she wanted. "All these years, you could have told me. Instead, you hid away, cowering behind your pain—"

"Of course I was in pain," he shouted back. "Do you think I don't feel my heart twist every time I look into my daughter's face and I'm not there? And how exactly was I supposed to tell you? In a letter? To your face? Perhaps I should've invited you to tea and we could have discussed their affair over a plate of lemon biscuits."

"Oh, don't be absurd..."

"If you're allowed to be angry then I'm allowed to be absurd! You're not the only one who was hurt, Julia!"

"But you've known for years!" she countered. Years for the pain to lose its edge, for it to transform into something dull and negligible, that would not slice into him anew every time he thought of it. "You've had time to—"

"To what?" A step forward from him and there was hardly any space left between them. "Accustom myself to my wife's infidelity? To the fact that my daughter was fathered by another man? The pain doesn't lessen. It changes, and it's shaped itself around my life, my every thought, but it never truly goes away."

It wasn't what she wanted to hear. She did not want hard truths and dire reality. She wished to be told that everything would get better, not that her very character would be shaped by all of the injuries, large and small, received from those around her.

"I can't do this." She dropped her chin to her chest, her teeth working at a cracked bit of skin on her bottom lip until she tasted blood. "I feel trapped." She looked up at him, her eyes wide and aching. "You've trapped me here. Because I don't want to leave you, and I don't want to leave Zora, but I'm not sure..." She sighed, heavy enough she feared she might fall through the floor with the weight of her troubles. "I will look at her, and I will see Frederick, and I will see the faces of all the children I lost. And I don't want to feel this way. It's not her fault. None of it is. And yet..."

QUENBY OLSON

Alexander placed his hand on her arm, a light touch above her elbow. Like a spark to tinder, it set her aflame. She batted him away, but then placed her own hand on his chest, above his heart.

"Don't," she hissed. "I don't want your comfort."

His gaze burned into her, twin coals in the stark wound of his face. He looked battered and raw, and she realized this was how he truly appeared beneath the mask he wore for Zora and others. This was the damage he took such pains to hide away, the agony he had never dared to show to her before now. "Julia, I'm—"

"No." And she pushed him a few steps back until he hit the wall, the letters falling from his grasp, scattering across the floor. Her hand remained on his chest, her fingers climbing upwards to the rumpled folds of his neckcloth. "I don't want to hear what you have to say. Not yet, please." She grabbed the fabric at his collar, holding onto it like a rope about to drag her up from the drowning depths.

She dragged his mouth down to hers and she kissed him. She kissed him because she wanted to taste the heat of his mouth, feel the thrust of his tongue against hers. There was the slide of his teeth on her bottom lip, and she urged him to bite, to send a shiver of pain through her.

"Julia," he said. Like it was a plea, like a prayer. "Do you want this?"

She nodded, her hands moving down, down, down. Over his chest, over his abdomen, wrenching at the buttons of his waistcoat, sending one of them to the floor while the others dangled from their loosened threads. She struggled with his shirt, pulling it out from the waistband of his trousers so that she could run her fingers across his skin.

He was hot beneath her touch, or maybe her hands were cold. But she wanted to wrap herself around him, wanted to submerge herself in him. It was either that, or continue to rail against the two people who could not be there to answer for their sins.

His waistcoat landed on the floor. The shirt went next. Julia took in the sight of him then, the bare planes of his back and shoulders, the shadow of hair across his chest, trailing down to where she could not see. For years, her husband had told her that one's naked body was a shameful thing. Adam and Eve absconding from the Garden of Eden, covered in fig leaves. But she wanted to look at Alexander. She wanted to revel in the sight of him, every inch of his skin bared to her, a statue of gold and shadows waiting for her touch.

She slid her hands over his ribs, then across his back. He turned away from her, guided by her fingers, by the scrape of her nails down the length of his spine. He groaned and leaned towards the wall, his head resting on his forearm, while she wrapped her arms around him, embracing him from behind. She wondered if he wanted this, needed this as much as she did. It wouldn't be gentle lovemaking. She had no need for soft caresses and whispered words. She wanted to hear his desire for her roar from his throat. She wanted to feel the slick of his sweat, the bite of his teeth. She wanted him to make her feel seen.

Her arms still around him, she reached down towards the front of his trousers, for the buttons there. He was hard and ready for her, so very ready. He swore as she slid her fingers up and down his length, as her thumb grazed his tip and the bead of moisture gathered there. When she leaned against him, his hips pressed back into hers, urging her to press harder in return. And still she stroked him, while her free hand moved down to the cleft at the top of his thigh, while she grazed her teeth on his shoulder and felt her nipples tighten as they rubbed against him.

"Dammit, Julia... Dammit!" He came with a jerk of his hips, his cock pulsing in her palm. She heard his heavy breathing, the litany of swears that fell from his lips, the soft thump of his head as it came to rest on the wall between his braced hands. They stood like that for a minute, Julia still holding him from behind, enjoying how well it felt to have his buttocks nestled so snugly against her front. She thought they might be done, that something of a reprieve had been earned by that quick burst of passion, but once Alexander had control of himself again, he turned around to face, moving so fast she couldn't catch her breath before he swept her up and carried her over to the bed.

She gasped as she fell back across the end of the mattress. He'd already pushed her skirts up past her knees by the time she levered herself up onto her elbows. She parted her thighs for him, arching her hips upwards as his hands burned a trail over the skin above her stockings.

The sound that came out of him at that moment, a low rumble in his chest, as though he'd gone feral. Onto his knees before her, his fingers spreading her open, and she felt his breath kiss her there before his lips, his tongue took over.

Her fingers tangled in his hair as he licked her, as he tasted her. She held him there, not wanting him to stop until he'd driven her over the edge. "Please," she begged, letting her head tip back as she gripped his hair so tight she feared it might hurt him. "God, please!"

And then... he stopped. She jolted in surprise, only to open her eyes and find him standing again, his knees resting on the edge of the bed as he pulled her hips towards him and settled his cock at her entrance.

"Yes?"

She nodded, and that was enough. Not even a hitch of her breath before he was fully inside of her, their hips joined together as he held her there, just for a moment.

"Alexander," she panted, and squirmed beneath him. The fullness of him embedded in her made her want to cry out her release right then and there. She looked up at him, and an understanding passed between them. She needed this as much as he did, this... untangling of something that had always been there, a shadow keeping them apart for the last dozen years. "Please," she said. "Don't be gentle."

He leaned down and kissed her. A soft touch of his mouth to

hers, at first. And then he drew her bottom lip into his mouth, biting down as he pulled his hips back and thrust into her again.

She reached up and gripped his shoulders, not only to hold onto him but to show that she trusted him, in a way that she never had with her husband. With Alexander, she could deliver herself into his power without fear, fear that he might use that power to control her, to hurt her against her will. To destroy her.

Even though she'd given him leave to be rough with her, there was still a carefulness underlying his every touch, a kind of safety net letting her know that should she fall, he would always be there to catch her.

His hands sought out her hips right before he came, and he urged her to wrap her legs around him, caging him in as his thrusts became more intense. She tightened around him, unable to hold off any longer before she broke apart, just a moment before he cried out and collapsed over her.

Julia held him tight, drawing him the rest of the way onto the bed with her. Beside them, the single candle on the nightstand still flickered, casting shadows on the walls and highlighting the lack of a fire in the fireplace. Alexander wrapped himself around her and she listened to the mingled racing of their hearts and the soft rush of their breathing, all while realization dawned that the household was still going about its evening business around them.

Did everyone know Alexander was in her room, that he had come to check on her after Zora had told him she was unwell? She pressed her cheek to his chest and closed her eyes, wanting to stretch out this moment while also batting away the fear that it would come to an end, and all too soon. But they hadn't been quiet, neither their argument nor their lovemaking afterwards. If no one had suspected there being something between herself and Alexander before, she doubted the same could be said now. He had been alone with her in her room, with the door closed, for an extended period of time. Had they been overheard? How many had seen him come in here?

No, no. She couldn't think about that now. She needed at least a few more minutes of peace before having to step out and face a world in which everything seemed to have tilted off its axis.

"I'm sorry," Alexander whispered against her hair. "I'm sorry I didn't tell you."

She placed her hand on his cheek, her thumb tracing the deep fissure of worry etched in the corner of his mouth. "You've carried it for too long on your own. I wish—" But she winced at that. As he had already said, there was no good in wishing for things to be different. The choices they'd made, and the actions of those around them — for good or ill — had succeeded in bringing them to this moment. With Alexander's arms around her, with Zora blossoming in her care.

"Will you be all right?" he asked. When she shook her head in confusion, he went on. "With Zora?"

Ah, that power he possessed to pluck at her thoughts without her having to say a single word about what was in her head at that moment. "I will be, of course. I hope you don't think that I would leave her because of this. That I would leave you. But I was angry. I still am." She had to say it, to acknowledge the rage that still coursed through her. "Not with you, not really. And certainly not with Zora. But... with everything else, I think. It was too much, all at once."

He swept her hair back from her forehead and kissed the path his fingers had cleared. "I hope you don't think I was calm and collected when I found out. I fear I was not myself for quite some time after learning my wife was carrying another man's child. But it wasn't until Zora was born, until I held her and she..." He scraped the back of his hand across his brow. "Christ, I was a lost man after that. I'd have done anything to protect her, to prevent her from knowing what a mess she'd been born into. She was this small person who wanted nothing more than love and care, and that — at the very least — I was able to provide for her."

Julia let her head fall back on the pillows. Now that it had been several minutes since they'd finished, she felt the lack of a fire, the chill seeping in from the corners of the room. "I shall have to apologize to her for missing our walk this afternoon."

"You can beg her forgiveness in the morning," he said, carefully sliding away from her and standing up again beside the bed. "You should probably take an evening to let your thoughts settle. Eat something, have a bath, or simply climb under the blankets and sleep for the rest of the night. I'm more than capable of taking care of my daughter for an evening."

Julia sat up on the bed, tucking her legs beneath her wrinkled skirt as she watched him sweep up his shirt and waistcoat from the floor. "Can I..." And she hesitated, because there was a deeper meaning to what she wanted to say, the answer to a question he'd already posed hidden inside her own query. "Can I spend the night with you? In your room?" she added, hoping he would understand her intent.

He paused while tucking the hem of his shirt back into his trousers. "Do you mean for the entire night? What if the servants—"

"I don't care." A bit of a lie, that. She did care, but not enough for it to deter her. "And whatever scandal might come of it, it should only be a temporary one."

The bed creaked as Alexander sat down. He reached out and took one of her hands. "What are you saying, Julia?"

"That I'm tired of being afraid." She laced her fingers with his. "That even though the very thought of marriage should send me running in the other direction, I know that I can't allow fear to continually keep me from what I want. And I want you and I want Zora and I want..." She paused, hoping to wait out the quaver in her voice, but she didn't think she would succeed. "I want happiness, and I want love. And I know it's possible, even if our own experiences might give evidence to the contrary. My parents were happy, and my sisters seem to love the lives they have now. But I love you," she said, and stumbled there, because she realized it was the first time she had dared to say it outloud. "And with you, I'm willing to try again."

He brought her hand to his lips. "Then I will do everything in my power to be worthy of you."

"No." She almost snatched her hand away, but she didn't want to alarm him. "Please don't say things like that. You make it seem as though I'm better than I am." She lowered her head, her teeth worrying at her lower lip until she feared she might set it to bleeding again. "Are you sure, though? About marrying me?"

"Julia." And he sighed, while he settled the palm of her hand against his cheek. "I've thought about having you as my wife for... too long," he admitted. "Since before it would've even been possible to marry you. I imagined what it would be like to wake up every day to your kindness, your beauty, your indomitable strength—"

"No, I'm not—" she started to interrupt, but her words faltered as he raised his eyebrows and looked at her.

"I remember when I first met you," he said, his voice low, mesmerizing. "At the vicarage. We caught you unawares, I think, not long after you and your husband had arrived. Anna wanted to pay a visit, and... Well. But there you were, flustered and doing everything in your power not to show it. And then you disappeared off to the kitchen and—"

"You followed me."

He nodded. "I wanted to see you." As simple as that, as though no other explanation was necessary. "You were bustling about, trying to put together a tray."

She smiled at the memory. "I couldn't find the tea, and I was out of sugar."

"And the biscuits were stale."

"Were they?" Her eyes widened. "Oh, I'm sorry. I was such a mess that day. You and Mrs. Halberd walked in, and I suddenly felt so... inferior."

"You were beautiful."

Her first instinct was to contradict him, but instead she let his words wrap around her, the touch of them as solid as his hands on her skin. Frederick had never told her that she was beautiful, but then, she didn't think her husband had ever seen her. And yet, she still hesitated, because there was still one more question she needed to ask. "But what about children?"

"What are you talking about?"

She swallowed. Already, her throat felt thick, like she might choke on her next words. "You understand that if we marry, I cannot give you any children. Not children of our own. We'll have Zora, but..."

"Julia, I know."

Oh, it was easy for him to say. But what about a year later? Ten years? Would he look back and regret choosing a wife who could not bear him a son or daughter? "I just... I don't want you to enter into this lightly. I don't want you to wish you'd rather have—"

"Julia."

She sniffed, and she realized her eyes were burning.

He shifted on the bed until he was in front of her, until she couldn't avoid looking at some part of him. "Yes, I was upset when I first learned that Zora wasn't mine. But that doesn't mean I'm not going to rest until I have a child of my own to carry on some great Halberd lineage. I'm not a Tudor king, ready to send you to the Tower if you're incapable of providing me with a son."

A laugh slipped out of her. "I know. It's only..." She shook her head. Why was all of this so difficult to say?

"Julia, I love you, and I want to marry you. That's it. There's nothing else. No footnotes or codicils. Only you. And it will make me the happiest I've ever been."

She lifted her eyes to meet his. He loved her. She saw it in his gaze, in his every feature. He loved her for her, and she couldn't put into words how that made her feel.

"I'm going to check on Zora," he said, and leaned in to kiss her forehead. "I left her with one of the maids, but no doubt she's bombarded the woman with so many questions she'll be resigning from her post first thing in the morning." He stood up, shrugged into his waistcoat, and fussed with a couple of the buttons before giving up on them. "But I'll see you tonight? Unless you'd—"

"Yes, tonight," she assured him. And every night after, she hoped.

Nineteen

J ulia was to be a married woman.

Again.

A night, a day, and another full night had passed since she'd found the letters from her husband to Mrs. Halberd, since she'd learned of their affair and Zora's true parentage. The pain of it had not retreated. It was less acute than those first few hours, changing now to a steady ache that curled up inside of her, like a dragon hoarding its anger as though it was a mound of treasure to be protected.

The most difficult moment had been in greeting Zora the next morning. Julia had steeled herself for it, thinking that if she simply grit her teeth and kept control of her breathing, all would be well. But she stopped at the threshold of the nursery, every part of her held still as she looked at the girl as if for the very first time.

There was her husband's jaw, she realized, as Zora clambered out of bed with a smile on her face. There was the tilt of his eyes, and the same curve in the shell of his ears that had been his, as well. She was amazed that she hadn't seen it before, now that the resemblance was so startlingly clear to her. But perhaps she hadn't wanted to notice it. Perhaps her own mind had been fighting to save her from the hurt it would undoubtedly cause. Perhaps—

"Good morning, Mrs. Benton!" Zora had padded over to her in her nightgown and bare feet, her dark hair sticking out from the back of her head like a bird's nest. "Are you feeling better today?"

Julia opened her mouth to speak and immediately felt her throat catch. Not because of any anger or hatred ready to spill over, but instead because of the love she carried for Zora, this little girl who so wished to share her own love and affection and curiosity in return.

"My head is still a little muddled," Julia confessed, as close to the truth as she would dare reach. "But I should feel well again soon enough. Let's get you dressed and have our breakfast together, hmm? And if the morning stays fine, I think we'll be able to fit in that walk I promised to you yesterday."

And so they had their walk, and their lessons, and then a respite in front of the drawing room fire with buttered toast and milky tea as the daylight waned.

Alexander returned that evening, and before dinner — with Julia's permission, and after a quiet talk with Zora (which was not quiet for long, once they told her the news) — an announcement was made to the household.

"Mrs. Benton," he said, his voice carrying over the heads of the assembled staff. "Has agreed to be my wife."

A cheer went up as drinks were passed around, and toasts and shouts of congratulation to the happy couple followed. Julia was overwhelmed by the attention, but Alexander's arm around her waist buoyed her up, while Zora clung to her hand, the girl's smile bright enough to light up any room without the aid of a lamp or candle.

The announcement had been made not out of any desire to rush the proceedings — Julia and Alexander had both agree to allow the banns to be read in church and all of the usual formalities to have their time — but rather to stave off any of the gossip that might have already begun to circulate about their relationship. Should they be seen together now that they were officially betrothed, any scandal that might erupt from the sight of one of them slipping into the other's bedroom in the middle of the night would be muted by the knowledge they were to be married soon enough. And they were older than most couples planning a wedding, with both of them having been married before and Alexander with a child. No doubt most people assumed they were marrying for companionship in their declining years, and so that Zora would have a mother in her life as she matured. Julia wagered few would believe they'd spent the last two nights together in Alexander's room, giving and receiving pleasure from one another in ways that made her blush to think about, even hours later.

And so Julia awoke that next morning as the acknowledged future Mrs. Halberd. Word, she knew, would travel quickly. No doubt the news of their betrothal was already circulating through the houses of Barrow-in-Ashton, swirling over their breakfast tables like the steam rising from their cups of coffee and bowls of porridge.

She didn't care what they said, or at least any of it that pertained to her. She had already endured countless rounds of gossip throughout her marriage to Frederick. What were a few more words sent into the air on wasted breath? The important things were Alexander's and Zora's happiness. And her own, of course. She'd spent too many years attempting to shape her life into a role that wasn't ultimately hers to fill, and all it had brought her was misery and grief.

"No more," she whispered to her own reflection, and went to the nursery to wake up Zora for the day.

They breakfasted downstairs in the dining room together, Alexander greeting Julia with a brief kiss to her cheek before they all seated themselves at the table. Julia didn't blush at the open display of affection, and she glanced over at Zora to see the girl smiling at the both of them, her eyes sparkling with some inner excitement.

They ate and spoke as though nothing had changed, and yet everything had. The servants, even, treated Julia with greater deference than before, fully aware that she would soon be transitioning from governess to head of the household.

But it wasn't the behavior of the servants that hovered like a storm cloud over Julia's thoughts. Instead, she wondered what Mrs. Holland's reaction to the news would be. The housekeeper had been present for Alexander's announcement, but Julia had barely seen her since then, only flashes of her here and there as they'd both gone about the business of their lives. Now that Julia was more informed about Mrs. Holland's history, her beginnings as a maid to the former Mrs. Halberd before rising to the rank of housekeeper after coming to Langford, Julia feared there might be an increase in animosity towards her from the other woman, as though she was seeking to wipe out all traces of Alexander's first wife from existence.

"I should be back this afternoon," Alexander said as all three of them left the dining room after breakfast. "It looks like rain this afternoon, or perhaps a little snow if the temperatures stay low. Perhaps some backgammon, Zora? Along with toasted sausages over the drawing room fire for a light supper?"

Zora clapped her hands together. "And we can make plans for the wedding! I think it should be outside, and at sunset. And Mrs. Benton could have her hair down—"

"We'll see," Alexander said, before Zora could have them planning a search for the ancient remnants of Camelot as part of the ceremony.

Julia and Alexander had both agreed they didn't want a large wedding. A simple affair was more to their liking, a small service at the church followed by a modest wedding breakfast primarily for the servants and tenants of Langford. Neither of them had a desire to entertain their neighbors by making a lavish show of things, but the prospect of readying the house for the dozens of guests they anticipated was still a large affair, especially since there had been no such parties or celebrations since Mrs. Halberd had died.

"Will there be music?" Zora piped up again, while Julia tried to wipe the last of the jam from the corner of her sticky mouth. "And dancing? Or maybe a juggler! We were reading about weddings in the time of the medieval kings and queens, and they would have jesters and acrobats and even sword swallowers! Do people still swallow swords?"

"I believe good food and maybe some music will be enough of an ode to our royal forebears," Alexander said, and kissed the top of Zora's head before he straightened and dropped a light kiss on Julia's lips. He grinned at the widening of her eyes, and laughed outright when she bussed the side of his jaw in return. "This afternoon, then," he promised, leaving them to fetch his hat and coat as Mrs. Holland strode from the rear of the house to meet them outside the dining room. The housekeeper's gaze narrowed on Julia in such a way that made it clear she'd witnessed the open display of affection between her and Alexander and did not approve.

"Mrs. Decatur is here," Mrs. Holland announced without preamble. Or warmth.

"Oh! Are the rest of the gowns finished already? Surely it's not been long enough for so much work to be completed."

Mrs. Holland sniffed. "She wishes to speak with you, Mrs. Benton. I did not think it my place to inquire as to the specific reasons behind her visit."

Julia suspected Mrs. Holland very much thought it her place to interrogate every visitor to any and all reasons behind their visits to Langford, but she refrained from saying as much. "To speak with me? That's all?"

"From what I understand, it has to do with your impending marriage to Mr. Halberd."

If lemons could grow mouths and speak, Julia thought while

surveying Mrs. Holland's change in expression as the word "marriage" passed her lips. "Very well. Is she...?"

"I've put her in the drawing room. I didn't take the liberty of sending for tea as it's so close upon the heels of breakfast. A bit of an impertinence, to show up so early in the day, but as she's in trade, no doubt she assumes she can come and go whenever it best suits her working hours."

Julia bit down on her tongue until the first flash of her ire dissipated. "I think a tea tray will be in order, along with any biscuits or tarts the cook might have available at such short notice. As Mrs. Decatur is in trade, as you put it, she has most likely been up for several hours already and is in need of some refreshment. Zora," she said, and turned to find the girl crouched down on the floor, tracing a pattern in the polished wood with her fingers. "Why don't you go up to the nursery and begin on your French? I can go over your sentences with you when I've finished with Mrs. Decatur."

Zora raced towards the stairs, darting up them two at a time before Julia could call out after her not to run in the house.

"She is still showing little signs of improvement," Mrs. Holland said from her place behind Julia. "I had hoped to see some change in her by now, but if anything she is even more feral than before. A few new gowns will not be enough to hide her misbehavior. I assume you will be hiring a new governess once you and Mr. Halberd are wed?"

Julia pressed her palms flat against the front of her thighs. "I hadn't given the matter any thought," she admitted, her jaw set, teeth clenched as she spoke. "But I see nothing untoward in Zora's behavior. She has an eager, curious mind, and an abundance of energy. In other words, she is a child." She turned around to face Mrs. Holland, and her hands found their way to her hips, her fingers digging deep into the fabric of her gown to better keep her temper in check. "But be assured that when Mr. Halberd and I come to any decision about her upbringing, it will have absolutely nothing to do with you. Good morning, Mrs. Holland."

She kept her breathing steady as she walked away, even as her heart hammered inside her chest. She was not accustomed to speaking so boldly to someone else, to putting voice to the thoughts she normally would have smothered in her head before they could make themselves heard. Her hands were still trembling as she opened the door to the drawing room and stepped inside. Mrs. Decatur was standing and waiting for her, her long face brightening with an easy smile as soon as she saw Julia enter.

"Mrs. Benton!" The dressmaker took an eager step forward. "I hope you will excuse my prompt arrival this morning, but I assumed that with a young child in your care, it followed that you very likely kept to a young child's schedule. And I wanted to see you as early as possible, considering that there is not much time to waste!"

"Much... time?" Julia hesitated beside one of the chairs, then remembered her manners and gestured for Mrs. Decatur to take a seat.

"Well, um." The dressmaker's hands fluttered in her lap. "I hope you do not think it presumptuous of me to mention it, but word has already reached me that you are due felicitations on your recent betrothal to Mr. Halberd?"

"Um, yes?" Julia's words carried the same gentle upswing of Mrs. Decatur's voice, shaping everything into the form of an unnecessary question. "Yes, we are to be married. Is... that what brings you here today? Or are the gowns we've ordered...?"

"Oh, the gowns will be done very soon!" Mrs. Decatur chirped, hands still floating about as though caught on an errant breeze. "Be assured you and your... should I say future step-daughter?"

"Uh... you may? Yes?" Julia fought the urge to glance over her shoulder and make certain the door — her nearest escape route — was still present and accounted for.

"Well, be assured that the two of you are my full priority right now. Which is what brings me here this morning!" She reached down into a small bag she'd brought with her, pulling out a small notebook and pencil and a collection of fashion plates and patterns displaying all the latest styles in ladies' gowns and accessories. "Now, some of these you've seen before, but I've brought several others with a more..." She twirled her hand in the air. "... bridal flair. Since I'm not certain if you've given any thought to your trousseau, I wonder if—"

"My trousseau?" Julia hated this constant feeling of being two steps behind in the conversation.

"Of course! I must admit, I had the pleasure of styling several gowns for... um, the previous Mrs. Halberd, and I think if you were to—"

"No." How Julia managed to throw out that single word with the snap of whip's crack, and all while keeping a polite smile pinned to her face, she would never know.

"No?"

"I beg your pardon, but I will not be needing a wedding trousseau."

Mrs. Decatur sagged with obvious disappointment. "But...oh. Well, surely for your bridal tour. You will be embarking on a bridal tour? Places like Rome and Athens are so much more pleasant than England this time of year. So a few new pieces—"

But Julia shook her head. "We're not planning a bridal tour, either."

"Oh." Mrs. Decatur's hands stilled over her notebook. "I had thought... well. I guess I had assumed, since the previous Mrs. Halberd had always—"

"I am not the previous Mrs. Halberd," Julia interrupted her again. Her tone was still polite. She could tell there was no malice in Mrs. Decatur's questions or assumptions, simply a woman hoping for additional business now that there was to be a new mistress at Langford. But she had expected this, the comparisons to Alexander's first wife, the expectations that she would follow the precedent already set out for her, to be fashionable and sociable and to hold dozens of dinners and parties every year.

But she was not Mrs. Anna Halberd. She had spent too many years wanting to be someone like her, someone who made their life and happiness appear so very effortless. And it had all been a carefully constructed sham.

"This has nothing to do with your skills," Julia added, not wishing to offend her. "The pieces you've already delivered for Miss Halberd and myself are of the most stunning quality. And I give you my word that you will always be our first choice when we are in need of a dressmaker. Keep in mind that Miss Halberd is a growing girl, and no doubt we will be calling upon your services many, many times in the years ahead."

Mrs. Decatur beamed at this proffered olive branch. Gathering up a few of her sketches, she passed them into Julia's keeping before she could protest. "In case something catches your eye, for yourself or Miss Halberd," she said, smiling. "I have some lovely ermine back at the shop that would make an exquisite muff. Oh! And a very fine printed muslin just came in that would look beautiful with Miss Halberd's complexion."

The tea arrived then, and Julia realized with a frisson of apprehension that she was expected to slip into the role of hostess, despite the fact she was not yet officially married to Alexander. So she poured the tea and inquired about milk and sugar, and she shared out the little dish of biscuits that had been provided. And all throughout, Mrs. Decatur fell into a comfortable rhythm of recounting all of the latest gossip from Barrow-in-Ashton and its immediate surroundings, the dressmaker apparently laboring under the assumption that this was the best way to win a friendship with the future Mrs. Halberd.

Julia didn't make any effort to disabuse her of the notion. Her mind was still awhirl from Mrs. Holland's earlier behavior, with the realization that this — sitting down to tea and biscuits with people suddenly displaying a newfound eagerness to earn her favor — would be expected of her in this new life. It was what had been expected of her when she was still married to Frederick, with the vicarage as her home, but her health had always been an impediment, and so she had shirked those duties and allowed Mrs. Halberd to step in as the social ruler of their parish.

But now...

When she had agreed to marry Alexander, she hadn't given a tremendous amount of thought to this aspect of her future life. That she would be visible now, no longer shunted aside like a forgotten pair of old slippers.

When the biscuits were nothing but crumbs on a saucer and the teapot was empty, Julia said goodbye to her guest, promised to look through the sketches — at least for Zora's sake — and sent her on her way. She stood in the drawing room then, alone. She looked around at the furniture, at the paper on the walls, at the keepsakes and figurines scattered about on the various shelves. She would be the mistress of all this. Not merely a visitor or a subordinate, but a woman with an entire household filled with servants to manage.

She pressed her hand to her abdomen and tried to quell the flutter of anxiety there, trapped beneath her ribs like a frightened butterfly. Everything around her seemed to serve as a reminder that she was not the woman who had last welcomed guests in this room, who had decorated the shelves with simpering shepherdesses and gilt-edged miniatures. But Alexander wasn't marrying her because she knew how to smile and make polite small-talk with their neighbors. He wouldn't want her to push beyond the boundaries of her own comfort and anxiety in order to assuage the gossips and matrons of their village. She could run the household however she liked. She could fill the role of mistress of Langford in whichever way best suited her.

If only she could so easily make herself believe it with only a few repetitions of those same words.

* * *

"What are you thinking about?"

Julia rolled over in Alexander's arms. She looked up at him in the darkness, only the faint glow from the dying fire allowing any play of light and shadow across his features.

"Too much," she admitted, and slipped her arm around his bare chest. They were both naked, the blankets tangled around their legs, the both of them still too warm from their most recent sexual exploits to want to cover up again.

Alexander ran his fingers over the curve of her shoulder, making her shiver. "Anything you wish to share? Or are you content to think on them and let me be a silent support to your troubles?"

She was tempted not to speak. It seemed the easiest route, the most comfortable one, as she had spent a good portion of her life holding onto her troubles in the belief that no one else would want to hear of them. But she shifted nearer to him, her head resting on his chest as she drew in a breath and said what she wanted to say. "I suppose I never considered how differently everyone would treat me once people learned of our engagement."

Congratulations had begun to arrive at Langford like waves lapping towards the shore. If the inhabitants of Barrow-in-Ashton felt any disappointment at Alexander's new choice of bride, if they had hoped he might choose from amongst the younger ladies of the town in the hope of having more children and adding to his family, they did not make a show of it. Invitations had arrived — to dinner, to afternoon teas, to hastily cobbled together musical evenings during which the highest tier of the village's mediocre talents would likely be on display. Even a little sampling of cakes had been delivered from Mrs. Cutler, a quite unsubtle display of her talents should they desire more intricate delicacies than Langford's cook might be able to provide for the wedding breakfast.

"And how are they treating you?" He kissed the top of her head and slid his leg between her thighs.

This was the bit that had troubled Julia for the previous day. "I think they see me as... Well, I think they want me to be like your wife. Like Anna, I mean."

His nostrils flared at the mention of her name. "Of course they do," he said, his bluntness surprising Julia. "They want what is most familiar to them, and so they expect my new wife to host parties and plan balls and to ride through the town like a queen deigning to smile and wave to her loyal subjects."

Unbidden, Julia's mind again went back to the first time she had met Mrs. Halberd, how she had glided into the vicarage and seated herself upon the finest chair like a woman possessed of the power to drag the sun and the moon and the planets along by the hem of her gown.

"But I'm not—" She closed her mouth, cutting off the rest of her protest.

"I know you're not," he whispered across the crown of her head. "You're Julia Benton, the woman I love. I'm not marrying you because I want to fix you in my cap like a feather, a prize to be won and flaunted but without any true feelings attached."

She detected a faint edge of bitterness to his words, and she wondered if that was how his wife had viewed him, as nothing more than a jewel in her crown, one she used to fund the lifestyle she wanted while harboring her affection for another man.

Her fingers skimmed over the hair on his chest, her thumb teasing his nipple until it peaked beneath her touch. "I love you," she told him. She enjoyed saying it, because of how true it was, how it tapped into the very depths of her heart every time those three syllables left her mouth.

Alexander reached down for the edge of the blankets, tugging them up until they were both snug beneath the covers. "And I will never stop working to earn that love."

"Don't say things like that." She sat up, the blanket slipping back down to her waist. "You don't have to earn my love. It's freely given, without anything expected in return." She looked at him earnestly, wanting — needing him to understand how important this was to her.

For years she had thought that if only she was a better wife, if she could provide her husband with a child, if she could attain that perfect portrait of motherhood, she could succeed in gaining his affection. But all she had done was make herself miserable, striving to win the love of someone who had already parceled it out to someone else.

"Would you apply the same thinking to Zora?" she asked. "You said you loved her from the first moment you held her in your arms. She didn't have to do anything for it. It came without cost, and that is what makes it so precious."

He reached out and pulled her towards him, and she braced her hands on his shoulders as she slid a leg over him, straddling his hips.

"Alexander." Her voice was low as her fingers skimmed down his chest, over his abdomen, down to where his cock twitched against her thigh. "Kiss me."

He kissed her, deep and hungrily, despite the lateness of the hour and how tired they would be if they didn't soon sleep. He kissed her as she raised her hips and slid down on his length, as her breathing hitched and her heart hummed with how very much she loved him.

Twenty

J ulia woke to find a steady rain had settled in, the kind that made her glance at the edges of the puddles and wonder how quickly they might rim with ice. Because of the weather, she didn't expect many of her pupils to show up for their Sunday lesson. Even the service at church had boasted a sparser attendance than normal, not many wanting to combat the ice and the chill for a reward of three hours in a hard pew with even the threats of hell-fire in the vicar's sermon not enough to drag them from their homes for that description of warmer climes. And yet minutes before her class was to begin, the rows of benches in the school-house were filled with over a dozen chattering, giggling, dripping girls.

It didn't take long for Julia to discover what had inspired such dedication from her students to their studies. Less than a minute after taking attendance, the first hand went up.

"Yes, Miss Donaldson?"

The little girl stood up, her slate clutched between her hands, the damp ends of her braids soaking the shoulders of her plain gown. "Is it true you're going to marry Mr. Halberd?"

Julia smiled. Ah, this was how it was to be, then. "Yes, Mr. Halberd and I are engaged to be married. You may sit down now," she added kindly, when Miss Donaldson showed no initiative to immediately return to her seat.

Another hand shot up. Julia bit her lips. Better to get it all out of the way at the beginning, she supposed, rather than let their curiosity prove a distraction for the entirety of the afternoon's lessons.

The school, she realized, wasn't something she had considered now that she was about to marry again. Not that she had any plans to quit teaching, and neither would Alexander wish or expect her to give it up. But with her status as mistress of Langford and the power that would come with it, she could do more for the school. More than merely better materials and books and the occasional bowl of flowers for painting. Her influence would mean a greater acceptance of its very existence. Perhaps more families would be willing to see their daughters educated. Perhaps—

"Now that we are finished with our questions," Julia said, having seen the last of the girls satisfied with a brief discussion of what kind of cake might be served at the wedding breakfast. "Let us move on to our spelling. Miss Thompson, if you could oversee the younger girls with pages nine and ten of their primers?"

The rain had not let up by the time school ended for the day. Once Julia saw the last of the girls sent back to their homes, she finished tidying up the schoolroom, wrapped herself up in her coat and gloves and bonnet before winning a brief tussle with her umbrella and setting off back to Langford.

The walk was slow and should have been miserable, but she enjoyed the sound of the downpour on her umbrella and the cold air as it slid in and out of her lungs. She had promised Zora a late afternoon of learning to bake rye biscuits sweetened with molasses, and then there would be the first of their piano lessons together after dinner.

It was a comforting thing, to see her days stretched out before her in a mingling of domestic routine, plans for the school, and the unanticipated freedom that a new marriage would bring. During her years with Frederick, their union had felt like little more than a noose around her neck, tightening slowly and incrementally as she failed again and again to live up to the role sketched out for her by everyone, including herself. That she was to be obedient and subservient and shape herself into what she thought her husband's idea of a wife should be.

But it had been all wrong. Frederick had never truly wanted her for a wife, regardless of her inability to provide him with children or to be the dazzling social butterfly his chosen love had been. Julia would have killed herself, she realized, in trying to attain a child because she thought that somehow — somehow! — it would ignite a small measure of affection in their relationship. And it would have given her someone on whom to shower her love when her husband so openly found her attempts to care for him as unwelcome.

And yet with Alexander, there was no need to break herself in order to be rebuilt into a form that would suit him. She simply had to... be. And that, she realized, was what had frightened her all along. To come face to face with who she was, a near stranger she had tried to hide away for so very long that she wasn't entirely certain she truly knew the woman she saw in the mirror each morning.

She shook out her umbrella as she walked up the front steps of Langford, then realized she would most likely have to change entirely before taking Zora to the kitchen for their baking lesson. In her bedroom, a fire had already been built for the evening, though she could feel the chill from the windows fighting for dominance. She quickly stripped out of her wet things, draping the worst of them over a rack near the fireplace so they wouldn't drip in a heap on the floor. Into dry clothes, and with her hair taken down, brushed out, and pinned up again, she went to the nursery first in search of Zora.

She wasn't there.

Julia hadn't fully expected her to be. No doubt she was curled up in some corner of the drawing room or the library, dragging feathers along the floor for the kitten to chase, or feeding her too much cream in the kitchen. Downstairs then, to the library first and then the drawing room. She popped her head into Alexander's study, but that was empty as well. After searching three more rooms and the kitchen, she stopped a servant in the hall and asked if Zora had been seen outside. Julia wouldn't have been surprised to learn the girl had donned her boots and was splashing in puddles, or had perhaps taken herself off to the warmth of the stables for the afternoon.

"No, Mrs. Benton. I've not seen her since your return from church."

"Oh." Julia set her hands on her hips and blew out a breath. "Well, can you ask Mrs. Holland if she—"

"I beg your pardon," the maid interrupted, shifting from foot to foot. "But Mrs. Holland is out. She said she had to run an errand in town and she hasn't returned yet."

There was a twinge in Julia's abdomen, but she tried to ignore it. "Well, when she does return..." She shook her head. Surely they would happen upon Zora, no doubt tucked into some nook or windowsill long before Mrs. Holland came back to Langford. "Nevermind. It's not important."

Julia returned upstairs and performed a thorough search of the rooms she had passed over before. She glanced into the nursery again, but the room was still markedly empty, as though the space was determined to announce its lack of anyone within its four walls. Alexander's room was empty, as were all of the other rooms along the corridor. At the end of the hall, she paused outside of Mrs. Halberd's bedroom. She didn't want to step inside, but she knew she would not be able to count her search as complete until she'd looked through every room at least once.

The bedroom was not as bright as the last time she'd been there. The rain and the lateness of the afternoon edged everything with a gloom that sent a slight chill up Julia's spine.

"Zora?" she called out, because she needed to break the unnatural silence that lay on everything like years of collected dust. She was about to turn away, to shut the door behind her, when she noticed something different about the room.

Her gaze settled on the dressing table, where the jewelry box with its hidden stash of love letters had been. Except it wasn't there anymore. And neither were several other items that Julia remembered, a hairbrush and a mirror, and a matching comb.

The absence made her breath catch. There might have been other things missing as well, but Julia had no idea what had been hidden away in the various drawers and the wardrobe, so she wouldn't know what to look for. She backed out of the room, then rushed down to the kitchen again and snagged the attention of one of the upstairs maids as she passed through.

"When did Mrs. Holland leave? Do you know?" She kept her voice steady, unwilling to let any fear creep in.

"Hmm, a little while after you left?" The young woman, named Helen, screwed up her features in thought. "Yes, I think it was around then. You went off to teach and I saw her in her coat and hat not long after."

"Did she give any clue as to where she was going? When she would be back?"

Helen glanced up at the kitchen ceiling, as though Mrs. Holland's itinerary might be scrawled across the rafters. "No, not that I recall. Though it's not really our place to question her, if you know what I mean."

Julia nodded. She could well understand the reluctance of the staff to interrogate the housekeeper about any matter she didn't choose to share with them first. "Has she ever been gone this long before on an errand? And on a Sunday?"

"No, Mrs. Benton. To be honest, I was surprised when she said she'd be going into town. Usually when she wants something, she sends one of us to fetch it for her, especially with the weather today being so awful and all."

Julia smiled, even though her face fought against the expression. "Thank you, Helen. Um..." She touched the girl's arm before she could turn away. "Do you think you could... Well, would it be too much trouble for someone to go out to the stables and some of the other buildings and see if they can find Miss Halberd? I worry she's wandered out in this weather and might be hiding somewhere, waiting for the worst of it to pass before returning." It was true that Julia wanted the stables and various outbuildings searched before she would allow herself to panic. Even the rest of the house needed to be looked through, in case Zora was reading beneath a table or setting up a battalion of soldiers inside a linen closet.

And so she began a quiet, methodical search through every room on every floor, checking wardrobes and cupboards and even asking for help with a ladder to climb up into the attics. By the time she was finished, the day had grown dark and the men who had gone to search the outbuildings and the surrounding grounds returned with a report that Miss Halberd was nowhere to be found.

"Right, um..." She stood in the middle of the drawing room, two maids and a footman standing in front of her, waiting for her to tell them what to do. "Where is Mr. Halberd? Has he returned yet?"

James, the footman, shook his head. "If he's anywhere, he's still at Markham's farm. Trouble with their sheep, or something like. I can send someone—"

"Yes." The word slicing through the air quick enough to make one of the maids wince. "Tell him... Tell him his daughter is missing and he needs to come home right away."

In the meantime, she decided to search Mrs. Holland's room. She didn't have a key, and the door was firmly locked.

"Mrs. Holland has the only key I know of," Helen told her when they ventured down to the servants' quarters.

"Fetch James, then," Julia said. "He can open it for us."

The maid gave her a confused look, but when she returned with the footman a few minutes later, he showed no hesitation when she told him to break the door open.

She walked into a cold, dark room. "A light," she ordered, and Helen ran to fetch a lamp.

At first glance, the room appeared untouched. The bed was made, the shelves bearing Mrs. Holland's books for the keeping of the household tidy and dusted. Julia went to the wardrobe first and flung the door open. Emptiness greeted her. Half the drawers were the same, cleared of their contents.

"She's gone," Julia said, staring at the depths of a desk drawer where only a few broken quills and dried spatters of ink remained. "She's packed up and left." She pressed her palms against her forehead, as though the pressure of her hands was a dam set against the chaotic workings of her mind. Mrs. Holland was gone. So was Zora. The two could not be a coincidence, no matter how much she wanted them to be.

"Family," she said suddenly. She turned around. Helen and James both stood there, watching and waiting. "Does Mrs. Holland have any family? Where is she from originally? Does she come from Cornwall?"

Helen shook her head. "She came with Mrs. Halberd from London, as far as I know. But I couldn't say where she hailed from before that."

God, why couldn't she think? Why would Mrs. Holland take Zora? How did it benefit either of them? Or was the housekeeper's animosity towards her so strong that she would risk removing a child from the protection of her home and family merely to separate her from Julia's influence?

She walked out of Mrs. Holland's room, James and Helen trailing behind her despite the fact she hadn't asked them to follow. She returned to the nursery, Helen's lamp bobbing behind her like a drunken moon. The bed was rumpled from that morning, Zora's skills at tidying up after herself still leaving something to be desired. Her newest gown was missing, along with her finest bonnet and her best shoes. But all of her favorite things — her most comfortable boots, her book about King Arthur and his knights, her deck of cards — were all still where she'd left them. Julia went to the bed and slipped her hand beneath the pillow, her fingers wrapping around the ammonite fossil Alexander had given her.

She pulled it out and held the cool stone to her chest, her thumb rubbing over it as though it was a talisman. Zora was gone. Mrs. Holland must have taken her, must have packed up a few of her things and spirited her away without anyone noticing. Julia squeezed her eyes shut, wincing at the headache rapidly building behind her left eye. She had been away at the schoolhouse for several hours, while Alexander had been at the Markham's farm all afternoon, leaving ample opportunity for someone to slip away without it being remarked upon.

A sound from downstairs dragged Julia's attention from her own scattered thoughts. The slam of a door, followed by loud voices — Alexander's voice louder than the rest — and then the quick, heavy tread of footsteps on the main stairs. Julia rushed out of the nursery, meeting Alexander halfway down the hall.

"Where's Zora?"

Julia swallowed over a lump in her throat that hadn't been there only a moment before. "I-I don't know. But some of her clothes are missing, and..." She closed her eyes. Her teeth had begun to chatter, but she didn't feel cold. Instead, it was fear crawling under her skin, setting her very bones to trembling. "Mrs.

Holland is gone, too. She's packed up her things and left, and I think she's taken Zora with her."

His hands gripped her shoulders. She looked at his face, the anger and horror and fright doing everything in their power to tear him to pieces where he stood. "Are you certain?"

Julia took strength from his touch. She needed it to find her voice, to keep from tumbling into an incoherent heap on the carpet. "No one has seen either of them since after I left this afternoon. It's been hours now. Zora hasn't disappeared for this long since I came here, especially not since she has Ellen to care for. And Ellen is still here, down in the kitchen. She would not have left for so long without her."

"Has the house been searched?"

His voice. She prayed she would never have to hear such agony from him ever again.

"Yes." She said it from between gritted teeth, her jaw clenched so tight she thought it might crack from the pressure. "And I sent people out to check the stables and other buildings, but... nothing."

Alexander pushed his hands through his hair, the ends still soaked from his ride home. The rest of him was coated in mud and dripping onto the carpet, but she knew she wouldn't be able to convince him to change his clothes or even to dry himself by the fire until Zora was found.

"When did she leave? Mrs. Holland, I mean." His gaze darted from Julia to James to Helen, anticipating an answer from anyone who would speak.

Julia told him what they knew, the servants filling in what details they could as Alexander was apprised of everything that had occurred during his absence.

"So she left here on foot? The both of them?" Alexander asked as they quickly returned downstairs.

"No horses are missing," James said. "And no one saw any kind of coach or carriage make its way up to the house."

"She must have gone into town first, then," Alexander remarked as they turned and entered his study. A fire had already been lit, and Helen and James both worked their way around the room lighting candles for additional illumination. "I want to know of any coaches that came through town and if Mrs. Holland — with or without a passenger — found a seat on one."

"I'll go," James volunteered. "And I'll take a few men with me, spread out a bit and get the work accomplished faster."

"Good man. And you," he turned his attention to Helen. "I want you to go into Mrs. Holland's room and gather up every letter, every scrap of paper you can find. Maybe she's left something behind that will give us a better idea of where she's disappeared to."

Helen stepped out as hurriedly as James did, leaving Julia and Alexander alone. Beyond the walls of the study, they could hear orders being relayed, the bustle of footsteps and of doors being opened and slammed shut again.

"Julia."

She took a step towards him. When he raised his eyes to her, he looked stricken. "Do you really believe Mrs. Holland's taken her?"

Julia looked down at her hand. She still held the ammonite fossil, clenched hard in her fingers. "I do."

"But why?"

It was the same question she had already asked herself a hundred times. "I don't know," she said. But she did know. Or at least she had the semblance of an idea.

She thought back to the last conversation she'd had with Mrs. Holland, and her breath froze in her chest as every one of the housekeeper's words transformed into a premonition with the power of Julia's memory fueling it. "No, wait. When we last spoke, she said... She declared that Zora had shown little improvement since my arrival. She asked if there would be a new governess after we married, and I,... I told her it was no business of hers what we did."

Alexander's breath hissed between his teeth. "She said that? To your face?"

"Yes," she admitted. But she didn't understand why it upset him so much.

"Julia." He placed his hands on her shoulders, squeezing slightly before his arms went around her, pulling her closer. "Why didn't you tell me?"

"Because..." But she faltered, because she wasn't certain why she hadn't told him of Mrs. Holland's behavior towards her.

Because it felt familiar, she realized. Expected. Because after years with Frederick, she believed it was as much as she deserved, to be spoken to with open disrespect.

"I didn't think it was important," she confessed. "I'm sorry."

"This is not your fault," he said, as though he could already sense the direction of her thoughts. "Something this drastic... I fear it may have been planned for longer than we can imagine."

Julia stepped back, out of Alexander's embrace. She needed to move and to fidget and to roll her shoulders before the frustration at not being able to immediately do anything overwhelmed her. "I always assumed Mrs. Holland didn't care for Zora. That she regarded her as a trial, a nuisance. She so often complained of her behavior, I thought she would've wanted to be well rid of her."

But even as she spoke, something dawned on her. A facet of the housekeeper's conduct that she had failed to see before.

"No," she said, and covered her mouth with her hand. "She wanted Zora to be her mother, a little dress-up version of her. She didn't like that I wasn't raising her to be another Mrs. Halberd." And as soon as she said it, she knew she was right. All of the times Mrs. Holland had mentioned Zora's prospects, the future the housekeeper seemed to have sketched out for the child in her mind. "It must be why she took her, to remove her from our detrimental influence."

Alexander cursed under his breath. "If we can't raise Zora the way Mrs. Holland believes she should be raised, she'll simply do it herself? Is that what you're saying?"

Julia threw up her hands. "It doesn't make any sense! You're her father, does Mrs. Holland think you won't come after her and take back your own child?"

It was a brief hesitation. Alexander raised his eyebrows, while his mouth worked silently for a moment before speech finally came out. "Perhaps she thinks I won't care, since I'm not Zora's father."

"But you..." Julia stopped while her mind tried to catch up to the rest of the conversation. "Does Mrs. Holland know?"

"Of course she does. She was my wife's maid first, remember?"

Julia shook her head. "But anyone who would see you and Zora together would know how much you love her."

Alexander laughed. It was not a happy sound. "Do you think love matters to people like Mrs. Holland? No, she sees blood, she sees pedigree. And no doubt she assumes that's how everyone else sees the world, as well. Why should I care if Zora is taken from me if she's not mine to keep?"

There was a low hum of anger carrying his words, but running through all of it was an overwhelming tone of resignation. And Julia wondered how many times these same arguments had sounded in his head, had kept him awake at night, had made him feel as though he wasn't enough. Enough of a father, enough of a husband. Enough of anything.

"We'll get her back," Julia said, standing in front of him. Her hands hovered over his, yet she refrained from touching him, afraid that a single brush of her fingers might shatter him like crystal.

She turned and walked out of the study, needing to move. To run, to scream at nothing. Alexander followed her. In the hall, they ran into Helen, already returning from her search of Mrs. Holland's room.

"I didn't find much," the maid confessed. "A few receipts and letters and things Nothing seemed very important, but I gathered up everything for you." She passed the small stack of notes and papers into Julia's outstretched hands.

"Did she ever write to anyone?" Alexander asked as Julia began flipping through the mundane papers, nothing offering any real clue as to where Mrs. Holland might have gone. "Were there any letters that regularly came for her, or that she wrote herself? Sent to the same address, perhaps?"

"It's George who mostly handles the post," Helen said. "I can fetch him if you'd like."

Rather than fetch him, they followed Helen down to the servants' hall, passing the kitchens — where dinner preparations were still underway, despite the sudden chaos infecting the household — and through to the narrow dining area where the staff ate most of their meals. An older man sat at the end of the table, the light from the lamps shining off his bald head while his thick white brows twitched above a pair of spectacles perched on the peak of a sharp nose.

"George?" Julia approached the old man, Alexander right behind her. His shoulders were hunched forward over his work, which appeared to be a clock torn to pieces and scattered across the end of the table.

He looked up at the sound of his name, his misty gaze switching from Julia to Alexander and back again. "Yes, ma'am? Sir? How can I be of help?"

"You handled some of Mrs. Holland's letters, did you not?"

"Aye." He knuckled his spectacles back into place and sat up straighter, though his shoulders retained their forward slope even with his elbows off the table. "I've taken care of Langford's post for near forty years. Thousands of letters have passed through these hands," he boasted, holding up a pair of gnarled hands that wriggled with a deceptively quick energy.

"And the housekeeper's letters as well," Alexander said, keeping the conversation steered in the direction they wished it to travel. "She trusted them to you?"

"Of course she did, every last one."

"Did she keep any regular correspondence with anyone in particular?" Julia asked. "Letters coming and going to the same place over and over?"

George wrinkled his nose, which made his spectacles slide down, which made him push them up again with the side of his thumb. "Now, I'm not good with my reading and writing. Only learned to sign my own name a few years ago, rather than just an X like my father before me. But when you see the same words written, they do have a way of sticking in the mind a bit."

Julia held her breath. She wanted to reach out and shake the old man, but she realized that he would work his way around to what he wanted to say at his own speed and there would be no hastening him along if he showed no inclination to rush. "Were there words you saw written more often than others?"

He sniffed. "I never liked that Mrs. Holland. Always acting like she was better than ev'ryone else here, just because she had her fancy London ways. But she wasn't from London, was she? Wrote to Cornwall more often than she ever wrote to anyone in the city, especially these last few months. Must have taken a dozen letters from her hand or more, and delivered just the same back to her."

"Cornwall." Julia looked at Alexander, an entire conversation passing between them in that instant. Both Frederick and Anna had been from Cornwall, where they had lived and fallen in love with one another before...

Well, before.

"Do you know where Mrs. Holland was from? Before London, I mean."

Alexander crossed his arms over his chest, for a moment appeared as though he wanted to curl up inside himself. "No," he said after a moment of thought. "I know her family hired her, though. That's all."

"But if she came from Cornwall originally?" Julia stressed. "If she has connections with your wife's family, her parents..."

"Do you think...?" He trailed off, but a spark of hope glimmered in his eyes.

Julia shrugged. "We could be mistaken. We might be looking in entirely the wrong direction."

"We could," he agreed. "But so far, it's all we have. And right now, I'll take something that could be wrong over nothing at all."

After that, they could only wait for James to return along with any news he might have gleaned from Barrow-in-Ashton. Julia pressed Alexander to eat something, and she did the same, though the both of them finished their small meal with plates and glasses still half full.

It was after eight o'clock before the footman returned, his hat still dripping and his boots leaving a trail of muddy water on the floors as he tracked the two of them down in the kitchen.

"They were seen," James said immediately, instead of wasting time on any kind of formal greeting. "Mrs. Holland hired Tommy Dickson to take her to the Root & Crown in Oakley. A coach runs through there on Sundays, bound for Dorchester. Tommy said she had a girl with her, though he couldn't describe her with the weather being so awful."

"Zora," Alexander said, a mere whisper of sound from between parted lips.

"From what I could gather, the coach left Oakley about four hours ago, though it's supposed to stop for the night somewhere around Stockbridge or thereabouts."

Alexander pushed away his plate and stood up before James had finished speaking. "Saddle my horse. I want to be on my way in a quarter of an hour. Less, if possible."

"I'm going with you!" Julia followed him from the kitchen as he headed for the servants' stairs.

He turned around with his foot on the first step, his shoulders brushing against the narrow walls. "I can make better progress on horseback."

"I know you can," she agreed. "But they're stopping for the

night. It's not as if they'll outrun you in the next few hours. And when you find her, what are you going to do? Tuck her into your coat and ride all the way back in the rain? In the dark?"

He hesitated, his breathing sharp and his teeth set. "Fine," he surrendered. "I'll have them prepare the carriage instead." He abandoned the stairs and took another step towards her, bending down to drop a quick kiss on her lips. "And Zora will need you when we find her. We both will."

Twenty-One

The roads were nearly impassable in places. The rain had stopped not long after their departure from Langford, but muddy ruts and holes caught at every turn of the carriage wheels, and more than once they were forced to turn around and find a different way that hadn't been flooded out by the heavy rains. After two hours with what felt like little progress, Julia began to despair that they would make better time if they simply climbed out and walked the rest of the way to Stockbridge.

"If the roads are difficult for us, they'll be difficult for everyone else." This was the assurance Alexander offered as they sat beside each other inside the carriage, Julia gripping the seat with white-knuckled hands while he bounced his leg as rapidly as though he was about to leap out the door and keep pace beside the horses.

They stopped at the first inn they came to, a dreary establishment made even less inviting by the flooded yard behind it. Alexander went in to inquire if anyone matching the description of Mrs. Holland or Zora had been seen, but he returned to the carriage with a dismal shake of his head.

"No sign of them inside, though the innkeeper said the

Dorchester coach had passed through here no less than three hours ago."

"We're catching up," Julia said, trying to inject some enthusiasm into her voice. "We'll find them, I'm sure."

They set off again, hardly speaking to one another as the carriage creaked and rumbled around them. Julia couldn't stop thinking about Zora, worrying about whether she was frightened or confused, worrying about whether or not Mrs. Holland was treating her well. She would miss her nightly story, she realized, and her eyes began to burn at the thought. And with only one more night before Julia finished the tale of the dragon with his heart made of coal.

Time slipped away in odd fits and starts. Alexander pulled out his pocket watch so often, checking it by the waxing light of the moon through the window that Julia worried he would wear away the engraving on its surface before the night was at an end.

"We should be there soon, I hope," was all he said a few minutes past midnight, before they fell into a taut silence once more.

They arrived at the next inn, near Stockbridge, over an hour later. Julia had been sitting with her head resting on Alexander's shoulder, her eyes wide open, too anxious to sleep. When the carriage shuddered to a halt, they both sat up, Alexander already on his feet and with the door flung open before the wheels had finished settling into the mud. He leapt out first, then turned around and held out his hand to her.

"Here we are," she said, and slipped her gloved hand into his. Even if Mrs. Holland and Zora weren't to be found here, she needed to at least stand up and stretch her legs or risk not being able to unfold herself from the carriage ever again.

The night was cold. Julia looked up at the sky and saw the gleam of stars beyond the brim of her bonnet, the clouds from the previous day's rain long cleared away. Together they picked their way across the inn's waterlogged yard and up to the path that led to the door. Alexander knocked loudly enough to shake the dead from their graves, and in less than a minute there was the mumbling of a voice behind the door before it swung open to reveal a squinting man in a cap and nightshirt, surveying them from behind the light of a single candle.

"What d'you want?" came his sleep-slurred greeting.

"I'm looking for a lady and a young girl." Alexander stood near enough to the innkeeper that he loomed over him like a specter. "They would have stopped with the Dorchester coach. The lady is about sixty years of age, tall and slender, gray hair and eyes. The girl is eight years old, dark hair, either very quiet or very talkative. Most likely the former, in this situation."

The innkeeper coughed into the sleeve of his nightshirt and cleared a rumble of something unpleasant from his lungs. "And how important is it to you if they do happen to be staying here?"

Alexander leaned forward. He stood taller than the innkeeper by several inches, so when he placed his hand on the doorjamb, there was nothing for the smaller man to do but quiver a little and take a faltering step back. "The girl is my daughter. Now, you will tell me if they are here, and which room they are staying in if they are, or else I will tear this building down to kindling around you."

"Ah." The innkeeper cleared his throat again and moved out of Alexander's path. "This way, then."

They followed him inside. The inn was mostly quiet, though there were a few footsteps and the murmur of voices from the floors above, guests who had yet to settle down for the night. They passed through the common room and the warmth that still lingered there and up the stairs, the boards creaking beneath their feet as though the entire building protested at this late intrusion.

"Here we are." The innkeeper kept his voice low once they arrived outside a door on the second floor. But before Alexander could reach for the knob, the innkeeper stretched his arm across the space. "Now, I'll have you know she promised me ten shillings for keeping her presence here a secret. A fine gentleman such as yourself would surely be able to double or even triple that amount for all the help I've given you."

Alexander fixed the innkeeper with a hard stare. "Why would I give anything to a man who so easily broke a contract with one of his guests? You should've made her pay you the ten shillings up front," he scoffed, and raised his fist to knock on the door.

There was silence, at first. A few seconds passed, and then there was a voice — Mrs. Holland's voice, Julia realized, and clutched Alexander's sleeve — complaining about the ungodliness of the hour before the door opened an inch and a sliver of Mrs. Holland's face appeared in the gap.

Her gaze fell on the innkeeper first, and her mouth opened again to speak. And then Alexander shifted into her line of sight, and her skin blanched.

"Oh." That little sound, dropping from her lips, before she tried to slam the door shut in their faces. Alexander was too quick for her, however, and blocked her attempt with the toe of his boot.

"I beg your pardon, Mrs. Holland," he said, his words carried on a tightly strung thread of menace. "I believe you took something of mine? I would very much like to have it back."

Mrs. Holland staggered back, leaving the door to swing open the rest of the way. Julia shouldered past them all and rushed into the room. It was dark, the light from the innkeeper's candle behind her. But there was enough moonlight streaming through the windows for her to make out the small figure of Zora curled up in the bed, sound asleep.

Julia stopped, her legs pressed against the side of the mattress. She was torn between the urge to bend down and pull the girl into her arms, which would startle her from her sleep, or to simply remain where she was and take in the glorious sight of her, apparently well and unharmed. So instead she carefully sat down on the edge of the bed, forming a kind of wall around her without doing anything to disturb her. Zora made a faint sound, her eyelids fluttering and her lips working around nothing before she rolled over and nestled against Julia's side, quickly falling back to sleep again.

"...take her to another room," she heard Alexander say. He was still caught in the doorway with Mrs. Holland and the harried innkeeper. "Away from her clothes and any of her other belongings. I'll deal with her in the morning."

Mrs. Holland was pushed out of the room, still in her nightdress and bare feet, a few words of protest trailing from her mouth before Alexander silenced her with a single glance. And then he slammed the door shut between them. He sighed heavily, then pounded his fist once against the wall before he joined her by the bed.

"Is she well?"

"She seems to be." Julia shifted so that he could sit down on the other side of Zora. "You should try and rest. It's been a long night." Though she doubted either of them would manage a wink of sleep before sunrise.

The bed creaked with his weight, the mattress sagging with an ominous groan, but the structure held the three of them without fear of collapse.

"What will you do about Mrs. Holland?" Julia canted her voice into a low whisper.

"I don't know," he admitted, his own voice more of a growl of tempered frustration than anything resembling a whisper. "I fear the majority of the night will be spent separating what I *wish* to do to the woman from what I *should*, seeing as how the former would have me absconding to the continent to avoid prosecution."

Julia looked down at Zora. Her heart ached so much with the leftover fear of having lost her that she thought her ribs might not be able to contain it. "But she's safe now. And will no doubt be utterly confused when she wakes to find us here." She wanted to laugh at that, but instead she bit at her lips and wondered what might have happened if...

There were too many ifs. If they hadn't learned which coach Mrs. Holland and Zora had boarded. If the weather had been different. If Mrs. Holland hadn't stopped for the night...

"Oh, God."

She glanced up at Alexander. Before her eyes, his face crumpled, a portrait drawn and wadded up again with careless fingers.

"I was so scared," he said, he breathed, his voice no louder than the rush of air carrying his words. "I thought..." He shook his head. "I didn't want to think. If we were too late, if we were wrong about where she was going, which coach they were on. I just..."

She slipped off her gloves, and she wiped the moisture from his cheeks with her fingers. He fell against her then, his head on her shoulder while sobs wracked his frame. She let him cry, let him release all of the fear and worry of the last several hours. And she held him, her fingers in his hair, her lips on his brow, and his child — their child, sleeping peacefully between them.

* * *

Julia did manage to sleep, for at least an hour or so before dawn. She woke to find all three of them still somehow clinging to the bed, though Alexander had swung a leg down to the floor to keep from tumbling off entirely. Between them, Zora squirmed awake, alternately burrowing herself further beneath the blanket and alternately stretching out an arm and then a leg from under the covers like a seedling bursting out of the ground.

"What...?" Zora mumbled. And then she looked at Julia, and she looked at her father, and her mouth formed a perfect little 'o' of surprise. "You're here," she said quietly. "You're here!" And she launched herself into Alexander's arms, nearly knocking him the rest of the way off the bed. "I knew you'd come!"

Julia scrubbed at her cheeks, wiping away the quick burst of tears before Zora could see them and worry about her.

"But how did you find us?" Zora still had her arms around her father, her fingers digging into the sleeve of his jacket as though she could weave herself into its threads. "I wanted it to be like Hansel and Gretel, leaving a trail behind me for you to follow. But I couldn't find anything to throw out the window, and Mrs. Holland wouldn't let me sit beside the window anyways. I had to sit beside a man who smelled like onions and kept telling me I was pretty." Her features curdled, as though she couldn't think of anything worse for an onion-scented man — or any man — to offer as a compliment.

"It was Mrs. Holland who left the trail," Julia explained, then went on to tell her about the housekeeper's correspondence with people in Cornwall and their being seen boarding the coach for Dorchester.

"Oh, I like that," Zora said, releasing her father long enough to roll towards Julia instead. "The witch leaving the bread crumbs instead of the children."

Julia choked on the laugh that burst out of her, but stifled it quickly. She glanced at Alexander who looked to be balanced on a knife's edge between apoplexy and hilarity.

"Where is Mrs. Holland?" Zora peered at the corners of the room, as though the housekeeper might be lurking in the shadows like a recalcitrant spider. "Did you dispatch her with your sword? Like a real dragon in all the stories?"

Alexander bent forward and kissed the top of her head. "I feel I should be worried about your fascination with dangerous weapons and monsters to be defeated." But he smiled as he said it, and Julia felt as though she could draw in a full breath for the first time since the day before.

"I'm hungry," Zora announced, her immediate concern over Mrs. Holland's whereabouts swiftly eradicated by the contents, or lack thereof, of her stomach. "Will there be breakfast?"

There would be breakfast. Alexander promised to go downstairs and fetch it for them, while Julia helped Zora to wash up and dress. Taking great care, Julia eased the truth from Zora about how Mrs. Holland had managed to take her from Langford without anyone knowing.

"She sent me out to play," Zora said, while Julia scrubbed behind her ears with a ragged flannel and the cold water standing in the pitcher. "She said I needed to run off my energy before the rain started. Then she came out and said you were to meet us in the village, at Mrs. Decatur's, as the gowns were done and we were to pick them up and bring them home. So I went, because I thought I was supposed to. And then she told me we were going to go in Tommy Dickson's cart out to the Markham's, that we would see Papa there first and then come back around for the gowns afterwards, rather than carry them with us the entire time." And by the time they made the transfer to the Dorchester coach, by the time Zora realized something wasn't right, they were too far from home, too far from Langford, from her father and from Julia, and so fright set in.

Zora twisted around after Julia had finished buttoning her gown, looking up at her with wide, pleading eyes. "I thought it would be all right. I didn't know I shouldn't have gone with her."

But Julia shook her head. "She lied to you, dear. You couldn't have known of her deception, and you had no reason to question it. You only did what you thought you should at the time."

"Even after it started raining, she kept saying the coach would take us back home, that it was only because the weather had worsened. But then the coach didn't stop, and Mrs. Holland wouldn't let me out, and she told me she was taking me to visit Mama's family, that I would be staying with them for a little while." She swallowed, her hands twisting the fabric of her skirt. "She said Papa wanted me to go."

"Oh, but—"

"Of course, I knew she wasn't telling the truth." Zora straightened her shoulders and tugged at the end of her braid while was still trying to tie a ribbon around the end of it. "Because you and Papa wouldn't have wanted me to go away, especially not before the wedding. Not when you're about to become my new Mama, and—" she added, with great emphasis on this point in particular, "—especially not without Ellen."

Alexander returned a few minutes later, and with a maid behind him bearing a large tray filled with what was apparently their breakfast.

"How is... everything?" Julia asked, trying to keep her questioning vague, in case he wanted to be careful of how they spoke of Mrs. Holland in front of Zora.

"We should be on our way back home after we eat," he said, pulling out the small, rickety wooden chairs from the equally rickety table. "Mrs. Holland will not be joining us on the return trip."

Julia thanked the maid and began filling the plates herself. There were potatoes and sausages and toast that was burnt on one side, but at least the food was hot and there was plenty of it. "So there will be no repercussions?"

"Mrs. Holland will be continuing on her way to Cornwall. To Truro, if I'm not mistaken." Alexander picked up his fork and stabbed a chunk of sausage. "And there she will remain. In fact, if I ever receive word that she has left Cornwall at any future date and for any reason, I will drag her in front of the magistrate and have her charged with abduction."

Zora looked up from her plate, where she had been carefully separating her foods so they would not come in contact with one another. "I wouldn't have liked to visit my Mama's family," she said, scooping up a piece of potato and surveying it with a suspicious eye. "She said I was to have dancing lessons and that I wouldn't be able to climb trees because ladies don't climb trees." She popped the potato into her mouth and made a face as she chewed.

They finished eating and Julia gathered up Zora's things to be taken down to the carriage, while Alexander helped his daughter into her coat and bonnet before leading her down to see the horses before they were off. Julia slipped into her own coat and was tugging on her gloves as she left the room, her attention so fixed on how quickly they could return to Langford that she almost didn't notice the door open to her left as she walked towards the stairs.

"Mrs. Benton?"

Julia halted, one glove still hanging from her fingertips.

Mrs. Holland stood in the doorway, still clad in her nightdress, looking as though she'd done nothing but pace the length of her room the entirety of the night. Julia couldn't bring herself to speak, or to even blink in acknowledgement of the sight before her. And so Mrs. Holland opened the door a little wider and took a single step over the threshold.

"The child belongs with her family," she said, the words short and sharp, as though each one had been carved out of the air with a knife. "I know Mr. Halberd has no claim on her, no blood claim. I had hoped that he would see fit to raise her in a way that would be beneficial to her class and fortune, but I fear I put too much hope in him. He is a man, and he does not know what a girl should need. But since she is her mother's daughter more than anything, I believe that she should be raised by her mother's family. It would be for her own good."

Julia pressed her lips together. She told herself not to say a word, to walk away. She would not even give the woman another glance. So she continued to pull on her gloves, her hands shaking, her legs feeling strangely like water as she took another step towards the stairs.

"He'll grow bored of you, you know."

Her breath stopped. She shouldn't listen. She shouldn't. But she stood there, tethered to the spot by the resemblance Mrs. Holland's voice had to the one that repeated the same words to her in her darkest hours.

"He needs a younger wife. A healthy wife. Someone who can give him children. Children of his own," Mrs. Holland stressed. "And not merely an illegitimate girl he's failed by letting run wild about the countryside, by bringing in someone like you to see to her care."

Another step. Mrs. Holland's bare feet barely made a sound on the floor. "If he's going to insist on keeping her, then you would do better to leave him, to leave Langford. Let him hire a proper governess, one who can see to Miss Halberd's education. A proper education, not one that allows her to dig in the dirt and play with toy soldiers like a little boy. An education befitting her status, one that will see her take her place in society and find a suitable husband, someone who is her equal."

"Like her mother?" Julia turned around, her fingers flexing inside her gloves. "A woman who deceived her husband? Who bore another man's child because instead of learning how to sacrifice for what she wanted, she simply took and took with the belief that she could have everything?"

Mrs. Holland's mouth drew into a flat line. "I will admit, I was disappointed in her for that. I never approved of her infatuation with Mr. Benton. I told her to leave him be, that no good with come from her dalliance with him—"

"It was more than a dalliance," Julia was quick to point out. "They were together for years."

"Oh." Mrs. Holland raised her chin, a movement that highlighted the shadows beneath her eyes. "And do you think I never noticed the looks between you and Mr. Halberd while you were both still married? The attention he paid to you? I knew what would happen when he decided to hire you as Miss Halberd's supposed governess. I'm not a fool, Mrs. Benton. I knew you'd end up in his bed, like some common whore, and I was right. But perhaps if you'd spent the years of your marriage paying attention to your own husband rather than lusting after someone else's, he might not have seen the need to carry on with Mrs. Halberd for so long."

No. No. Julia would not listen to this. She would not let anyone tell her that she was at all to blame for her husband's infidelity, for his cruelty towards her. And she would not let such poisonous speech reinforce her own guilt and fears, would not let it destroy the brilliant shard of happiness she had found with Alexander.

"I will not wish you a good day, Mrs. Holland," she said, her voice polite enough for the grandest of drawing rooms. "Or safe travels, or any of the trite and meaningless words etiquette would dictate I offer to you in farewell. I will simply wish you gone."

She turned and walked down the stairs, determined not to look back, not to give the housekeeper another second of attention than she deserved. When she stepped outside the inn, it was into near-blinding sunlight, the air so bracingly cold it made her feel as though each breath was scraping away something old and dismal from inside herself and allowing a newer, brighter portion of her thoughts to shine through.

She spotted Alexander and Zora at the other side of the yard, Zora busy trying to catch a chicken and spattering the hem of her new gown with slush and mud in the process while Alexander did nothing to stop her.

"And just what are you doing?" She tried to inject a touch of admonishment into her tone, but the sun was too bright and the day full of too much potential for her to stifle the grin teasing the corners of her mouth.

Alexander turned to her with a smile of his own, though it dimmed at the sight of her. "Are you all right? You look—"

She waved away his concern, not wanting to speak about it in front of Zora, to spoil the joy of the scene before her. "I saw a shadow, and I was startled. That's all."

He slid his arm around her waist, pulling her closer to his side. "The carriage will be ready in a few minutes. If the roads are a bit better this morning, we should be home again in only a few hours."

Home again...

Her chin quivered, but she brushed the back of her hand across her jaw, hiding the movement from sight. "To Langford," she said, as Zora squealed and the chicken squawked to fly away from her. "Home."

Twenty-Two

The last of the wedding guests did not leave until well after sunset. Julia and Alexander saw them off from Langford's front steps, the stars sparking to life overhead as they waved away the cart bearing Mr. and Mrs. Cowper and their five children (along with enough leftovers from the meal to feed the family for a week).

Once the cart had rumbled down the drive and out of sight, they stood there beneath the clear, open sky, a light breeze picking up the ends of Julia's shawl and teasing the ends of Alexander's hair.

Julia breathed in deep, noticing the mossy smells of earth and new growth carried on the wind. It was still winter, but its hold over the land seemed to have loosened over the last few days, even the rain they'd had earlier in the week carrying a tentative warmth that spoke of spring flowers and green grass carpeting the lawn. Still, she wrapped her shawl more tightly around her shoulders, the evening chill raising goosebumps on her arm after spending so many hours entertaining dozens of guests indoors.

"It was a good day," Alexander said, wrapping his arms around her and pulling her against him.

She laughed, low and deep in her throat. It had been a good day. And an exhausting one. There had been the wedding in the morning and then immediately on to the wedding breakfast at Langford, which had extended into an all-day celebration hosting Langford's tenants as well as guests from the village and the surrounding county, including many of Julia's pupils and their families.

And there had been gifts and messages of congratulations. Though the best of them were the letters from her sisters, including a promise from both that they would come to Langford with their families once the weather improved. For an extended stay.

"We should go in," Alexander said, still holding her. His hands found their way beneath her shawl to settle snugly beneath her breasts.

"We should," she echoed, but without any true conviction behind the words. The night was cold, but Alexander's embrace was warm. The servants were inside, cleaning up from the party — and a party it had swiftly become, once Alexander had the wine and ale brought up from the cellars and a portion of the floor had been cleared of furniture for an impromptu bit of dancing. "But not yet, I think."

She turned in his arms, working her own embrace to fit beneath his jacket. He was her husband now, Mr. Alexander Halberd. She tipped her head up to kiss his chin, and then the side of his jaw, and then the corner of his mouth before he twisted his head to claim her lips completely.

He kissed her slowly, but with an undercurrent of yearning. It was a kiss meant to remind them both that they had the rest of their lives together for such kisses and embraces. No, they weren't as young as most newly-married couples. Julia brushed her fingers through Alexander's hair, sporting its streaks of gray. Yes, she could lament the years they'd lost, years spent desiring one another from the periphery of their own lives, but the past was a thing that couldn't be changed. They had each other now, and they had Zora, who had already brought so much happiness into their lives.

"Where is Zora?" Julia asked, pulling away from Alexander to speak before he could kiss her again. "The last I saw her, she was trying to feed Ellen bits of fruitcake."

"Under one of the tables, asleep with Ellen curled up beside her. She retreated under there not long after the dancing began."

Julia smiled and tucked her head against his shoulder. "We should go in then, if only to take her up to bed. Surely she can't be comfortable on the floor of the ballroom."

Alexander laughed. "You'd be surprised to see where children choose to sleep when left to their own devices. In the middle of the floor, on the stairs, tucked behind the potatoes in the root cellar—"

"What?" Julia laughed. "Behind the potatoes?"

"She was four years old at the time. We were playing hide and seek." He laughed at the memory. "She was already snoring by the time I found her."

They held hands as they returned inside, Alexander's thumb brushing over her knuckles in a way that could have been perfectly innocent, but ignited such a feeling of need in Julia that she wondered how anyone could glance at her in that moment and not know exactly what was on her mind.

Their wedding night.

She wasn't a young maid about to approach her marriage bed for the first time. She and Alexander had spent nearly every night together in the weeks leading up to the wedding. But this felt... different, somehow. It would be their first time together as man and wife. There would be no secretly slipping into his bedroom or his study after Zora was asleep and most of the household had turned in for the night, or rushing back to their own rooms before the maids came back to light the fires. They were Mr. and Mrs. Halberd now, and there was no reason to hide their love for fear of scandal.

They made their way to the ballroom, which had been opened up and cleaned in preparation for the wedding, after sitting in stifling silence for years. A few servants still roamed the edges of the room, clearing away dirty plates and leftover food, one maid even draining the dregs of a serving of wine before adding the empty glass to her collection of dishes.

They found Zora asleep beneath one of the long tables, the end of a tablecloth drooping over the edge and serving as her blanket. Ellen sat on her hip in a curl of orange fur and twitching whiskers, so Julia gathered up the kitten — who was soon to outgrow the title of kitten in the next few weeks — while Alexander reached under the table and scooped Zora up into his arms. She murmured something unintelligible and slung her arms around his neck, then settled back into sleep as they walked out of the ballroom and up the stairs.

"She'll rest well tonight," he said as he laid her on her bed and fit the pillow under her head. Julia set Ellen down — who promptly began walking in a circle at the foot of the bed and kneading the blanket with her paws — and took off Isadora's shoes before tucking her feet and legs under the covers.

"And most likely be awake before dawn tomorrow," Julia added, leaning down to kiss her cheek. "So we shouldn't stay up much longer ourselves if we're to get any sleep."

"Sleep?" Alexander looked over at her, confusion written across his features. "It's not late yet. Surely you don't mean to—" He trailed off, realization smoothing the lines from his brow. "Ah," he said. And his gaze darkened, his grin becoming an invitation. "Then what are we waiting for? I wouldn't want you to wake up too tired in the morning."

"You're terrible." She teased him. She liked teasing him. She liked that she could tease him, that there was such comfort between them that she never worried she might say or do the wrong thing. That he would ever think less of her for any reason.

"I am terrible, yes. Pity you should only discover it tonight, now that everything is legally bound by the church and the law." His hand slid over her ribcage, and she felt the heat of him through the layers of her clothing. "Divorces, I hear, are awfully difficult to acquire."

She laughed as he opened the door to his room, as he led her inside. But despite the levity, her heart fluttered in her chest when she realized they were alone together, that the day was at an end and she was retiring for the night with her husband.

Her husband.

Julia never believed she would be able to utter that pairing of words without panic assailing her. For a moment, her thoughts whirled back to her first wedding night, over a dozen years before. How nervous she had been then, how willing to oblige and do everything that was asked of her, without requesting anything in return. And then Frederick had climbed on top of her, finished within three minutes, and rolled away from her, leaving her alone on her side of the bed for the rest of the night.

And she had thought that was how it was supposed to be. That to want more, to think she deserved more was akin to believing in fairies and dragons and happily ever afters.

So she had spent those years following Frederick's death, after coming to terms with the fact her marriage had been a misery, and that she would never be able to bear a child... Well, she had spent that time wanting and wishing for nothing. Because she was still alive. And she had her little place with Mrs. Cochran. And she'd had her school on Sundays, as ill-supported a venture as it was by the majority of the townspeople, though she would never stop teaching, as long as she still possessed the ability to do it.

And she had believed herself fortunate to have those meager comforts and liberties, to be able to exist without having to fully throw herself onto the charity of her family, to be stored away like last season's coat — or last decade's coat, if she was to be honest with herself — and promptly forgotten.

But Alexander saw her. And he always had, since their very first meeting all those years ago.

To be seen was a remarkable thing. It didn't depend on what she could provide for him, children or money or status. Instead, she suspected he saw her very much as she saw him, as someone who made her feel safe, and loved, and wanted, simply for who they were.

She walked into the middle of the bedroom, her arms folded over her chest and her hands sliding up and down the long sleeves of her gown as though she was chilled, regardless of the heat emanating from the fireplace. Alexander was behind her. She heard him light a candle, heard the strike of his boots on the floor as he carried it over to the nightstand. When she finally turned to look at him, he stood beside the bed, the knot of his neckcloth already undone, every mark of his features limned with anticipation.

"No," she said.

A line appeared between his eyes. "No?"

She smiled. "Come here."

He turned away from the bed, crossing the room to stand in front of her.

She didn't know where to begin. To kiss him? To touch him? To strip him down until he was naked and wanting before her? He had given her so much control in their relationship, and she wondered if he knew what a marvelous thing that was.

"Alexander," she said. Saying his name, watching the fire burn in his eyes and the thrum of his pulse beneath his jaw.

He swallowed, and there was the rise and fall of his throat, the sudden tension in his jaw as the prospect of the night ahead vaunted into the realm of the overwhelming. Without looking down, he took her hand, his fingers lightly circling her wrist, and brought it up to his lips. He kissed her fingers, and then her palm, the tip of his tongue tracing one of the lines on her skin before his teeth nipped at the soft flesh on the inside of her wrist.

That alone was nearly enough to undo her.

She brought her hand down to the front of his trousers, to the hard length of his cock already pressing against the fabric there. His buttons were easily managed, her fingers working as quickly as their trembling would allow. He gasped when she touched him, her skin on his, her hand wrapped around the base of him. She stroked him once, so slowly she knew what torture it was for him, just as maddening as it was for her when he drew out the pleasure of his fingers and his mouth between her legs.

A quick tug at the hem of her gown, and she lowered herself to her knees before him.

His exhale came on a shuddering breath. "Julia."

She licked her lips, unsure of what to do now that she'd brought herself to the cusp of it. But keeping her hand wrapped around him, she drew him into her mouth. Only the tip of him, at first, but even that was enough to make his entire body flare up, as though lit by a fire sparked to life with that first touch of her tongue.

She let him guide her after that, his reactions, his words, the gentle thrust of his hips as she took him deeper. Her own hips squirmed as she pleasured him, as she imagined him filling her up down there, driving into her with all of his need and his passion until they both burst apart at the seams.

"Not yet," he ground out, and dragged her back up to her feet before he finished, no matter that he had seemed close to coming in her mouth and her hands. He guided over to the bed, turning her away from him. She knew what he wanted, and she bent forward over the end of the bed, tilting up her hips as he pulled up her skirts, as the chill air of the bedroom touched her bare thighs and her bottom.

"Please," she said, wanting him inside of her with such desperation she was almost in tears. "Now, please!"

He placed his hands on her waist, just above her hips. He pulled her back to meet him as he thrust forward, burying himself inside all the way to the hilt.

It wasn't a gasp that slid out of her. Instead, it was a long, breathless keening of want as she gripped the blankets, as she tipped herself towards him. He released one of her hips to reach around her waist, to dip down and find that hot, throbbing place between her legs. A few flicks of his thumb and she fell over the edge, crying out into the blanket as his own release slammed into him behind her.

He fell onto the bed beside her, pulling her towards him so that her back was tucked against his chest.

"Dear God," she said, when she could dare to speak again. "Surely it cannot always be like this, can it?"

He laughed softly and kissed the back of her neck. "Let's see where we are in ten years, shall we?"

"Ten years?" She rolled onto her back to look up at him. He was all disheveled and sweaty, and bearing that heavy-lidded gaze he always wore after their lovemaking. And it made her want to pull him back on top of her all over again. "We'll both be worn out from exhaustion by then."

"No." He shook his head and kissed the tip of her nose. "You give me a strength I've never had before. I'll live to be a hundred if only so I can keep waking up with you beside me."

"So young?" Her fingers grazed his jaw, her thumb at the corner of his mouth coaxing a wider smile from him. "I would've wagered our having at least another eighty years together."

He laughed and kissed her full on the lips. Her hands slid up between them to grasp the collar of his shirt, to tangle in the loose remains of his neckcloth.

"This infernal thing," he growled, and pulled the length of the fabric free from around his neck. "I should take on the guise of a cantankerous old man, aged beyond the rules of dress and etiquette required for everyone else."

Julia plucked up the discarded neckcloth and slowly drew the fabric between her hands. "We can use them to sew new gowns for

Zora's dolls, or make a lead for Ellen so she can be taken out on walks across the lawns."

Alexander teased it from her fingers, pulling it taut while his expression took on a pensive cast. "I think we could find a few uses for it, if we're creative enough." He looked at her with a new light in his eyes, eager and lustful. "That is, if you're not already tired out for the night."

She swallowed. Inside her gown, her breasts ached, and the muscles between her legs tightened again in anticipation. "What did you have in mind?"

He wrapped the cloth around his wrist, holding it tight before he released it and let it slip sinuously from his arm. "Do you trust me?" he asked, his eyes sparking with fire, his grin irresistible.

"Always," came her reply, before she leaned forward and kissed him.

Acknowledgments

I know that I'm going to forget someone, so I will start off with a vague and generic "Thanks to everyone who helped during the creation of this book! You know who you are!" *wink*

Now, onward toward specifics: Thank you to Kay Villoso, for listening to me work out this story, for egging me on, for making up silly placeholder titles halfway through the story that still make me grin. For putting together the lovely cover that graces the front of this book. For being not just a fantastic writer friend, but a great friend, full stop.

To C.M. Caplan and Krystle Matar for their never-ending enthusiasm and cheerleading. You called yourselves the reverse Statler and Waldorf, and I cannot think of a more fitting title.

To my Patreon readers who were the first to read an early draft of this book and fall wholeheartedly in love with it, thank you so much, and I hope you know how much motivation you gave me to keep writing.

To the Terrible Ten, for their constant support and writing (and life) wisdom, thank you.

To my family, for always being there, for letting me love you and — for some reason — loving me in return. Without you and your support, this book would absolutely not exist.

To my readers, thank you for being such a wonderful audience.